Anna Adams wrote her [first story] in wet sand with a stick. These days she uses pens, software, or napkins and a crayon to write the kinds of stories she loves best—romance that involves everyone in the family, and often the whole community. Love, like a stone tossed into a lake, causes ripples to spread and contract, bringing conflict and well-meaning "help" from the people who care most.

Anna J. Stewart is a born and bred California girl. Raised in San Francisco, she discovered romances early in her parochial high school education and from then on knew what she was meant to be: a romance author. An English graduate of California State University of Sacramento, she's held a variety of jobs and, for the past seven years, she's been honored to work as *New York Times* bestselling author Brenda Novak's personal assistant, helping run her annual online auction for diabetes research. In ten years, the auction has raised over $2.3 million. Anna lives in Northern California with an overly attentive and affectionate cat named Snickers.

Melinda Curtis lives in California's arid central valley with her husband—her basketball-playing college sweetheart—who has a man-crush on Duke basketball legend Coach K (admit it, your man does, too!). Their three kids are all in college, and the only grandbabies they have are of the four-legged variety. Melinda loves cross-stitch, needlepoint and quilting, although since she started writing she hasn't completed a single project. She writes sweet contemporary romances as Melinda Curtis and red-hot reads as Mel Curtis.

HEARTWARMING

Christmas, Actually

Anna Adams
Anna J. Stewart
Melinda Curtis

HARLEQUIN® HEARTWARMING™

PLEASE RECYCLE
THIS PRODUCT IS RECYCLABLE

ISBN-13: 978-0-373-36702-3

Recycling programs
for this product may
not exist in your area.

Christmas, Actually
Copyright © 2014 by Harlequin Books S.A.

The publisher acknowledges the copyright holders
of the individual works as follows:

The Christmas Gift
Copyright © 2014 by Anna Adams

The Christmas Wish
Copyright © 2014 by Anna J. Stewart

The Christmas Date
Copyright © 2014 by Melinda Wooten

This edition published by arrangement with Harlequin Books S.A.

For questions and comments about the quality of this book,
please contact us at CustomerService@Harlequin.com.

® and TM are trademarks of Harlequin Enterprises Limited or its corporate affiliates. Trademarks indicated with ® are registered in the United States Patent and Trademark Office, the Canadian Intellectual Property Office and in other countries.

Printed in U.S.A.

™ www.Harlequin.com

CONTENTS

THE CHRISTMAS GIFT
Anna Adams

Dear Reader,

Sophie Palmer is confused when the pregnancy test comes back positive, but one thing she knows for sure—she already loves her unborn child. She doesn't expect former army surgeon Jack Banning to break all contact, though. He's promised financial support, but he wants no other involvement with her or their coming child.

He must have a reason. She's known him and loved him for two years. At Christmas, she follows him to Maine to tell him she's putting his name on the birth certificate.

She'll never let their daughter believe she can expect more than her father's name. Still, Sophie can't forget the soldier who has lived by the code of Leave No Man Behind, the doctor who has cared more for his patients than himself, the man who shouldn't know how to be dishonorable.

Fatherless herself, Sophie doesn't care about the financials. She'll take care of her own. She wants only to understand why Jack has become an impossible-to-love stranger.

I hope you'll be as moved by Jack and Sophie's story as I am.

Wishing you warm and loving holidays,

Anna

To Steve, for always being at my back. To Karen Whiddon and Debby Giusti, for reading so much. To Melinda Curtis and Anna J. Stewart for spending this holiday with me, and to Victoria Curran and Dana Grimaldi for working so hard to make this a Christmas Gift.

CHAPTER ONE

SNOWFLAKES HIT THE windshield and splayed into star shapes while Bing Crosby crooned his dreams of a white Christmas. Sophie Palmer tried to sing along, but her mind was already racing up the icy interstate to Christmas Town, Maine, where the father of her unborn child now lived.

That *Charlie Brown Christmas* song came next, with talk of happiness and cheer and families drawing near. Sophie stared at the road, as frozen as the world she was driving into. The closer to Christmas Town she got, the more humiliated she felt.

But she wasn't going to ask Jack Banning to love her again. He'd rejected her and their child—love wasn't a possibility.

She dropped one hand to her slightly rounded belly. "You deserve better. You deserve the chance to have a father, if he can remember he's a decent man."

Overhead, a sign warned that the exit for Christmas Town was a quarter mile ahead.

Time to embark on possibly the most foolish fool's errand of all time.

She veered off at the exit, pausing to yield, and then turned onto a two-lane road bounded by primeval forest.

Another car was coming toward her, but it shimmied in its lane, as if the driver was asleep. Sophie slid her foot to the brake and lowered her speed, edging to the right, but the other car seemed to follow. It crossed the line. And sped up.

Sophie slapped at the steering wheel to find the horn. She hugged the edge of the road, screaming at the oncoming driver as she tried to stay out of the ditch.

Time yawned as the driver's face came into focus. A young woman—looking up from her phone. Her face screwed up in horror, and Sophie realized she would see that woman's expression in nightmares for the rest of her life.

The little blue car swung away, rocking, but then skidded back as the driver tried to steady it.

In the time it took to gasp, Sophie hoped they would have a near miss. Then the back of the girl's car smacked the front of hers, and they spun away from each other.

That quickly, it was over, and Sophie found herself staring up at snow-covered trees. While the clash of metal echoed in her ears, Nat King Cole's "Christmas Song" made the silence surreal. Sophie whipped off her seat belt and splayed her hands across her stomach.

Nothing. She felt nothing.

At eighteen weeks, she might not. The baby was small. She still had plenty of cushion. Her unborn daughter might be okay. Everything might be okay.

Sophie looked back at the other car.

Everything was not okay.

The girl's vehicle was on its side in a spray of snow. The teen lay on her back, spilled onto the road, denim-covered legs out straight, hair splayed across the car's skid marks.

Sophie tried to open her door, but it wouldn't budge. She shoved as hard as she could and then tried the other side, which also refused to open.

The window.

She tugged at the bottom of her coat until she could pull it over her head, and then leaned against the console and kicked the driver's window with all her strength. Two kicks and it crashed through, hanging on to the door by a corner, all in one jagged-edged piece.

Sophie slithered through, careful to avoid the glass, and hit the ground, taking her weight on her hands. Pain shot through her wrists to her fingers and up her arms. Ignoring it, she leaned back inside for her phone, tucked away in the console.

Punching 911, she ran the thirty-forty steps to kneel beside the young woman.

"Christmas County Emergency Services. How may I—"

"I'm putting you on speaker." Sophie tossed her coat over the girl's torso. "I've just been in a car accident. We're east of the Christmas Town exit, not even a mile. I have a female in her late teens, ejected from her vehicle, probable broken arm. Unconscious. Probable broken right leg. She's got a gash on the head, just beneath her temple. Thready pulse."

"What's your name, ma'am?"

"Sophie Palmer. I'm easing her arm out from under her body—"

"Don't move her, Sophie."

"I'm an E.R. trauma nurse. I think she's lacerated an artery." Sophie recognized her own growing shock in the wave of nausea that surged through her as she assessed the gaping wound on the young woman's upper arm. She whipped off her cotton shirt and tore it with adrenaline-fueled strength. "I'm applying a tourniquet," she said, shivering in her tank top.

"We're sending a helicopter," the operator said. "Is she breathing?"

"Yes. Low and fast." Drops of blood had appeared on the teen's chin. "She has a— Oh." It wasn't the girl's blood. Sophie didn't dare stop winding the shirt to check her own injury.

No pain in her abdomen. *My baby girl.* Eighteen weeks. Plenty of cushion.

"Are you hurt?"

"Some pain in my wrists, and I have a laceration somewhere on my head or face. I'm eighteen weeks pregnant, but I don't think I'm bleeding, and I have no abdominal pain. Please hurry."

"They're lifting off. Shouldn't be more than five minutes."

The girl struggled as if she were trying to breathe, and then—nothing. Sophie felt for a pulse with shaking fingers. "She's stopped breathing. I'm starting CPR."

She began compressions, while her wrists screamed for her to stop. The operator's voice went on in the background, but Sophie barely heard.

This girl had left some other mom's home this morning, with her whole life just waiting to be lived. She'd be going back if sheer force could make her breathe again.

Tears leaked from Sophie's eyes.

A new sound made her want to look up. The whir of blades. So many times Sophie had waited on the landing pad in Boston, but today would be different. Her own baby and this girl were both going to live.

Chaos descended. The helicopter landed close enough to lift her hair and the teen's. Papers fluttered past. One, titled "Biology," imprinted itself on Sophie's eyes. The girl's Christmas break assignment.

Feet appeared around them. One crushed her phone on the road. A pair of legs in dark blue uniform pants eased her out of the way.

Someone else helped her stand, but she felt as fluid as water. The EMT supported her when she began slipping back to the ground.

"Are you in pain?" He looked younger than the girl she'd been helping.

"A little in my wrists but I don't think they're even sprained."

He tilted her chin up with his finger and then pushed her hair out of the way. "You have a small laceration." Producing an alcohol wipe, he cleaned it.

A nurse in a flight suit applied a cervical collar to the patient, while the first EMT was still doing compressions. Sophie watched his hands, stronger than hers.

Sophie slid her arms around her stomach. "I'm pregnant," she said. "Eighteen weeks."

The EMT helped her to sit down on the road, out of the way of the others.

The man's colleague, still working on the girl, looked back. "I have a pulse. Let's get her in the chopper." He helped the others strap their patient to a backboard.

Sophie's EMT touched her arm. "An ambulance is on the way for you. She'll be fine. Are you bleeding?"

Sophie shivered as the cold cut into her. "I don't think so."

"How hard did you strike your head?"

"I'm not sure."

"We'll check for concussion at the hospital. For now, follow my finger." She did. "How old are you?"

"Twenty-five."

"Where do you live?" he asked. "Street address?"

"Nine-ten East Portland Street in Boston."

"Good enough. Can we call your husband? I think I stepped on your phone."

Jack's face, expressionless, flashed in front of her. She tried to breathe. "No husband. No one to call." She stared across the road at the pieces of glass and plastic and a hot-pink phone cover, instead of looking into her own thoughts.

With any luck, Jack wouldn't be on duty today.

CHAPTER TWO

JACK BANNING MET the chopper, where the patient had gone into arrest for the second time from loss of blood. After the crew resuscitated her, he took a report from the flight's RN. Running beside his patient's gurney toward the E.R. entrance, he was forced to veer out of the way of an incoming ambulance.

When the doors opened, he saw Sophie.

It wasn't really her, of course. Since he'd left Boston, Jack had seen her face everywhere he went. Guilt, he figured.

Not that guilt would change his mind.

Sophie would have to accept his financial assistance and hope a better man came into her life.

Jack looked back at his patient, assessing on the fly. He couldn't help glancing at the ambulance.

It was still Sophie.

Staring at him, white with shock, blank.

Nausea hit him so hard he was almost sick

on the cement. He took deep breaths that didn't provide nearly enough oxygen.

Was she hurt? And her baby... He didn't let himself think of the child. Another doctor would take care of Sophie and the—her—baby. What was she doing here?

"Dr. Banning." The trauma nurse assigned to his team spoke his name. No one ever had to focus him, and she sounded alarmed.

Sophie had come after him when he'd rejected her and the baby—it was completely out of character. He pushed thoughts of her aside, clearing his mind and hardening his heart.

Emotionless, capable, in charge, he knew what to do next.

"O.R. Two is waiting for us."

"YOUR BABY LOOKS GREAT." Dr. Everly glanced up from the ultrasound, where Sophie's unborn daughter appeared to be practicing for a future in Olympic diving. "Your blood pressure and pulse are a little elevated."

"Natural, considering I was just in an accident."

"And you're bruised. I'd like you to stick around town for a few days. Were you headed home for the holidays?"

Relief helped to calm Sophie. Dr. Everly

wasn't worried about the baby if she was going to let her leave the hospital. "I'm visiting."

Sophie tried to wipe away the tears she couldn't hold back. Who knew if they were tears of joy or sadness? All this time, she'd been stunned at Jack's sudden exit from her life. She'd been unable to believe the man who worked miracles in the operating room could be so cold to a woman he'd professed to love, who'd loved him.

"Stop worrying." The doctor squeezed her shoulder. "I wouldn't lie to you, and someone told me you're an E.R. nurse. You'd know if you were in trouble."

"I'm happy." *Happy* didn't exactly describe everything she was feeling. She pulled the sheet up to her chin. The doctor whisked a tissue out of a box on the counter and passed it to her before reaching for the switch on the ultrasound machine. Sophie caught her wrist. "Could I listen for a few more minutes?"

"No problem. Where are you staying?"

"I have a reservation at a B and B. Esther's House?"

"Esther is an old friend of mine. She'll send someone to pick you up." The doctor began inputting notes on her tablet at the counter. "Is your car drivable?"

Shrugging, Sophie discovered her muscles

were as tender as if she'd thrown herself into a blender. "I don't even know what happened to it. An EMT told me the tow truck driver would be in touch with a bill."

Dr. Everly smiled ruefully. "My brother-in-law owns a body shop. I'll see if they towed it to him. They might have impounded it, but impound at the police station consists of the two farthest spaces in their lot." She made a note on the palm of her hand with her pen, but then looked up. "I'll ask him to let you know if he has the car."

After a quick grasp of Sophie's hand, she went to the door. "I'll call Esther's to check in with you later tonight. Unless you'd rather stay in one of our fine rooms?"

"Not a chance." Forcing a smile, when she was still fighting the urge to cry, Sophie swallowed hard. Naturally, she was emotional. Her baby had survived that crash. Sophie was a walking cesspool of hormones, and the man she'd been driving for hours to see had just looked at her as if they'd never met.

A fatherless daughter herself, she'd believed her child had a right to know her dad. Maybe she'd been mistaken.

"Why don't you get dressed?" Dr. Everly suggested. "Esther's car will be here by the time we discharge you."

"Thank you, Dr. Everly."

"Georgette. And that young lady in surgery should be thanking *you*. Word around the landing pad is you saved her life."

Jack's sharp features swam in front of Sophie's eyes. Thank goodness the ultrasound only measured the baby's heartbeat.

She pulled herself together. Coming here might have been an impulse she'd live to regret, but she could leave at any time. "My shirt got torn." She plucked at the neck of her borrowed scrub top. "Do you think I can wear this out of here? I'll wash it and return it after I get home."

"No problem. I'm sure you can keep it." The other woman opened the door, but then turned back. "Sophie, do you have anything else on your mind?"

She pressed her palms to her stomach, ignoring the slight tenderness in her wrists as she took consolation from the rapid heartbeat echoing in the small room. "No."

"Call me if you have any problems. I'll have your nurse put my cell number on your discharge instructions."

TESSIE'S SURGERY WAS a success. No problems. Nothing unexpected.

Jack explained to her parents that their daughter would live to celebrate many more Christmases if they confiscated her phone. They went to see her, and he was left alone. Taking a deep breath, he tried to figure out what to do about Sophie.

Coming out of that ambulance wrapped in a blanket, she'd been pale with terror. The physician who'd taken oaths to help the sick and injured wanted to go to her.

The man, who knew what he had to do, didn't want to get near her. She was the last person Jack had expected. Proud and strong and self-contained, Sophie would never chase a man who'd rejected her.

So what was she doing here?

He went back to the E.R. and checked the board to see if she was listed as a patient. Oddly, in the computer age, Christmas Town's hospital still used a whiteboard. It was large, easy to read, easy to update.

He found the palest outline of "Sop" where someone hadn't completely erased her name after she was discharged. The pregnancy meant that Georgette Everly would have been her attending…unless Sophie had come to Maine to tell him she'd lost the baby.

She could have lost the baby in the accident.

Georgette opened the door of a treatment room almost directly across from where he stood at the nurses' station. With her eyes on her tablet, she was already moving on to the next room.

Jack headed for the doctors' lounge.

He showered and dressed in jeans and a blue button-down shirt, then grabbed his coat from his locker before heading for the E.R. exit.

Georgette was leaning on one elbow at the nurses' station, making notes. She looked up with a smile. "I heard your surgery went well."

In no small part because Sophie had treated the girl while she was still lying on the road.

"Tessie Blaylock's fine." Jack should walk on. He should make sure he knew nothing about Sophie or the child. He didn't want to ask, but the words came out of his mouth. "How's your patient?"

"She's good. Eighteen weeks pregnant, and the baby has a strong heartbeat. Lots of movement. Lucky for Tessie, she hit an E.R. nurse with trauma experience."

"Are you keeping her overnight?"

"She's staying at Esther's House. I called to have someone look in on her before bedtime, but I'll phone her, too."

Esther Underbrook was like Mrs. Claus, opening her home to tourists seeking a potent shot of holiday spirit. Sophie had made fun of his hometown, with its blatantly commercial name.

"No use confusing anyone about Christmas for sale," she'd teased him.

He'd been so busy keeping his life with her in Boston apart from his real life that he'd never explained Christmas Town wasn't like that. She'd had no need to know that he wasn't the man he'd been in Christmas Town. He'd avoided mixing his two worlds and the people in them.

She had no need to be here at all.

Nothing would change between them. Nothing. He didn't care what plan nurturing, dreamy-eyed, yet practical Sophie Palmer had made.

Jack drove through the softly falling snow. Already, the sun was heading downward and the blue-gray sky darkening. He parked at the square and walked a block north to the Federal-style family home Esther had managed to refurbish by taking in customers.

She'd started her business by turning her dining room and parlor into a restaurant frequented by foodies from all over the world, but a house built when George Washington might reasonably have been expected to stop for hay and victuals required a formidable amount of upkeep. Naturally, she'd turned the restaurant into an inn.

Esther was carrying linens between her two busy dining rooms when he opened the door, stomping snow off his boots. "Hello, Jack," she said. "You should be at work or asleep."

Usually, he teased back. She'd been a fixture of kindness since his childhood. Tonight, he had to finish the last conversation he and Sophie would ever have.

"Actually, I'm working. I thought I'd drop in to check on an accident victim who came to the E.R. today."

"Isn't that nice of you?" Esther was so pleased his conscience quivered, but he instantly shut it down. "Sophie's in room eight. Let me give you a pitcher of cider for her."

He waited. Esther brought a tray with hot cider, scones straight from the oven and two delicate cups and saucers that had never been intended for a man's use. Nevertheless, he negotiated the stairs and knocked at Sophie's door.

She opened it immediately. Her smile reminded him of the old days—days and nights they'd shared just a few months ago—when her smile had been for him, and he'd never imagined being without her.

"I thought for a minute you didn't even recognize me," she said.

He moved toward her, and she had to step

back. "Why are you here?" he asked. "I made myself clear."

"When you packed up everything you owned, quit your job and moved home because I was pregnant?"

Her tone, as sharp as a scalpel, sliced into him, but he and Sophie and her child would all fare better if he withstood the wounds. He set the tray on a table between two armchairs in front of the fireplace.

This might go more easily if she'd only shown up to extract a pound of flesh.

"Nothing's changed," he said. "What did you expect?"

She shut her eyes, and her face seemed to smooth as she breathed her stress away. He hardened his heart. He could not be around a child. Would not.

She opened blue eyes, more beautiful than he remembered. Two months, and seeing her made him as eager as a starving man contemplating a table groaning with abundance.

"I hoped to find the man I loved for nearly two years." Her voice dragged his gaze from her eyes to her mouth. "The doctor who gives his all to save lives, the friend who never, ever walks away."

"I walked." He turned toward the door. "If that's all…"

She followed, grabbing his arm. He would not shake her off. He wouldn't risk hurting her.

"Sit down," she said, her confusion a painful stumbling block. He was determined to stick to his decision, but he didn't want to hurt her more than he had to. "For a few minutes, listen to me."

Whatever she said wouldn't change anything, but maybe, after he said no again, she'd go away.

Cold sweat raced down his spine.

CHAPTER THREE

SOPHIE POURED CIDER into both cups and took one, mostly to keep her hands occupied. "Let's get this over with. I'm not even sure there's a point in talking."

Except she'd been nobody's daughter all her life. Not even a name to peg her hopes or her resentment on.

"You're finally hearing me," Jack said.

She put one hand to her mouth, resting her index finger along her upper lip as her stomach heaved. She had yet to conquer morning sickness. Some women had it from conception to delivery. Hers seemed to be connected to stress. "You know that my mother kept my father's name off my birth certificate?"

"I don't want my name on the baby's papers."

Was he trying to make her despise him? It might work, if a small voice in her head would stop insisting he must have lost his mind. He had to have a reason.

"I came to tell you I won't do that. It's not

best for my baby. I know nothing about my father or whatever family he might have had, except that clearly he was either ashamed or married or a coldhearted—"

"Those are the stories you've told yourself," Jack said. "You can't prove any of it."

"Exactly. But when you're the one who's been rejected, it's harder to pretend it doesn't matter. If something happens to her later in life, if she needs medical records or—I don't even know what—I'd like for her to have a name. I don't know the man you've become, but I'm putting your name on the birth certificate."

"You could have asked me that on the phone."

She sipped the cider. It still burned her lips. "I said 'tell you.' I'm doing this, and you can live with it."

"Don't encourage her to dream up comforting stories about me," Jack said, standing. "You'll only make sure she'll be hurt."

Sophie tried to equate this guy with the loving, witty man she used to know.

Bringing her a pot of purple violets on a Tuesday evening just because he thought the color would look nice with her eyes. That pot still held pride of place on her nightstand.

"I don't know how you can leave your own

baby." She went to the door and opened it for him.

"I've already spoken to an attorney about child support. I'll be setting up the payroll deduction as soon as you deliver."

"What a good idea. Once it's set up, you won't have to think about your daughter ever again."

Despite her anger, she only wanted to know one thing. *Why?*

The question echoed inside her head. She heard it, but she must be holding it back. He didn't even blink. He just walked away. Again.

She slammed the door so hard the whole house must have shivered. Nice pregnant women didn't run at implacable men and pound their fists on feelingless backs. Nor did they break Esther Underbrook's house.

Sophie bit her fist to keep from crying. As soon as her car was repaired, she'd get out of Christmas Town.

"ESTHER, I NEED to buy a new coat." The next morning, Sophie had gone downstairs to breakfast, nibbled on a slice of toast and decided she'd walk off her frustration. No need to lurk around the B and B, whiling away the hours before her car was repaired. "Mine didn't survive the accident."

Esther refilled Sophie's herbal tea. "There's Dockery's. Go around the courthouse and follow the green, where they're starting to put up the decorations. You won't be able to miss it. Dockery's doesn't put up their Santa until after Thanksgiving, but he's been waving from the top of their pediment for a week now."

Sophie's hard heart softened. Maybe she could use a little Santa after last night's dose of rejection. "Is the distance walkable?"

Esther looked over Sophie's thick sweater and purple knitted cloche, mittens and scarf. "Maybe on the way back. I'm going to call you a cab for the drive over. " She motioned for Sophie to follow her to the reception desk, where she shuffled among the pages for a map of downtown, and then drew in directions for walking back from Dockery's. "Now you be careful. The sidewalks might be icy."

The cab arrived in no time, and Sophie rode in the backseat, staring out the windows at the lighted snowflakes blinking on street lamps and the people attaching holly to a white picket fence around the long town green.

At Dockery's, a tall Victorian brick department store that oozed decorum, Sophie hopped out. She was drawn to the Norman Rockwell–type window displays. The first showed a family around a tree decorated in rich reds and greens and the other, a family around the fireplace, popping corn to string on their still bare tree.

Sophie couldn't just walk past. She ran her hand over her belly, promising her daughter she wouldn't lack for love because she didn't have a father. Sophie's mother had probably made the same Christmas wish, and that hadn't come true. Every child wanted to be wanted by her parents.

On the store's third floor, Sophie rummaged through the racks until she found a coat she liked. While she was paying for it, she breathed in the fragrance of a fir tree tucked into the corner of the checkout desk.

"You hardly ever see real ones anymore," she said to the woman running her credit card.

"Fire hazard, I guess, but we got special permission to use one on each floor for our elf trees."

"Elf trees?" Sophie noticed the small white tags hanging from the branches.

"The children whose parents can't afford much this Christmas were asked to fill out a card with their wishes." She handed Sophie her receipt and pointed at the tree with her pen. "Each one of those cards is a wish."

"If I buy something now, can I turn it in before I leave the store?"

"The collection boxes are supposed to show up sometime today, one at all the exits, but if you don't find a box before you leave the store, bring your gift back to me, or drop it at Customer Service."

"Thanks." Sophie took a tag that said "Red coat with black buttons" in a childish scrawl. Someone had written on the corner of the tag that this was for a girl, size 4T, and jotted a code, which must identify the child.

Sophie remembered being annoyed with clothing when she was small. She'd wanted toys—a treasure trove of toys, stacked like a pyramid around the tree.

A bit embarrassed, she smiled at the cashier and headed for the escalator, where a sign directed her to the children's section, on the second floor. She found a beautiful wool coat, cinched in at the waist, with a swirling skirt and a black collar to match the required black buttons. She added mittens and a scarf, in red with black trim.

In the toy department, she found a doll in a similar coat and jaunty hat. She picked up a notepad and crayons and a toy cell phone, a miniature pewter tea set and Lincoln Logs, which she would still play with herself if she had them.

There were no collection boxes on the ground

floor, so she headed to Customer Service, where a man behind the desk eyed her pile of gifts with doubt. "You picked up a lot of tags," he said.

"Just one. Can I get these wrapped?" Maybe it was guilt. Maybe it was her own grief. But one little girl, size 4T, who was so mature she'd asked for a coat instead of toys, was going to receive a mini pyramid.

"Sure." He leaned over the counter, pointing to the right. "Just around that corner."

"Thank you."

She persuaded the resident wrapper to do each item and then put them all in a bigger box, which she also wrapped in gorgeous red metallic paper that glittered each time the box moved. Sophie chose a white taffeta ribbon, and the woman performed a miracle of looping with it. The finished gift was so beautiful Sophie was tempted to believe in Christmas again. She meant to leave it at Customer Service, but the man behind the counter had disappeared, and she hated to leave the package just sitting there.

Maybe the collection boxes had shown up by now.

She was just in time. The store security guard was pulling a box covered in Santa-figured wrapping paper toward the revolving doors. Sophie carried her package to him, peering over the top to make sure she didn't mow anyone down. "Will this fit?" she asked as the guard held out his hands.

"I think so. Good thing you got here first, though."

"I know it's a lot to ask, but could you make sure the bow doesn't get crushed?"

"No problem. I'll arrange it myself, and we empty the box every night at closing."

Together, they set it inside.

"That was some wish," the guard said. "What was it? A horse?"

Sophie laughed. "Just a coat."

"In Kevlar?" He glanced up as the door behind her opened, and a familiar voice called out a greeting. "Jack, your first wish came true."

Sophie whirled. "You're collecting toys for children?" she asked. The irony tasted bitter and felt like poison.

Jack barely even blinked. "It's a family tradition."

"It's a Banning trait," the guard said. "I saw your brother, Nick, splicing wires on Main Street for those stars they hang on the lampposts, and your sister stopped by to round up my granddaughters for their first Christmas choir practice about an hour ago. Who's your friend, Jack?"

"We're not friends." Sophie pushed past both men and hit the street. Let Jack explain her exit. All the better if he couldn't.

Something about those toys had pushed her over the edge. She felt betrayed again, as if she still loved him. It wasn't going to be enough, telling him his name would be on the birth certificate.

She'd thought she'd known Jack Banning, but that man had been a lie. A soldier who lived by the code of "Leave no man behind," a doctor who cared more for his patients than himself, a man who didn't know how to be dishonorable.

Sophie didn't need his infuriating promise of financial support. She'd take care of her daughter, with love and everything else her child might need. But she might lose her mind if she couldn't understand what had turned Jack into a stranger no sane woman could love.

CHAPTER FOUR

JACK STARED AFTER her, his only thought that she shouldn't be walking on icy streets.

"You know the lady well?" Gary Cook asked.

"We've met."

Sophie had him pegged. Except for one thing—she didn't know that every time he touched one of those boxes, he heard the echoes of a child's cry.

He opened the door and went after her. "Sophie."

She didn't stop. She didn't look back. He'd tried to make her see her best choice was to stay away from him. Now that he'd succeeded, he couldn't let her hurry through icy streets while she was so angry she might forget she was working with a different center of gravity.

"Sophie, let me give you a ride."

"No, thanks." She pulled a kind of beanie from her purse and tugged it onto her head.

He caught up with her. "You should be more

careful. At least walk on the other side of the street, where the ice has had time to melt."

She turned. Her anger hit him like a burst of heat, full in the face. She crossed the street, but she wasn't trying to be safer. She just didn't want to be near him.

Jack stopped abruptly. He'd succeeded at last. Since the night they'd discovered she was pregnant, he'd had one goal. Make Sophie happy to stay away from him. Make her forget him.

When he'd seen her after the accident, concern had surprised him. Fear had ripped through him, when he'd thought he'd turned off his emotions.

But now he'd made sure she knew nothing had changed. He hadn't changed.

A car honked, and he discovered he'd stepped into the street. Jack waved at an angry Santa behind the wheel of a vintage VW van, and hurried to catch up with Sophie.

Santa ground his gears and honked again as he passed them. Sophie looked up, as startled to see Jack as she was to be harassed by Santa's clown horn.

"What do you want?" She tugged at her mittens. "Need these, too? Maybe you don't feel I should dress warmly, but you can hand out my clothing to your Christmas Town neighbors. I hope they're not all hypocrites like you."

"Hardly any of them," he said. "Except Santa. Will you slow down?"

"I'm cold."

"You're pregnant. You might fall."

She turned her face to his, rage sparkling like ice in her eyes.

Jack held up both hands. "Given the current... situation, the last thing I want to do is take toys to children, but it's tradition. I can either do it or invite my brother and sister to diagnose me like you're trying to."

"That does make me feel like one of the community." Sophie edged away from him. "I didn't ask for your company, and I don't want your help. Go back to putting on a show for the people here—they obviously don't know the real you."

"You don't know me, either," he said.

"Which works out for both of us, since you want to be alone." Without another word, she whirled into a store and turned back to close the door in his face.

Sophie was wrong. When he was alone, memories crowded in, sharp-edged, growing ever more dangerous.

"ARE YOU SURE you'll make it home for Christmas?" Marisa Palmer asked. Her concern was the first real warmth Sophie had enjoyed all day.

"I'm positive, Mom. There wasn't that much damage."

"But you're sure you and the baby are all right?"

"Absolutely no sign of a problem."

"You could always ask Jack to drive you home. A few hours in the confines of a car, and you might be able to extract the truth from him."

"He'll never explain," Sophie said, "and I've spent too much time trying to understand. Maybe he was just the wrong guy for me, but I'm starting to think he's definitely the wrong father for my baby."

"I don't want to believe that's true," her mother said. "He's been a good man, but something's happened. Well, keep me updated on when you plan to return, and drive carefully in the snow, okay? We don't want another accident."

"Uh-huh." Sophie stood as a clatter and loud swearing outside dragged her to the window. A man was dusting himself off as someone else righted a fallen ladder. Bystanders were checking on another man, who seemed to be wearing one of the metal-framed Christmas stars that were going up on light poles all over town.

"Everything's going to be all right. I raised you on my own. You never felt you were missing a father."

The truth quivered on the tip of Sophie's tongue, but she held it in. Her mom couldn't change anything now, and admitting she'd felt abandoned—how much she'd envied her friends who'd casually talked about their dads—wouldn't help anyone. "I'll have you, too, Mom. We're all going to be fine."

"The three musketeers," Marisa said, relief in her tone. "Don't forget your seat belt. I have some research I need to do, honey. I'll talk to you later. Or tomorrow."

Her mother was head of the psychology department at Gaudy University, one of Harvard's sister schools. In Sophie's elementary school days, her mom had always been working and didn't have time to join the class trips or show up bearing baskets of cupcakes. But she'd tried to make Sophie understand she could count on herself. She'd reminded Sophie she was loved.

And she would always find time for Sophie's daughter. Better to be one of a group of musketeers than a lone ranger.

Sophie turned back to the dressing table and

tucked her new cell phone and her electronic reader into her purse. She wanted to check on Tessie Blaylock.

SINCE JACK HAD arrived at the hospital, he'd performed one surgery on a collapsed lung and another to relieve pressure from a subarachnoid hematoma. After consulting with the physicians who'd be taking over his cases when they reached the treatment floors, Jack showered and started his rounds.

He was eager to check on Tessie. She'd be going home the next day, as long as her blood work improved.

Outside her room, Jack heard a familiar voice—light, sweet, melodic. A voice that refused to vacate his mind.

Sophie was asking Tessie a question, and the young woman responded.

"I think I remember you," Tessie said. "You're the lady I ran into. You're a nurse."

"I should have introduced myself when I came in. I'm Sophie Palmer." She sounded different. More certain.

"My parents tell me I owe you my life."

"We don't need to go that far. Dr. Banning did the real work."

"But you were there first, because of me, and you saved me anyway."

Tessie's tearful voice made Jack pause in the doorway. He couldn't un-hear Sophie's estimate of him. She had every reason to hate him, but she'd been professional.

Sophie sat beside Tessie's bed. She was just pregnant enough that the chair forced her to sit at an uncomfortable angle. Funny, they expected patients' family members to sleep in those chairs. She pushed one hand behind her back to brace herself, but her attention was on the girl, who was finally regaining her natural, healthy color.

Tessie reached out and Sophie put the girl's palm in her own. "You don't have to thank me. Just say you won't ever text and drive again. Promise you'll leave your phone in your purse."

Tessie's bandage was stark white against her skin, a reminder that she and Sophie had escaped serious consequences. Despite himself, Jack felt the tug of fear.

"I promise I will never touch my phone while I'm driving. I've been lying here wishing I could take back that one second when I picked it up, and thought I could type a quick text."

For a moment, Jack returned to the heat of his own personal hell—possessing only one pair of hands, which couldn't do half enough work in time to save his friends and soldier comrades.

Sophie let go, and he saw empathy in her eyes. He'd always admired the caring she brought to her work, to her life. "I'm glad you realize how bad it could have been, Tessie."

His patient nodded, her gaze more somber than any seventeen-year-old's should be. "I might have killed you and your baby. The police came by. They said they could charge me, because I admitted I was texting. My mom and dad are getting a lawyer."

"That's not Sophie's problem," Jack said, going into protective mode without thinking.

Sophie looked up, so startled she didn't even seem angry with him. She reached into her purse, pulled out a silver case—so small and delicate one of Santa's elves might have crafted it—and plucked out a business card.

"This has my cell number. If you need me to speak for you, I'll tell them what I believe— that you're sincere."

Tessie's face blanched. "Right now I don't ever want to get behind the wheel of a car again." She glanced from Sophie's stomach up to her face. "My mom said you risked your baby's life."

Jack felt pain like thunder in his head. His mouth went completely dry. His spine seemed to lock in place, while his legs protested at being used.

He shot a glance at Sophie, but thankfully, she didn't notice the perspiration dripping from his temples.

Without acknowledging him or his impulsive comment, she tucked in Tessie's bedding with a nurse's economy of movement. "I was in no pain and you needed help. Honestly, if my baby had been at risk, I would have chosen her over you without a second thought."

A massive, unseen fist squeezed Jack's rib cage. Of course she'd choose her child. He was counting on it.

Tessie sank against her pillow. "Thank you. That makes me feel less guilty, and I promise I won't ever forget about the texting thing."

Sophie took the girl's water bottle. "I'll get this refilled," she said, staring him down.

Jack pushed away from the doorjamb, moving to the computer mounted near the bed. "I need to check your wound, Tessie, when your nurse arrives."

SOPHIE MADE IT to the nurses' station and set the bottle on the counter. "Can we get this refilled?" she asked. In her hospital, there was filtered water available. They must have something similar here, because a woman in green scrubs took the container away.

Sophie leaned on the counter, breathing. She didn't allow herself to embrace the hope hovering at the edges of her awareness.

Jack's defense of her had come out of left field, but it didn't mean he'd changed his mind about being a father to their child. He'd broken a sweat as Tessie talked about the baby.

Was he concerned about their baby? Or any baby? He'd lost an eleven-month-old girl in a surgery in October. That was when the dreams had started.

"Here you go," the nurse said, handing over Tessie's water.

Sophie collected herself. No need to get confused about what she wanted, either. Jack might have tried for a second to protect her, but even if he'd meant it, even if he still cared for her, he could abandon her in the next breath.

It didn't matter, but before she put Christmas Town in her rearview mirror, they both had to be certain what kind of man he'd become. Would Jack be a name on a birth certificate? Or would he come to his senses and understand the magnitude of the unexpected gift he was throwing away?

When she returned to the room, he was finishing Tessie's dressing. Jack was one of the few surgeons Sophie knew who didn't turn that duty over to the nurses. He smoothed the tape.

"That should do you, Tessie."

The nurse gathered up the supplies. "Anything else, Doctor?"

Jack shook his head. "We're good," he said. The nurse left the room, closing the door behind him.

"Dr. Banning, my mom and dad are stringing lights on the green tonight. Do you think I could help them?"

He looked at Sophie as if she'd asked the question. "We all help decorate. A few years ago, the town council had to choose between fewer decorations, including canceling the pageant on Christmas Eve, or volunteering in shifts so we could cut the labor budget." He made his notes on the screen beside Tessie's bed. "I think you need to stay here another night. We had to transfuse you. We'll do blood work again this evening and in the morning. If your levels are rising, you can go tomorrow."

"I hate this place." Tessie shifted in the bed, but grimaced as her arm pulled, reminding her of the life lesson her recklessness had taught her. "Not that I'm not grateful you fixed me up."

"But the food is horrible, and you can't have a nice hamburger or a chicken wrap or whatever teenage girls eat these days." He touched a button that darkened the monitor. "You're a week early for Santa's daily visits, although I hear the nutritionists are lobbying for him to distribute fruit this year."

"Fruit?" Tessie's show of disgust betrayed her. She wasn't a forbearing saint or an adult. The child who didn't care for healthy holiday goodies lingered inside her.

Sophie laughed, relieved to find a normal adolescent had survived her trauma.

"What do you like, Sophie?" Tessie smoothed her hospital sheet. "At our house, we dip strawberries in dark chocolate. And then we dip everything else we can find in the kitchen. Even bacon."

A hint of morning sickness rattled Sophie. "Chocolate-covered cherries," she said. "My mom gives me a beautiful box every year because her parents gave her one. The good ones with cordials and liqueurs, which I will not be enjoying this year."

"That's a waste of good chocolate. I'd take the fresh fruit over chocolate liqueurs."

"Or bacon," Jack said.

Tessie laughed. Sophie concentrated on not looking startled that he'd try to be funny with her in the room. But putting on a show might be his second best skill.

"You two are finicky," he said. "I prefer those chocolate oranges my mom used to put in our stockings. You crack them against a table and they separate into slices. I could eat one of those now," he said.

"I could eat anything." Tessie sniffed the air. Out in the hall, the rattle of silver and serving trays predicted the arrival of lunch. "Except whatever they're bringing me."

"You'll be out of here in twenty-four hours," Jack said as Sophie realized she was still holding Tessie's bottle. "In fact, you can talk your parents into taking another shift on the green tomorrow."

"I will. I could help when the other cheerleaders do their shift, but I think my parents need me more right now."

"Or you could do both. You know what they say about idle hands."

"I know what my grandmother says," she answered sharply.

"I guess you're feeling more like yourself," Jack said. "But please do as you're told and rest today so you can work on the holiday decorations tomorrow. You're a lucky girl, Tessie."

"I know."

The girl's guilt touched Sophie. "You have to learn from this, but you don't have to mourn surviving," she said.

At the foot of the bed, Jack turned to her with a look of accusation on his face.

"Jack, I took a cab over here," she said. "Mind giving me a ride back?"

He gave a reluctant nod. "Will you wait while I change out of my scrubs? Tessie, take it easy. I'll see you in the morning."

"Don't lose my card," Sophie told her. "I'm glad you're feeling better."

CHAPTER FIVE

Sophie waited near the E.R. entrance. She felt a little light-headed as she searched for the words to ask Jack if his tours of duty in Afghanistan might be part of the problem between them. Between him and their unborn daughter.

She had so little time. Tact wouldn't suffice.

He came out of the elevator, having traded his scrubs for jeans and a black sweater. He shrugged into his lined bomber jacket and met her at the doors, leaning down to speak to her.

"What do you want?" he asked. "Tell me now, and we won't have to ride back to the square together."

"It's going to take that long. Jack, I really need to talk to you."

He looked at her with pity in his eyes. Poor little stalker ex. She can't take a hint.

"Put up a wall," she said. "You think if you're rude enough I'll back off?"

"What more do you need to know? I walked out without looking back."

"That might have worked if we'd had some casual relationship, but we were friends for how long before it grew into something deeper?" Her patience dwindled and bitterness crept in. "Of course, you were lying to me about who you really are."

"Knowing that, why are you still here?" He didn't make the slightest effort to deny what she'd said, or defend his own actions.

"What happened to you in Afghanistan?"

Jack's eyes instantly glazed in a convincing show of indifference. "Nothing happened." He started for the physicians' parking lot, and Sophie followed.

"Something did, and the fact that you can't talk about it means you aren't handling it on your own. I've seen the symptoms—cold sweats, a startle reflex at loud noises.

He opened the door. "You're quite the diagnostician."

"And the dreams? The fact that you reacted to Tessie's mention of my baby? You're still upset over the child in October, but you know you couldn't save her."

"I believed I could or I wouldn't have done the surgery." Jack unlocked his rusty blue truck. He'd told her about the vehicle before.

"This was your grandfather's?"

He opened the door. "He gave it to me because I helped him work on it. I probably didn't do as much as I remember."

"But the memory makes you happy."

"You're a good nurse, Sophie, but you are not a psychologist, and I don't need to be analyzed. I will not be creating memories with your child," he said. But he couldn't hide his unexpected confusion—an expression that made her look into his eyes the way she had before, when they'd cared for each other, when his gaze was a reminder that they were together among everyone else in the whole wide world.

Jack walked around to the driver's side and got in, staring straight ahead while Sophie climbed in and put on her seat belt. "I abandoned you," he said. "What kind of mother would risk having me in her baby's life?"

"A mother who never had a father, but once believed with all her heart that her child's dad was the most decent man she'd ever know."

He didn't answer. She'd been too honest. He probably thought she was making an argument to save their relationship.

At the square, Jack parked on a side street that wasn't blocked off for holiday decorating.

They were walking toward the inn when he stopped. "There's my sister."

"Don't worry," Sophie said. "I won't make trouble for you."

A young woman with flying hair and a distracted, sweet smile paused in midstride, her arms full of wrapping paper, ribbon spools around her wrists like multihued bracelets.

"Callie," Jack said, and his guard went down. His affection for his sister drew Sophie in his wake. "Who are you rescuing today?"

"I have a few gifts to wrap, and I'm preparing for choir practice." Callie smiled at Sophie. "You must be the nurse from that car accident."

"Sophie Palmer." The name obviously meant nothing to Callie.

Sophie wished they could have known each other. Maybe if she'd been able to talk to Callie and Nick, they could have found a way to help Jack.

But at least they'd never have to know they were losing a niece. Sophie shook hands with Callie, ribbon spools and wrapping paper and all.

"I'm happy to meet you, but I'm about to drop all this."

"Let me help you," Jack said.

"If I hand you something, I'll drop everything else. Are you working on the decorations on the green later?"

He nodded. More than ever, Sophie felt like an outsider.

"Maybe I'll see you there," Callie said. "I put a doll in your donation box on my way out of Dockery's this morning, Jack."

"Thanks. Callie," he said, his tone deep and serious, "have you heard from Mom and Dad?"

"I got a text when they were in Yosemite."

"Mom with the trees? I got that one, too." He sounded wistful. He never allowed himself to sound like that in front of Sophie, likely thinking it made him seem weak, but she admired a man who could acknowledge his feelings. "Our parents are touring the country in an RV," he said to Sophie as if she were a stranger and he was trying to include her in the conversation.

"Jack suggested a cruise to Hawaii," Callie said, "but they wanted time all to themselves."

"I thought Mom might like the chance to be pampered," he said.

"When did you ever meet a Banning who could stand a steady diet of pampering?" his sister asked.

Jack tapped the wrapping paper tubes sticking over her shoulder. "I did have another text from them. They asked me if you were having fun, Callie. How many presents are you wrapping for your neighbors this year? If you won't slow down and enjoy the holidays, Nick and I could help you."

"I'm fine, Jack. I don't suggest you stop helping where you can."

He turned his face to Sophie's, and she remembered every word they'd spoken to each other, each argument and each laugh. There was so much between them, but he'd never mentioned her to anyone he loved, and he'd given her only the barest bones of information about himself.

He maneuvered an arm around his sister's shoulder. "I don't do enough," he said, and though his voice was teasing, he looked at Sophie with a trace of confusion, as if talking to his sister reminded him of the man he'd pretended to be with Sophie. Here, his heart seemed softer. He was less glib. He cared about the people who loved him, even as he tried to prove he didn't care about Sophie or their baby.

She tried to steel herself, but she felt as if she were sinking through the snowy air, melting into the frozen sidewalk.

"I'm not like you and Nick, Callie." Jack kissed the top of her head. "But I am trying to do the right things."

His sister's confusion made the situation more awkward.

"I'm so happy to meet you, Callie," Sophie

said. "And nice to see you, Jack. I think I'll check out the construction."

A stranger would naturally offer a brother and sister privacy. Sophie walked toward the green, where a wooden stage was being built. She stopped at the back of a slowly growing crowd.

The Jack she loved still lived inside that cold man, but she couldn't allow herself to pretend the love they'd professed for each other had been real. She'd had enough of being rejected. No matter what his motivation, she deserved better. She just wanted to be sure how he felt about their child. Maybe if he knew he'd never have to deal with Sophie, he could be a good father to his daughter.

Standing at the white picket fence, Sophie glanced back as someone called a hello to Jack.

"I'm so glad you're home," a beautiful auburn-haired woman said as she shooed her two little boys toward the green. "We still have the same number. Call us so we can all catch up."

Sophie turned away, trying not to hear his answer. She wanted that smile, the way he used to look at her as if she was all he needed to be happy. And yet, if he'd been so happy with her, why hadn't he shared his life back home? They'd visited her mother, in D.C., many times.

Why hadn't he wanted Sophie to meet his friends and family?

Somewhere, deep inside, she must have known something was wrong. She'd pretended not to notice the nightmares and the panic he tried so desperately to hide. He wouldn't talk about it, so what else could she do? She'd explained away his lack of connections, assuming it had something to do with his service.

But seeing him in the town square, she realized he'd never tried to live in both worlds. Her Jack had lived in this happy little Santa town, too. His neighbors and his family greeted him the way their colleagues in Boston had, with respect and warmth. No one would be that happy to see a man who abandoned his daughter. And he obviously didn't want anyone from Boston tainting his life here in Christmas Town.

CHAPTER SIX

JACK WAS TACKING twinkly lights onto his Victorian porch when Fred Everly strolled along the sidewalk in oil-stained overalls and a peacoat with his company logo stitched on the back. Everly Body Works. Simple. To the point.

Jack got straight to it, as well.

"Fred," he said, aiming his staple gun down as he leaned over the rail.

The other man turned. "Need a hand with that, Doc?"

"No, no. I've got it." Jack set the gun and the strand of lights on the porch railing. "How's work going? Are you busy in the run-up to the holidays?"

Fred grinned. "Is your granddad's truck in danger of failing inspection?"

"I'm not sure why everyone acts as if my truck is likely to disintegrate in the middle of the road." He stopped. Honesty was such a relief after lying or pretending, or just dancing around the truth, that he could go on about his truck for hours. "I wondered how you're doing with that nurse's car. From the wreck the other day? I happened to see her in Tessie's room at the hospital, and I realized she's stranded here."

"I'm having some problems with a few of the parts, and some of my suppliers don't push themselves so close to Christmas."

Jack imagined Sophie waking on Christmas morning alone in the B and B, in a town where he'd never mentioned her name. No one even knew they'd been together.

He'd felt bad about that, with Callie treating her as a stranger. He'd been closer to Sophie, given more of himself, trusted her with more of his secrets than he had with anyone.

He'd tried to start a new life in Boston, and when that hadn't worked, Christmas Town was waiting for him.

Why had he treated Sophie like that? And why hadn't she exposed him when she'd realized Callie didn't know about her? She had to be angry, but she'd said she wouldn't make things worse for him.

"You will finish it in time?" Jack asked. "You know she did Tessie Blaylock a huge favor?"

"Saved her life, I hear," Fred said, "but that doesn't change my deliveries. I'm going to try,

Doc, but it's Christmas. She may need to rent a car, or maybe take the train or fly."

"That's not a bad plan. And then after the New Year, you'll have her car ready and she can come back?"

"Honestly? I wouldn't be surprised. Do you know her well enough to suggest she'd be happier doing that?" Fred asked.

"We talked a little today. I could speak to her about making the most of her holidays."

"Good idea, Doc. I'll suggest it, too."

"CAREFUL OF THAT staple gun, Nurse Palmer."

She whirled and shot a staple over his shoulder. Sophie's mouth dropped open in shock. "Jack, I'm sorry. I could have hurt you." Her eyes welled with tears.

"I'm fine." He eased the tool out of her hand, nevertheless. "Don't worry."

"I'm not used to you talking to me."

"I know." He took up the holly she'd been stapling. "I've been brutal, but I wish you'd accept that I'm right."

"I'm getting there." She tugged at her hair, which was stuck in her collar. "You never meant for anyone here to know me. A man in love wouldn't pretend the woman he cared for didn't exist."

"I should have told my sister and brother," he

said. Because Sophie did matter to him. She'd been his family when he couldn't explain himself to Nick and Callie. "But maybe it's best for everyone that I've behaved unfairly from the beginning."

"You turn everything inside out." She lifted the rope of holly attached to a thick strand of jute and subtle lights that would twinkle in the darkness. "But I promise not to shoot at you again."

She'd already finished a long series of holly loops, which were wafting back and forth with the heavy breeze. "How did you end up manning the fences?" he asked.

"I had nothing else to do. Dr. Everly's brother-in-law came to the B and B at lunch and told me my car might be delayed."

Jack didn't bother with subtlety. "Maybe you should let it go for now and come back after the holidays."

"Rent a car from now until after the New Year? That's crazy," she said, and then understanding dawned. "You talked to him. You're that desperate to get me out of here?"

"He passed by my house and we spoke. He said the car might take a while, and I suggested going home could be a good idea. Your mom would be glad to see you."

"When did you become so comfortable, try-ing to manipulate me?"

"Maybe I'm tired of hurting you."

Through the snowy afternoon's green-gray light, he saw faces watching them.

Sophie turned to see what had caught his at-tention. The air wafted a dizzying scent around them—the fragrance of her shampoo. He had to be a desperate man, because that scent took him back to moments of closeness, his kiss in her hair, her whisper in his ear, feeling as if he belonged.

"People are watching us."

Anger tightened her mouth, and he couldn't help staring.

"Sophie," he said, his throat aching, "I'm thinking of you. And your baby."

"I don't care." She lifted her hands and did half a spin, as if inviting everyone in sight to join them. "I'll be gone from here. You'll be the one answering questions."

"Why didn't you tell my sister?"

Sophie's lips softened again. Her mittened hand lifted as if she was going to touch him, but at the last moment, she drew it back. Then she turned to her work on the fence. Loop the holly, hit it with a staple. "I'm angry with you. If it were just me, I'd wallow in rage that you

dumped me. I certainly wouldn't have humiliated myself by coming here."

"Why doesn't the baby make you feel that
even more strongly?"

"I told you. I don't even know my father's
name. My mother would never tell me. We
don't talk about it anymore because we want
to get along, and she's been a supportive, wonderful mom."

"And you think my name could change
things for your child?"

"Our child."

A compulsion to look down at her slightly
rounded belly was difficult to resist. "Tell me."

"You'll always have a way to find her. When
she's old enough, she can look for you, and if
you want to tell her to her face that she doesn't
matter, that's your choice. She'll have me to
lean on, and I won't have controlled her op-
tions, or made the decision for her."

Jack saw that moment in his mind. A beautiful tall girl with his dark hair and Sophie's
blue eyes confronting him because he'd stayed
out of her life.

"Jack, are you all right?"

He came out of the scene where he let down
the one child who had a right to his loyalty. "I
would've been if you'd stayed away. Why do

you need her to be mine? I told you I'd be responsible for her."

Sophie looked around them. No one was close. Hammering went on at the stage and power stapling rang out as if everyone on the green was doing target practice.

"Our baby girl deserves all the love both of us can give her."

"You don't understand." He wanted to shout, to rip down the holly ropes, to persuade Sophie to give up this ridiculous fight and get out of his town.

"And you refuse to explain. But I have to be the best mom I can be, so I'm doing what I believe is right for my daughter. I've seen you with patients, with friends' children. You're gentle and kind. You talk to them as if they matter. You can give that to kids who walk out of your life the next second, but you can't give yourself to your own daughter?"

"Now you understand. But you still haven't explained why you didn't tell my sister."

"I don't know what goes on when you're like this." Sophie gestured toward the perspiration that was cold at his temple. "But I do know my child will have family here, and I don't want your sister to think badly of you."

"I didn't tell my family about you because I never planned to come back here."

"What?" The word left her mouth in a whisper. She turned back to the fence and resumed working in silence. Jack followed. He could have walked away, but realized what he was doing to her.

He didn't have enough courage to risk loving the baby they had made together. How could he do that when he was already fighting every day to be sane, to look normal because of another child?

"Why did you come back here after you left me?" She tugged more holly out of his tight grip. "I was so sad after you walked out, I would have screamed at the first jaunty caroler."

"They don't sing all year." He couldn't explain his need for familiar faces, for the love of his brother and sister, if he couldn't have Sophie's anymore.

"Sophie Palmer," a man called out. Tessie's cousin, Otto Taver, must have heard enough about Sophie to recognize her, a stranger helping out like a Christmas Townie.

Uncharacteristically shy, she nodded, stepping closer to Jack. Did she even realize she'd eased his way for support? He didn't move. For this moment, he wouldn't abandon her, even though Otto meant no harm.

"Just wanted to thank you." The other man

yanked off his thick gloves and shook her hand, hard. "Tessie's my cousin. I hear she might have ended up in big trouble if not for you."

"Thank you, but she only needed a tourniquet. Jack did the hard part."

"That's not true," Jack said, unable to stop himself from putting the story straight. "That tourniquet saved Tessie's life."

"I'm glad you were there to tie it." Otto shook her hand again and nodded at Jack. "Doc, good to see you." He strode off, heading toward the stage with his tool bag.

Sophie pushed her hands into her coat pockets. "You were the one who saved her life," she said.

"She wouldn't have had a life to save if you hadn't stopped her bleeding."

"How do you manage their expectations?" she asked, looking around. "Don't you know you could fail them, too?"

"I'm trying not to mess up."

She was silent for a moment and then shivered. He took the stapler and balanced it on the fence. "Are you cold?"

"A little."

"You shouldn't let your core cool. Why don't you head back to the B and B?"

"I'm fine if I keep moving."

"Georgette told you to rest, didn't she?"

"I haven't been overdoing it." Sophie's low, intense tone and the pulse beating just above the collar of her coat dared him to express concern about the unborn infant he was so intent on abandoning.

"I'm not an animal," he said. "I don't want you or the baby to be at risk. I'll walk you back to Esther's."

"I'm capable of walking by myself."

"I'm walking with you, Sophie."

She gave in. He handed the stapler to one of the other helpers and turned back toward Sophie.

She had already started across the green, but Jack caught up in a few steps. "Will you please consider taking Fred Everly's advice and go home until your car's ready?"

"Your advice."

"It's a good plan."

"I'm not coming back here. When I leave, I'm gone for good." She pushed ahead of him. "Which means your clock is ticking, Jack."

He caught up again. "Stop running away."

She turned to him, her hair flying in a gust of snow. "No one has ever made me as angry as you."

Or as desperate. He saw it in her eyes. She

needed to understand, and he'd never explained what had happened to him.

He watched the woman he'd loved desperately trying to avoid him, as if she couldn't bear to share the same oxygen.

If he told her, maybe they'd find a way. Maybe she'd help him see his future in a different light. He started to reach for her shoulder, then stopped himself and let her add to the distance between them.

WHEN THEY REACHED the B and B, Sophie said goodbye over her shoulder as she ran up the salted steps and into the house, shutting the door behind her.

In the foyer, people were laughing, anticipating a late lunch or an early dinner. Sophie nodded at Esther as she took off her mittens and stuffed them into her coat pocket.

"Hungry?" her hostess asked.

"Not right now. Maybe later."

"Do you want a menu to take to your room?"

Sophie shook her head. "No, thanks."

She hurried up the stairs. She'd threatened Jack with a ticking clock, but she was the one who felt Big Ben banging out the passing quarter hours in the back of her head.

Inside her room, she sat with a sense of relief, suddenly understanding Jack's ability to hide from the truth or the past, or whatever horrible moments had their claws in him.

Someone knocked on her door and she jumped. For a second, Sophie hoped. With all her heart, with all the foolishness of a pregnant woman who still cared too intensely for the man who'd left her.

But then she came to her senses and opened the door.

A uniformed policeman and a woman in a dark suit waited in the hall. The officer lifted his cap. "I'm Sergeant Reese. This is Celia Dane. She's a probation officer with Christmas County. You may not remember me, but I was at the accident scene after Tessie Blaylock struck your car."

"I remember." Vaguely. He'd taken a brief statement as the EMTs were checking her vitals inside the ambulance. "What can I do for you?"

"May we come in?" Ms. Dane asked.

Anxiety bloomed inside Sophie's chest. No nurse wanted to go to court. But it was a fact of life that came with her job. No one wanted to take anyone down, or prop someone else up, without good reason. Tessie's future was too much responsibility.

The same way a baby's future might seem like too much responsibility?

Sophie held the door open. "I don't have anything to offer you here, but could I call down to ask for coffee? Or water?"

"Just talk," Ms. Dane said.

They took the chairs at either side of the fireplace. Sophie sat on the tufted chest at the end of the bed.

"I know you've spoken to Tessie," the probation officer said. "I have to check on her, too. I've spoken to her teachers, her friends and her parents. I've even had a word with her doctors."

"Jack Banning?" Sophie hadn't asked him how he felt about Tessie's mistake.

"And her GP. I'd like to hear your version of the accident."

"I spoke to Officer Reese, and I wrote a statement for the police."

"But I need to hear what you remember now." Celia smiled. "We're not out to get Tessie. We want to do the right thing to make sure this doesn't happen again."

Someone else knocked at the door. Sophie stood. "Excuse me. You probably know Esther's a little protective of her guests."

She was wrong again. Jack stood on the threshold. He looked distracted and unsettled, but determined. "I thought you might need—" he looked past her, into the room "—something."

Baffled, Sophie let him in. "I'm fine."

"You act as if you're concerned, Jack," the officer said.

"Sophie's alone here. She doesn't know many people."

"Let me repeat what I told your friend," Celia said, and Jack didn't deny that they knew each other. "We're searching for the right solution for Tessie. We already know this accident was not Sophie's fault."

Jack backed down, but Sophie couldn't look away from him.

"Ms. Palmer?" the officer said.

She returned her attention to the visitors. "I already told you how it happened. I came off the exit ramp and saw Tessie driving toward me. She was weaving. She saw my car and tried to swerve." Sophie reached behind her neck to smooth out her hair. To breathe in and out. Her baby was okay, but those horrifying moments replayed in startling clarity. She glanced at Jack again. Was this what happened to him?

"Are you all right?" he asked.

"I'm fine." She turned to Officer Reese, her blood thrumming in her ears. "We collided. I saw she was hurt. I applied a tourniquet, and the emergency services arrived."

"Why did you feel the need to speak to her in the hospital?" Celia asked.

Sophie hesitated. "I think it's because I was so afraid she would die out on that road." She splayed her hands over her belly. "And maybe because I'm pregnant. I wanted to make sure she was all right. I wanted to know if she was remorseful, and I believe she is."

"You can't think she deserves a free pass?" Officer Reese asked, angry in the way of a man who'd seen too many injured drivers.

"I believe Tessie when she says she won't ever touch her phone again while she's driving. I believe in second chances. Don't you have driver's safety courses? Couldn't she speak to the children at her school—at all the schools near here?"

"That's what I'm considering." Celia turned to the policeman. "I think Sophie's suggesting that Tessie has already paid for her carelessness."

"She almost died," Sophie said. "And she was terrified that she'd hurt me and my child. That's a lot of responsibility for a teenager."

"If she remembers this. If she never forgets what might have happened," Reese said.

"You probably know I'm an ER nurse in

Boston. I've talked to a lot of people who pretend to feel remorse for things they've done. Tessie's relief when she saw me was real."

"Jack already gave us that speech," Reese said.

"He did?"

Jack shrugged but then moved so his shoulder touched hers. "Everyone in this room has faced people they have to trust or doubt," he said. "I need to know patients aren't lying about the meds they're taking, or the extent and location of pain. Reese, here, has to judge every word an offender says to him. And Celia—she has to know when a kid like Tessie deserves probation or when she needs to be locked away."

"You believe Tessie, too, Jack?"

"I'd put her on courses and community service to make sure she never forgets what might have happened, but I do believe she's sorry."

Reese's smirk worried Sophie. Celia nodded slowly, making notes on the pad she'd balanced on her knee. When she finished, she clicked her pen and rose, smoothing her skirt.

"That's it, Officer. Let's leave these people to their evening. I'll let you know, Sophie, if you need to come to court."

Sophie managed not to quiver at the thought she might still hold Tessie's future in her hands.

They walked to the white door together, but Jack stayed behind. Sophie tried not to look shocked.

"They came up to the steps as I was walking away," he told her when the two of them were alone. "I tried to leave, but I didn't want you to face them by yourself. Reese has a reputation for being hard-nosed, and he's not above bullying you to testify against Tessie."

"You tried to leave?"

He unzipped his coat. "Do you think I want to keep getting involved?"

"I'm glad you couldn't help yourself." She turned him toward the door. "But I'm tired and hungry, so I'll leave you to stew over the idea that someday our daughter might do something, accidentally, that involves the police. And I'll be her only defense."

His face paled.

"I was joking, Jack! I'm a responsible person with a good job. I'd call an attorney." As she eased him through the door, Sophie couldn't help liking the shock on his face. The most detached man in the world had suddenly seen a future where his child might need him. It was about time.

CHAPTER SEVEN

THE DAYS SLIPPED BY, and Christmas drew ever closer. Jack performed trauma surgeries, did his rounds and collected toys for children in the hospital, as well as those whose families needed a little help this year.

Each afternoon at three, Santa's sleigh, drawn by two massive farm horses, glided to a halt on the snow-covered green. Santa alighted from his seat and fell happily into the swarm of children demanding candy canes and chocolates as they offered gift ideas for themselves, their siblings and friends.

Jack had started parking his truck a few miles east to avoid Santa and the adoring youngsters. But he couldn't forget the old days, when he'd worked as an EMT during breaks from school. His ambulance had often sat on the green to be on hand in case of emergency. Sipping hot chocolate from a stand near his post, he'd enjoyed the shouts of *a puppy for my baby sister* and *a little brother* and *a fire engine that shoots water*. Some asked for video game systems with names that were already unfamiliar, because he was too busy to play any kind of game.

Now, his friends would be taking their own children to see Santa, and next year, Sophie would likely take their baby to visit a Santa in Boston.

Someday his little girl might be a pint-sized video game wizard.

In a few days he'd be playing Santa at the hospital. His grandfather had done the job until he couldn't drive the blue truck over there anymore. Jack's dad had taken over, but this year, Jack had to fill in. He dreaded it. Happy children who had no idea what existed in the world outside this town pretty much unmanned him, but he couldn't let them down.

He veered toward the green, parking close to the square. Listening to the sounds of Christmas might help him brace himself for an evening as the hospital's jolly old elf. It was the way he'd gotten used to being around families before he'd lost that little girl in surgery. He'd helped with rounds on the children's floor, walked through the common, even eaten dinner out.

He glanced at his watch. Five minutes before three.

He reached the holly-covered fence just as

the gates opened for Santa's sleigh. Jack was about to walk through one of the decorated arches when he noticed Sophie, one foot on the fence's bottom rung, laughing as the children surged forward in a line that snaked with their exuberance.

The Victorian carolers that strolled through Christmas Town from Thanksgiving until New Year's Day burst into "Here Comes Santa Claus."

Sophie's laughter was a temptation he couldn't resist. She included him in her joy, as if she'd expected to see him. "Could they be more on the nose?"

"The kids love it," he said. Best he could manage when he was breathing her in, like a man starved of oxygen.

"So do their parents. Look how happy they all are."

He always saw; it was part of his self-administered therapy. Families survived. Fate didn't draw a target on everyone who dared to be happy.

Sophie pointed to his scrub pants. "Are you headed for work?"

He nodded. "What are you doing out here?"

"I'm losing my cynicism," she said. "This is the most holiday-loving town in the world. You people are genuinely excited to embrace

Christmas." She gave him a teasing, sidelong glance. "Well, most of you, anyway."

"You want to hear something funny?" It didn't feel at all funny, with his throat closing up and his head aching every time he thought of it.

"I'd love to."

"I'm the hospital Santa night after tomorrow. We give the children on pediatrics a Christmas party every year."

"You're Santa?" Her surprise got under his skin, but he couldn't blame her. "I don't understand you," she said, stepping away from the fence.

Each time he saw her, he was more tempted to explain, but what if he said he'd try? What if he said that, deep down, he felt as protective of his child as she did, and that paternal compulsion had driven him to leave her and stay away? "Maybe I'll see you before you leave town." Cutting off whatever she'd been about to say, he headed for the truck.

"Jack," she said.

He turned back.

"I hope you imagine her face as you hand out each present."

He snapped his head away, to hide pain like

a blow to the gut. If he could stop imagining their daughter's face, abandoning her would be so much easier.

FROM THE MOMENT Jack had said he was going to be Santa, Sophie knew she'd show up for the toy distribution. She'd never felt a need to punish herself before, making her decision to go as inexplicable as Jack's own behavior.

But her car would be repaired soon. She'd never have to see Jack again, and maybe watching him playing Santa for children who had no claims on him would finally convince her he was right.

She offered to gather the last few toys out of Esther's collection box while she waited for a cab.

"Thanks for taking these." Esther piled them into a canvas shopping tote. She sighed as she patted the bag, smoothing it into a less lumpy shape. "I love this town. It's full of caring people."

"Do you?" Sophie didn't see the town in quite that way, but Jack's behavior had colored her view. He was saving himself by abandoning their daughter.

She wasn't like Jack. She couldn't turn her back on someone without trying to fix whatever had gone wrong.

"We try to help each other," Esther said. "Just look at the green. How many places in this world do you know where everyone in town donates a good amount of money and time every year to do something that's nice for the children?"

Sophie took the bag, smiling. "If you aren't head of the tourist board, they're suffering a great loss. The adults seem to enjoy it, too, and the tourists are growing ever thicker on the ground."

"You'll understand soon. You'll be even happier at Christmas once you're sharing it with your own kidlet."

If only Jack could see that. "There's my taxi." Sophie waved as she went through the door. "See you later, Esther."

"Sing extra loud for me."

The carolers in their Victorian finery were already making the walls echo when Sophie stepped off the elevator on the hospital's third floor. Dr. Everly came over to greet her.

"I didn't expect you. Everything okay?"

Sophie held up her bag as she shrugged out of her coat. "I had a few things to deliver," she said.

"Oh, good. Always room under the tree."

Sophie added her packages to the impressive pile. "There aren't this many children in the hospital?"

"Whatever we don't give out we take to the green for distribution later."

"Where's Santa?" Sophie focused on folding her bag.

"Waiting until all the children arrive. He doesn't dare show his face early. There'd be a riot."

"How did Jack end up playing Santa?" she asked.

"His grandfather used to play Santa, and now his dad does, but his parents are touring the country in an RV during the holidays. No one expects them back."

Sophie still didn't understand that. Instead of providing a polite answer, she waited in silence, hoping Dr. Everly would explain. Sophie was eager for any tidbit that might explain Jack's behavior.

"They took care of Jack's grandmother for years. She had debilitating epilepsy that couldn't be controlled by medication. She endured several experimental surgeries and I don't know how many drug trials. Nothing worked, and when she couldn't be left alone, the whole family pitched in. She passed away recently, and the elder Bannings took off for the first time since I've known them. I think they didn't know what to do with themselves."

"When did his grandmother die?" Sophie already knew. The "business trip" he'd taken in May. He'd disappeared for nine days, and when he came back, he'd been jumpy and moody, and had made excuses to avoid spending time with her.

If only she'd taken the hint then.

"I think it was just before…oh, I know. The week my children got out of school, end of May." Dr. Everly guided Sophie toward a table with punch and cookies set out on plates stamped with The Tea Pot's logo. "He'd hate us discussing him."

"I didn't mean to." Maybe her desperation, even for her baby, didn't make snooping acceptable, but at last his story was starting to make sense.

They both sipped punch, and Dr. Everly introduced her to members of the hospital staff, who'd also brought their children to the event.

Everyone sang. When a small group of pajama-and-robe-clad children began to recite "'Twas the Night Before Christmas," the festivities had started. Nurses and doctors drifted among the little knots of young patients, passing out treats and punch. Sophie joined in. Even her own little girl seemed to understand she was at a party. The fluttery sensations intensified, lending Sophie strength and smothering her guilt over badgering Dr. Everly.

The carolers offered a few more selections until the children began to fidget, growing impatient for the big arrival. Sophie couldn't blame them. What little child hadn't firmly feared Santa would never come?

CHAPTER EIGHT

IF HE HAD to hear one more Christmas carol…
The cheerful voices and hopeful lyrics were
bitter enough to make Jack want to cancel the
holidays. He couldn't wish anyone a merry,
merry anything, and he was sweating inside
the Santa suit.

All those children out there. Waiting to see
him.

Hopeful, happy, expectant.

They weren't waiting for him. Just for the
man he was playing.

As he'd played a strong, decent man for Sophie, until she'd actually needed him. If she
could see him now, she'd have to agree he was
right about keeping their child out of his life.
He'd worked himself into a cowardly sweat
over pretending to be a nonexistent hero for
sick children, kids who were depending on him
to be a plausible Santa Claus.

He shaped the pillows beneath his coat,
eased the furnacelike beard over his moist
upper lip and opened the door before he was

tempted to head back to Boston instead of doing one simple job that his family expected him to complete.

Jack saw twinkling lights, colorful presents beneath the tree and a red velvet bag bulging with the gifts the volunteers had gathered for him to distribute.

The singing stopped. The chatter stopped. The children stopped.

Their faces turned as one. Joy shone on some, disbelief on others. Most terrifying of all, some of these innocent babies looked at him with naked hope.

"Ho, ho, ho." It sounded pathetic and weak to him, muffled by his beard. No one else minded.

Cheers and shouts and laughter rang out, and the children flooded his way as if he were the best surprise ever.

The breath left his body in a gasp only he could hear. He was light-headed, but stayed upright by sheer force of will.

Laughter became the scream of rockets launching. Shouts became the whistle of tracer bullets passing by his ears.

He saw a face, small, bloody, in pain.

He reeled back, thankful to have his backward plunge stopped by the red bag he was supposed to haul around the room.

Again, the children didn't seem to notice, but, hyperaware, Jack witnessed the looks tossed between his colleagues. Georgette Everly looked at Sophie as if she might know what was going on.

Sophie didn't seem to catch the doctor's silent question. She'd already begun to weave toward him, through the knots of happy children.

"Did you forget your clves, Santa? I'll help you with these beautiful presents."

She rested her hand on his shoulder, gripping him in a way that dragged him into the present. He didn't even care that she must feel the perspiration soaking him underneath the jacket. He took the chair she pushed his way, and let her fish the first few gifts from the sack.

On each tag, a code noted whether the gift was for a boy or girl, and another sorted it by age range. He stared at the letter and numbers, unable to put it all together.

"Boy, seven to nine," Sophie whispered next to him, already diving for the next gift.

He called a boy up and handed it over, managing small talk that made the child laugh. Jack and Sophie kept up the act, with him avoiding his curious colleagues until he recovered his composure enough to focus.

Sophie stayed with him as he took the last

of the gifts to the children too ill to walk up to him.

After everyone received a gift and good wishes, he went to the goody table.

"I might take a couple of these delicious cookies for my reindeer," he said. "I'm sorry this hospital won't let them in to visit with you children, too. I hope you're all feeling well soon. Thank you for having me at your party today." He gave a much jollier "Ho, ho, ho" and returned to his makeshift dressing room, amid a chorus of goodbyes and Merry Christmases.

Sophie slipped in behind him, hugging the empty red velvet bag. "Are you all right?" she asked. "Are you ill?"

"I'm fine. You should go before I have to explain what you're doing in here with me."

"I don't care what anyone thinks. You're not safe to drive. Where are you going from here?"

"I'm fine."

"Who do you think you're talking to? Let me check your vitals."

He knew what she'd find. His pulse was sky-high and his blood pressure probably made a stroke seem like his next destination.

The memories he'd been fighting made him unsafe. Sounds and faces and pain he was keeping at bay by pretending he didn't hear, see or feel them. He just needed to look normal long enough to push Sophie out of his escape route.

"I'll take a ride if you can drive my truck."

"Are you kidding? I learned on a stick. My mom and I thought we were so cool, driving around in her old Rambler." Sophie nodded at his red suit. "Are you changing clothes?"

"Wait here. Don't go back out there."

"Whatever, Jack."

He slipped out the back door and headed for the bathroom. Sophie didn't understand. His neighbors in this small town tended to be nosy. They'd want to know why the nurse he'd never admitted knowing had followed him from the party.

He wrestled with the Santa costume, breathing deeply as he got his head out of the jacket. It wasn't just panic and memories. That getup was hot.

Sophie was waiting, her coat over her arm, when he went back to the office where he'd left her. They headed to the elevators. When the door opened, they joined two other surgeons already back in scrubs. As the elevator stopped at their floor, one of the men turned back.

"Good night, Santa."

"Ho, ho, ho."

Laughing, the two men went their separate ways and the doors slid shut.

"Feeling better?" Sophie asked.

"Yeah." Jack wasn't about to discuss what had happened.

"You're doing me a favor. I'd have to take a cab if I wasn't riding with you."

"Drive to the B and B. I'll be fine to go the rest of the way to my house."

"Oddly, the pregnant woman is steadier than you right now, and it's barely a block to walk." She held out her hand for the keys as they exited the hospital.

Once they were in the truck, she started the engine and reversed smoothly. Soon they were on the two-lane road back to town. She drove toward his town house near the square.

"This is a Christmas gift. A parking spot in front of your home."

Sophie's good cheer didn't quite mask her steely mood. Something was on her mind. He'd gone along with her wishes so far, but he was losing patience.

"Thanks for the ride." He held out his hand for the keys.

Sophie got out and met him in front of the hood.

"Why don't you leave?" he asked, his throat so tight it hurt to speak.

"I will, Jack. You just tell me why I'm going. Why I'm giving up when I loved you for two years, unconditionally. I didn't talk about it, but I noticed the way you dreamed. The odd way you reacted in the subway sometimes, or on the Common or at a play, when you'd suddenly break into a cold sweat and drag me out. I assumed the problem was enclosed places, or crowds."

"No." It was children. Always children. Laughing or crying. Happy or sad. Children being children.

She closed her eyes, all but begging the thin, cold air for patience, and handed him his keys. "Let me talk to you. If we can't sort out our problems tonight, I'll go home, and you won't see me or the baby until she's old enough to make a different choice." Sophie gripped her hands together. "A few minutes—not an expensive price to pay for the one thing you want."

He did want her and the baby away from him, no matter what he had to do. He couldn't face the kind of utter annihilation she was asking him to risk.

Not ever again.

"You have to tell me, Jack. I don't understand, and I can't walk away until you explain." Frustration made her so vulnerable he had to resist reaching out for her. Wanting to comfort her and push her away at the same time.

He walked to the narrow door of his town house and unlocked it. The foyer held a bench and a small sofa, just large enough for two. He turned on a lamp and took up a stance at the newel post on the stairs opposite.

She looked frustrated, as if she'd expected him to collapse in some sort of admission.

"I think I'm figuring it out." She pulled off her mittens and her cap. She unbuttoned her coat, and he went to the thermostat midway down the hall to make sure the house was warm enough.

To take his face out of the light, so she couldn't see him.

"I'm trying to do the right thing, Sophie. If I wanted you to know, I would have told you two years ago."

"Something's wrong with you. It's not just that one of the most decent men I've ever known suddenly became the most despicable." She stroked her belly as if tracing her hands over the baby, a habit she'd formed since he'd left Boston. Maybe she'd had to love this baby for two.

"That's why you should stay away from me. You shouldn't consider telling that little girl my name."

"I think it started when your grandmother died."

He froze. Ice seemed to form in the veins of his feet.

"Dr. Everly told me your family was helping her because of her illness. When she died, you could have asked me to come with you. We'd talked about marriage. We'd both said we loved each other. Were you lying?"

The temptation to lie now nearly killed him. "No."

"You came here for her funeral, and you made sure your family wouldn't know you were involved with a woman…"

"Let's stop this."

"Then you lost that baby in surgery, that little girl."

The ice started to prickle his scalp. "Stop it."

"I can't. It's all part of a pattern, and I believe losing your grandmother and that little girl took you back to whatever you're trying to forget."

"I don't know how to make it clearer that I'm through with you, Sophie. Get out of my house."

This time she didn't even flinch. Her determination was as strong as his. "I have to know, so I won't ever be tempted to come back here again."

He shook his head. He'd never told anyone about that night in Afghanistan.

"How can you believe you'll be happier without your own daughter?" Sophie asked, the wonder in her eyes pulling him deeper, because she'd loved him. She'd believed in him when he'd forgotten how to believe in himself.

"Rent a car and go back to Boston, Sophie. I'm trying to keep her safe. I don't want her to be in—"

"What are you talking about?" She stood, reaching for him, but her hands on his only triggered another cold sweat and a pounding heartbeat that ached in his head. "Why wouldn't she be safe? The surgery on that little girl was a long shot, Jack. You did it knowing you were likely to fail. Even the parents knew you were battling stiff odds. You can't still believe you did something wrong."

"I didn't do anything wrong." He raked his hands down his face. "That's the point. The surgery was a success, if you don't count the fact that the eleven-month-old girl died."

He'd been unsettled after his grandmother's death, suddenly reluctant to be as close to Sophie or anyone.

Being alone had come easier, because he didn't have to share any part of himself.

But the dreams had started again the night of the operation. Dreams that left him shaking, unable to breathe as he stared at the ceiling, sleepless and helpless. That little girl had reminded him of the boy. In the dark, he heard that child's cries, in a voice so weak Jack had had to lean down to hear as he ran, carrying his tiny weight.

Sophie wrapped her arms around herself. "Maybe I've asked for too much. I'm not sure I can talk about babies who don't survive."

"I'm getting out of here." He stood, ready to abandon her in his own home. "Call a cab, or try Esther for a ride."

"No." She sounded short. Unforgiving.

She hurried to the door behind him and caught him close, sliding her arms around his waist. "I've let you go over and over again. This time you're facing me and our baby, and you are going to explain yourself."

He shook his head, parting her hands and removing himself from warmth he didn't deserve.

"Yes," Sophie said, "because I don't want to wonder what else I could have done. I want you out of my head and gone from my heart, so I need the truth, if the truth will finally make me see why you're not worth a fight."

"If that's what it takes," he said. But if telling her was easy, he would have, months ago.

He eased her to the sofa and stalked around the room. He'd locked the words away so long.

He'd fended off the memories with activity and work and empty conversation.

Jack glanced back at Sophie and her swollen stomach.

"What happened to you?" she asked, bare and honest, no bravado. Just begging for the truth.

She deserved honesty. She was carrying his child.

"I'm trying to tell you."

She linked her fingers together, so tightly her knuckles turned white. "It happened in Afghanistan?"

He paced again, trying to produce the words.

"Were you on a base?" she asked.

He had to do this. Make her understand.

"One of our patrols was attacked," he finally spat out. "Everyone suffered injuries, but one man was critical." Jack rubbed the back of his hand across his mouth, which was as dry as that hard dirt and sand. "You wouldn't believe the terrain. The guy had six gunshot wounds, as well as shrapnel from a homemade bomb. They tried to bring him back to base, but the night was freezing." Even wearing a coat and boots and every conceivable item of protective clothing, Jack had shivered. He shivered again as that cold crept back into the marrow of his bones.

"The attackers didn't stop hunting them. One soldier made it to base, and he asked me if I'd go back out with him. They were afraid the injured guy wouldn't survive the night."

"That's the man I thought you were," Sophie said.

"They'd found a lean-to—a tarp spread out on posts. I treated the injured man. Around midnight we put him on a makeshift stretcher so we could carry him out as soon as we had enough light."

What came next stopped him. The hardest, most hellish night of his whole life—if he was lucky and careful.

His legs shook again, making him worry he was about to fall. He sat in front of Sophie, on the floor, as if he were back in that hut.

"An hour after I finished treating the rest of the wounded, we heard noise outside. The Special Ops guys surrounded my patient and me. We braced for another attack." His voice deserted him, along with all the air in his lungs. His throat swelled shut. Seconds ticked by. Seconds filled with gut-wrenching fear, the scratch of the canvas across his patient's chest, where Jack had thrown himself to protect the man from further injury.

"We heard children. Crying, but trying not to because they knew noise could get them

killed." Jack looked at Sophie, seeing the rag-
tag bunch who'd eased inside the lean-to, all
skidding to a halt. "Eight orphans, lost boys
and girls who couldn't find their families, but
they'd made one on their own, out there in that
desolation, and they clung to each other." He
needed water—as badly as he had that night,
when all he could taste was sand and terror.
"The oldest was thirteen, a girl who was carrying her little brother. He was three, and he'd
been shot during the earlier battle. The children had been hiding in a ravine, but a stray
attacker's bullet had hit this kid in the shoulder, and the little girl dragged those children
all over that wasteland, looking for the doctor
who'd be treating the soldiers, so he could save
her little brother."

A sound in Sophie's throat dragged Jack's
gaze off his feet. Tears blurred her eyes, making them glitter. Her bottom lip trembled, just
as that little girl's had when she'd held out her
brother to the hard men in uniform.

"The boy was bad. He'd lost a lot of blood.
I didn't know how to tell her the odds were
against us." Jack's voice cracked. "She helped
me calm him. She wouldn't leave his side.
When I saw the wound, I didn't want to op-
erate, but he wouldn't survive till morning if
I didn't."

The girl had begged him in words he hadn't understood, but he'd felt her love for her brother. "I removed the bullet, packed the wound. Our translator had barely told his sister the boy had a chance, when the second attack came."

Jack stared at Sophie, not seeing her, but the strange Christmas-twinkling lights of tracer fire.

"They'd followed my boy's blood trail. We had no choice. Stay there and be mowed down, or run." His heart pumped. "I picked up the boy. The Special Ops guys grabbed the stretcher and the other kids. We ran, as quietly as we could. Some of the children cried. The little guy I was carrying woke enough to whimper into my chest."

Jack closed his eyes, reliving that particular torture. Running, holding the boy protectively, leaving space for the toddler's troubled breathing. Jack had whispered words of comfort. For a second, he felt again the deep relief that came after the little guy passed out.

"We followed our leader. It seemed like miles. Eventually, all we could hear was gunfire and our gasps for air."

"Jack."

Was she begging him to stop? Trying to offer comfort?

The story would hurt as much to hear as to

tell. But this was the truth that would keep her and their innocent child out of his life, where they belonged.

He had to finish.

"Out of nowhere, we reached a camp. I don't know if our guys knew there was another patrol out there, but they found backup, and we were safe. We stumbled through those lines, and it was like winning a marathon. The soldier on the stretcher lived. He's still in rehab."

Sophie started and held her stomach. He looked up, interpreted the wonder on her face. His baby had moved. At this point, Sophie should be feeling feathery tickles. A flutter that no doubt comforted her in the middle of his nightmarish story.

"Do you think she can feel what I'm feeling?" Sophie asked.

"I hope not."

"That little boy…"

"We lost four of the children. Fifty percent. We carried their bodies with us. A little girl who was clinging to our guide's hand as she was killed. A boy who was too high on a sergeant's shoulder. Another boy who presented a clear target, even though the soldier carrying him tried to cover the child with his body." Jack closed his mouth. Bile rose to the back of his throat. If only he could vomit out this memory and rid himself of it forever. "And my little guy. Sweet and clean, wrapped in clothing the soldiers had donated to keep him warm and safe from shock. Gone. I thought he'd passed out from the pain of being jolted across that dark valley. He'd died. We couldn't get him back. His is the face I see in nightmares, feeling peace I couldn't give him. I hear him cry the second I'm alarmed about anything. His is the loss I began to live again when my sweet grandmother died, who thought she was a burden on our family, and when I lost that little girl in October."

Sophie didn't speak. Jack stood, going to the door, staring out at snow drifting on his porch, blowing down the street.

Clean, white, untouched snow.

"I cannot—I will not—lose another child."

"You didn't hurt anyone. You tried your best." Sophie sniffed hard, and he realized, in the strange, mundane way life had of intruding, that he didn't have a tissue in the house to offer her. "What else could you have tried?" she asked.

"I'm not getting involved in another child's life."

"That's crazy. You'd make your own little girl believe you abandoned her rather than risk losing her? You're throwing her away."

Sophie hadn't run through the night, willing that boy to live. "I was so grateful I managed to carry him to safety. But the second we stepped into the light, I saw he'd died."

"You need to talk to someone. That little boy's memory chased you all over Boston, and now it's happening here. You tried to handle it yourself, and it's not working."

His temper woke up. "Talking won't change anything. I can't face having this happen again. Not with my child." He met her gaze, his own a humiliating blur. "Not with your child."

She came to him, grabbed his hand and pressed it to her stomach. "This is our child. Yours and mine."

He yanked his hand away and stepped around her.

The truth had made her look like Sophie again, calm and certain.

"You know how to treat trauma, but not your own, Jack. Talk to someone who can help you learn to live with these memories."

"I know what any therapist will tell me. I do what I need to do, and I was fine for two years."

He would not be telling that story again. To anyone.

Heartache and empathy warmed Sophie's eyes, but she barely gave him a few seconds' thought before she made a decision. She stood, putting on her coat. "I should have talked to you when I knew something was wrong. This isn't a situation where a physician can heal himself."

"I can handle it."

Could he? How long had he pretended he was afraid of another child being hurt around him, when his real fear had been losing their daughter? For the first time since he'd left Boston, he let himself hope she wouldn't listen to him. She wouldn't let him push her away.

"You were right," she said, after all the arguing, all her insistence. "I can't let you be part of her life unless you get better. With the best intentions in the world, you could hurt her when she needs you most."

Despite all his ruthless work to achieve this end, her words cut into him.

"You are not some metaphysical lightning rod for danger," she said. "If our child ever needed your skills, you'd be the first surgeon I'd call. But you will abandon her again if you don't admit you have a problem you can't handle on your own."

She dragged her hair from beneath the collar of her coat. His fingers tingled as he remembered the silky slide of those strands against his palm.

"Here's the thing, Jack." Tugging on her hat, she went to his door. He followed her, no longer in control of his own body. "You just described a night that was so traumatic you never shared it with me. But you claimed to love me."

He couldn't answer. He had loved her. Loving her had helped him heal from that night, those weeks, those years.

She flattened her palm against his chest.

It took all his willpower not to cover her hand and beg her to stay.

"I feel different now that I've told you. Calm."

"Because you told me the worst thing you know about yourself, and it was something nightmarish that happened to you, not something you did wrong. You've made a start. You have to live with the past. Like that soldier is negotiating rehab. You have your own rehab to do."

"Thanks, Nurse Palmer."

She shrugged. "I sound pedantic? That's funny, because if I put your hand over my heart, you'd feel it beating as if I were in a race. I came to this town to give you a chance with your daughter because I thought I knew you better than you knew yourself."

"And now that you do know me, you don't want me?" His success didn't satisfy as much as he'd expected. His relief faded. She would not be coming back.

"My coming to you now only hurt me, because I can't seem to stop myself from caring what happens to you, but I can't go on creating opportunities for you to abandon our daughter."

He didn't say anything. The cold, hard earth had opened up again. They'd finally reached the same conclusion.

"After I leave, you might realize how much your choice will hurt her. One day she'll ask about you and find out you didn't want her because you were afraid. If that's the man you are, then that's fine." Sophie's voice broke, and she paused, straightening the tips of her mittens. "But if you're the man I loved, who'd carry an injured boy miles across a battlefield, shielding his body with yours, find a therapist who can make you remember real life is worth standing your ground and putting up the fight that will make you whole again."

Only habit stopped him from telling her he loved her still and he always would. The Jack she'd known would have said those words, and he would have tried to believe they fixed everything.

He shut the door at her back, leaning his

forehead on the chilled glass in the diamond cutout.

He'd told the truth at last. Sophie had helped him find some freedom. He could free himself if he found a way to live honestly, but he had to make sure she wasn't just another safe place to hide his secrets. She deserved a whole human being, not the wreck who'd wasted so much time trying to hide his broken pieces.

Jack sat on the stairs, burying his face in his hands. He didn't know how to cry, but he pictured that boy's face and he felt stillness, loss. His body heaved, but he didn't fight the horror. He let it shake him like a rag.

Or like a man who wanted to feel again.

CHAPTER NINE

HE'D TRIED SO hard to avoid Sophie, but Christmas Town felt empty now that she'd gone. He went about his rounds. He checked in with Fred Everly, who'd agreed to have her car driven to Boston when it was finished. Jack stopped for breakfast at The Tea Pot and dinner at Esther's.

The day after she left, he'd woken, hung over with emotion and regret. He called his friend in rehab and asked about the therapist who'd helped him. Dialing that number was almost as difficult as letting Sophie leave, believing they were through.

He'd had his first appointment that night and came out aching, angry, but grateful to Sophie for believing he possessed the courage to seek help. Jack had wanted to call her and tell her he was trying, but he couldn't think of living with their baby yet, and that fear would keep Sophie from letting him back into her life.

He kept going to his daily appointments.

About a week later, he was stumbling downstairs in search of coffee when he found a package on the floor beneath the mail slot.

Inside was a photo of his family. His parents and grandparents, his brother and sister. Secret Santa had struck. So far, Jack hadn't been able to face the thought of Christmas shopping, but he'd always loved this family tradition.

He rubbed the glass over his grandfather's face. Nathan Dresden had never given up on his wife, even when she became a hostage to her own body. After trying and failing with every traditional and experimental treatment for epilepsy, he'd simply loved his wife and thanked his daughter for caring for her mother.

And Lily Dresden had never given up on life, even when normalcy wasn't possible. She'd lived in the care of her family. She'd quilted and cooked and loved and suffered, and she'd taught Jack the strength that had forced him to survive.

Lily had never given up on trying to get well.

Jack set the photo on the kitchen counter.

He could have had a family photo like that, someday. Of his daughter and her children, perched around him and Sophie. That could have been a Secret Santa gift in the Banning tradition.

He stared at his own face in the photo,

searching for a hint of the weak man he'd become, but saw only a college senior's confidence. A new adult's belief that he was going to be the next Christiaan Barnard.

Jack smiled as his finger traced the plaid shirt he wore in the photo. A piece of that shirt—along with his Little League uniform, and that pair of jeans he'd ripped, coming off his first bike—had made it into the quilt his grandmother sewed for his graduation.

You don't want a quilt, Jack. You're a man, newly minted, and you think this is girlie and silly. But someday you'll have a baby, a little girl or boy, and you'll want to share your stories. The clothing I saved from your childhood, these bits and pieces of the past, will bring your stories back to you. Give it to your wife when you know you're ready.

He'd been so busy committing emotional suicide, he hadn't realized he was creating a loss for the daughter who didn't know him yet. If he tried hard enough, he could be a man she'd be proud to call her father.

CHAPTER TEN

ON CHRISTMAS EVE morning, Sophie took the exit to Christmas Town with a little more wariness than the last time she'd driven this way. But the road to town was free and clear, the pavement freshly plowed of a recent snow.

Her mother had cautioned her against returning. With not one word from Jack, Sophie had no reason to believe that he'd changed his mind about finding help.

But she'd learned something about herself as she'd driven, tight-lipped, to Boston two weeks ago. She loved Jack. He'd hurt her because he was hurt. She might not trust him to be a father, but she loved him, and she wouldn't turn her back on him if he'd let her into his life. If he'd make an effort to get well.

She checked into the B and B again.

"Good thing I keep a room open," Esther said. "Sometimes we get some fancy people looking for a place to stay on Christmas Eve."

"This year you got me," Sophie said.

Esther patted her cheek. "I'm glad you called. How's that baby?"

"Perfect. Growing as she's supposed to. I have a sonogram photo in my things. I'll bring it down and show you later."

"You'd better."

Sophie carried her bags to a suite at the top of the house. She sighed as she shut the door. With dormer windows on all four sides, she had a view of the snow falling on the courthouse steeple. On the green, Santa was lumbering off his sleigh, passing out candy canes and promises to small clinging fans.

Sophie took off her coat and scarf and mittens. She could eat first or take a walk.

Or she could call the man she loved and ask if they could meet. She dug her phone out of her purse. Jack answered on the first ring.

"Are you all right?" he asked.

"Fine. How about you?"

"Why are you calling?"

Her heart sank a little. Her mother was going to enjoy this "I told you so."

"I'm back," Sophie said. "Could we talk?"

"Back where?"

"At Esther's."

"I'm coming."

She hardly had time to reconsider being so

darned available. In mere minutes, Jack's firm knock rattled the thick oak door to her room.

She opened up to find him holding a box he hadn't wrapped. He looked worse, drawn, exhausted. Did that mean he'd decided he was his own best therapist? "I don't need a gift," she said. Not if he couldn't give her the one she needed most.

He glanced down at the box. "I'll tell you about this later," he said. "Will you let me in?"

She had so many questions, but she couldn't ask them in an open doorway. She stood back and he passed her, setting the box on a table. He came back as she closed the door.

Taking her shoulders in his hands, he searched her face as if he'd never seen her before. As if he were studying her through new eyes.

"Jack?" What was he seeing?

"I talked to my friend in Saco. My friend in rehab? He gave me his therapist's name."

She nearly melted into the plank floor. "I'm so glad."

"I'm grateful you made me talk, Sophie, but I didn't do it for you. I wanted to be the man I used to be." He turned away from her, nervous energy in every taut line of his body. "Or some mixture of him and the man I pretended to be. I wanted to love you, not to feel grateful that you'd pried that night out of me."

"That's the way I want it, too." She went to him, sliding the back of her hand along his jawline. "Talking must be hard work. Is that why you look so rough?"

He wrapped his hand around her wrist and opened her fingers so he could kiss her palm. "I look like I feel. Real." With a grin, he went back to the box.

"This is for the baby."

That startled her. "You don't have to prove anything."

"You can't tell fathers not to bring gifts for their babies. Baby gifts are traditional. Do what you want with it afterward, but I'm giving it to you. You just have to handle it carefully because my grandmother made it."

With no more fanfare or explanation, he opened the lid on a sea of blue. Dark and light, navy and pale, with other colors spearing throughout. A white stripe, a zigzag of yellow lightning. A school badge on a piece of polo shirt. And the *B* from a small Red Sox cap.

"She made it out of your clothing." Sophie touched the quilt with reverent hands. "This is your story."

"Until I was twenty-one," he said. "That's what Gran said when she gave it to me."

"I can't take it from you." Sophie looked into his eyes, drowning in memories of love, when this quilt would have been one more piece of the puzzle that made them.

"She suggested I wasn't yet bright enough to understand what it meant, and she was right. I thought a big fancy watch would be more appropriate." He smiled. "Gran told me to give it to the woman I loved, who'd be having my babies, so I could share my stories with my child someday. You're that woman, Sophie. I know I've hurt you, and I almost lost our baby, and I don't know how else to show you how sorry I am. Even if you leave, you are the woman I will always love, and that baby you're carrying is my family, so this quilt will go with you."

"What are you saying?"

"Didn't I say it?" His face was pale, but his smile she remembered from the good times, when every moment hadn't been filled with the danger of abandonment.

"I love you so much I'm gutted at the way I treated you. Why did you come back?"

"Because I kicked you around until you finally told me what mattered, and then I walked out on you." Sophie stood on tiptoe to kiss his pleasantly stubbled cheek. How she loved this man, whose scent was part of her brain, whose voice was healing her aching heart. "I'm sorry. I didn't know what to do."

"I had to do what came next."

"But is it real? Are you going to change your mind again?"

"I wouldn't offer you the story of my life if I wasn't sure I wanted you to be the most important part of it." He lowered his mouth to her forehead. His sweet kiss was heat and comfort and gentle persuasion. "A life that belongs to you."

"But are you saying that because you're unhappy?"

Shaking his head, he smiled at her with humor she hadn't seen in too long. He kissed her, teasing her mouth until she couldn't stand his playful touch and wrapped her arms around him.

Sophie kissed him with the longing of loneliness and the certainty that had made her risk everything to make him see the man he really was. She kissed him with love that would never find an ending, because each day she loved him more.

"I'm so grateful you found help," she said.

"Just in time," he replied. "What do you say about my quilt?"

"We can hang it in the baby's room, and you can tell her all your stories." Sophie clung to him. "But you look unwell. I'm worried about you."

"Forget how I look and tell me you want to marry me."

She shuddered. Half her soul sang in sheer joy. "What would your doctor say? Shouldn't you be a little further down the road before you make that commitment?"

He slid his hand between them, rubbing her stomach with the confidence of a proud father. "We could wait, Sophie, but I am sure. As bad as I feel, I'm also more free than I've been in two years."

"I'm asking if it's too soon."

"I want to be your husband when our child is born. I want to be with you when you meet this girl and tell her you're her mother. I want both of you to know I'll always be her father."

Sophie tried to speak but produced only a choking sound.

Jack leaned down to kiss the bow of her upper lip. When she gasped, he kissed the side of her mouth. She caught his elbows in her hands, and he brushed his lips across hers.

"Think," he said. "Take tonight and tomorrow. Take as long as you need. I know where Boston is. I'll come to you if you call."

With a last kiss, he walked to the door, powerful and effortlessly in control. Jack again, only better, because he was so certain.

From her window, she watched him walk

down the street. The moment he disappeared from sight, she came to her senses. What was she waiting for? He'd said everything she hoped he'd feel.

She only had to trust.

She'd asked him for something a lot more difficult.

Grabbing her things, she hurried downstairs and then through the streets, dodging late shoppers and laughing lovers and children dancing with excitement, until she turned in at Jack's gate. On his porch, she drummed on his door so hard she startled herself.

His footsteps came down the stairs. He'd shucked off his coat, but he lifted his cell. "My phone died again. I was about to charge it in case you called, but I like the direct approach."

"How can you be so sure, Jack?" She touched her stomach. "If you commit, you're committed for life."

"I ran because I thought I was keeping our daughter safe. I was messed up and hiding from my past and afraid of losing someone else, but loving you was never a lie."

"And you know that if things go sour again, you have to stay and fight?"

"I'll fight to stay out of the dark place I've been living in—which had nothing to do with you. You were my comfort, the only healthy part of my life."

She did know him. She always had. "Jack, will you marry me?"

Laughter roughened his voice. She trembled in his arms as he leaned in to kiss the sensitive skin just beneath her ear. "You know there's no waiting period in Maine? If we buy a license, we could be married in time to kiss beneath the mistletoe on the green on Christmas Eve."

"Yet another tradition?" Sophie asked.

He lifted her hands in his and drew them to his mouth. "It won't last long. About the time I pull you into my arms, my sister and brother will descend on us, demanding full explanations."

"That sounds like the kiss of a lifetime. We should practice so we get it right."

"Just one kiss." He tucked her hair behind her ears and slid his mouth to hers. "To start a lifetime of loving."

HEADING TOWARD THE green while Callie's choir wished the town a Merry Christmas, Jack considered singing himself. He'd hardly let go of Sophie's hand since they'd made their vows, but he loved watching her admire the simple gold band on her finger.

As they reached the first arch, he led his wife beneath the mistletoe, twining their left hands so that his matching band shone in the lights strewn from every branch and streetlamp.

"No regrets?" he asked.

"Not one." Her eyes glowed in the twinkling lights of stars and happiness and Christmas joy. "Just so much love I think I'm exploding."

"Sophie, I don't have a gift for you."

She freed her hand to caress his cheek. "What I want we'll have to wait a bit for."

He turned her hand to kiss her fingers. "The baby?"

"I'd like to name her after your grandmother."

His heart contracted. Tears sprang to his eyes, and Sophie brushed them away with wonder in her gaze. She was already in his arms, and he kissed her until they were both breathless with love made more intimate by the ceremony they'd shared that morning.

At last, he pressed his forehead to hers. "Our own Lily. How will I ever give you anything that compares?"

She smiled. "You already have. You gave me yourself today."

* * * * *

THE CHRISTMAS WISH

Anna J. Stewart

Dear Reader,

What happens when writing buddies chat on Skype after a major writers' conference? Anthologies...and magic happen. How do I know this? Because this is the story that fulfilled my lifelong dream of becoming a Harlequin author.

When Melinda, Anna and I came up with the idea for *Christmas, Actually* (inspired by one of our favorite movies), I'm not sure I realized how much fun I'd have helping to create Christmas Town, Maine. I've lived in big cities all my life and I'm a California girl to the core. Learning about small towns on the East Coast made me realize just how special places like this are. While writing an interconnected series of novellas featuring three siblings seemed daunting at first, for me, everything fell into place from page one. As if it was meant to be.

Just as Callie Banning and Dean Galloway are meant to be.

When some people meet there's that "thing"—magic, some call it. Love at first sight, perhaps. A true connection that grows into something remarkable. I'm a firm believer that the right people find each other at the right time, and in Callie's case, she and Dean have a bonus factor...a little girl crying out for help in an unusual way. Dean's daughter isn't the only one who needs healing and help. By working together, they're reminded of what's most important in life—family—and they learn that you can still hold those you love close even after they're gone.

I hope you enjoy Callie and Dean's story as much as I loved writing it. I'd be thrilled to hear from readers. You can contact me through my website at authorannastewart.com and through Facebook (Author Anna J Stewart/AJ Stewart), and you can follow me on Twitter (AJStewartWriter).

Happy reading!

Anna J. Stewart

To my personal Yoda, Melinda Curtis, for bringing me on board, and to Cari Gunsallus, who is always a text or Skype call away (except during tornadoes).

Thank you both for always being there.

CHAPTER ONE

CALLIE BANNING LAID her head on her desk and banged it three times, once for each of the phone calls she'd gotten in the past half hour. If one more person asked for her help...

"Miss Banning?" The baritone brogue that accompanied the knock on her second-grade classroom door should have been the last straw.

Callie shot up in her chair, the blush suffusing her cheeks blazing hot enough to set all of Christmas Town, Maine, on fire. It was all she could do not to mouth the word *wow* as a man stepped into—and took over—the room.

"Is this a bad time?" The combination of sympathy and amusement shining in green eyes, along with the tamed Irish lilt, called to mind fields of clover dotting rolling hills. She'd spent many a night and more than a few days dreaming of traveling to the Emerald Isle. Now it seemed as if Ireland had come to her. Shoulder-length, golden-streaked hair brushed the worn leather of the bomber jacket he wore over snug jeans, the hint of a plain white T-shirt peeking from under the collar.

"Mr. Galloway." Callie stood up so fast she sent math tests flying. The pages fell like scattered snowflakes to blanket the linoleum floor and Mr. Galloway's snow-dampened boots.

"Why do some Fridays feel like Mondays?" Callie bent to gather the tests. "But at least with Fridays, you get the weekend to recover." *Babbling, Callie. You're babbling.*

She did the crouch and scoop around the desk, holding math tests against her chest until she plowed headfirst into his knees. Strong, firm hands gripped her arms and pulled her up, holding her steady as she found her footing. "Thank you," she said as he placed the last of the tests on her desk.

"I have a feeling it's the least I can do." The soft smile that curved his lips tied knots of tension in her belly as she set her stack of papers down. "What's Eliza done?"

"Oh, well." Callie cleared her throat and tucked her hair behind her ears. She sat on the edge of the desk and crossed her arms over her chest. These conversations were never easy. "Mr. Galloway, let me start by saying she's absolutely delightful—"

"Most of the time," he finished, and the combination of pride and frustration shone on his face like her mother's tree-topper Christmas angel Callie had yet to display. "And it's Dean, please. I appreciate you trying to soften the blow," he continued, "but I've been anticipating this call since her first day."

"Ah." Callie tried to suppress a smile. She could only imagine how much of a handful the little girl was for this single father. "She has a mind of her own?"

"A creative one at that."

"Eliza definitely has an active imagination. But I think there's something else going on. And I think it's better if I show you." Callie led him to the back of the classroom and opened the supply room door. "I managed to hide it before the other students saw, but…" She sighed. "…I'm afraid our Secret Santa mailboxes are a total loss." Not to mention the hours she'd spent hot-gluing milk cartons together before wrapping the whole thing in Santa paper and sticking white pom-poms all over it. It hadn't been her best effort, but she'd stayed up until two in the morning to finish.

Now the twenty-five cartons lay squashed and mangled on the supply closet floor, as if a renegade elf had set Santa's reindeers stampeding.

"Eliza did this?" Dean's tone made Callie cringe. She hated this part of the job—

providing evidence children weren't the angels their parents believed them to be. Looking back on the five weeks since Eliza and her father had arrived in Christmas Town, Callie was forced to admit the little girl's behavior and anti-holiday mischief increasingly worried her.

"Mr. Galloway... Dean," she corrected. "Eliza was the last one in the classroom before recess this morning, and this is what I found when we returned. When I asked her about it—"

"She lied?" Anger flashed across Dean's face.

"She didn't lie," Callie said, wondering if she'd gone about this revelation in the wrong way. "Quite the contrary. Eliza readily admitted she'd destroyed the display. She told me she sat on it. Twice."

"Why?" Confusion mingled with disappointment as he looked from the mailboxes to Callie and back again. "Why would she do this?"

"I was hoping you could tell me." Callie placed a hand on his arm and drew him away from the closet so she could close the door. He'd seen enough. "Please, let's sit down and see if we can get to the bottom of this."

She guided him through the maze of desks, past the drawings of anemic Christmas trees and intoxicated-looking elves frolicking with snowmen. Her students might never reach the heights of the masters, but they made up for their lack of perspective with colorful and sometimes explosive enthusiasm. Painted foam ornaments hanging from the ceiling swayed as Dean's six-foot-plus frame passed under.

"I am so sorry," he said in such a low and disillusioned voice Callie's heart twisted. "I thought this time would be different, that whatever triggers this behavior wouldn't happen here. This is even worse than last year." He refused the chair Callie offered, plunging his hands into his pockets as he looked out the window at the snow-covered playground.

"I had a feeling something like this might have happened before." Callie reached out a comforting hand before she remembered the need for professional boundaries.

"The past two years," Dean said. "Always the week before Christmas. It's like a switch inside her gets flipped and I don't know what to do about it. I'd planned to be in the Southwest this year, someplace where she wouldn't be bombarded with the holiday—middle of the desert maybe. But when my editor suggested a photographic essay on Christmas Town, I took it as a sign. Obviously I was wrong to hope surrounding her with Christmas would fix the problem."

"Eliza's been vocal about all the places she's lived, and the adventures the two of you have shared." Living in a motor home, even the extravagant one Callie had seen parked near the Pine Tree Inn, couldn't make for an easy life. Though their unusual situation certainly explained Eliza's maturity, despite her recent behavior. Still, moving from town to town, state to state, had to take a toll.

"It suits both of us," Dean said, a little of the tension melting from his voice. "Eliza's mother died when she was four. My work has me traveling all over the country."

"You don't have any other family? Grandparents? Siblings?"

"Both Maura and I were only children of older parents. Since she's been gone, it's been Eliza and me. And our grand adventures." He let out a breath that seemed to deflate him. "I'll pay for a new display, Miss Banning. And make sure Eliza apologizes to the entire class before we're on our way." He started for the door.

"Wait, you mean leave town?" Callie bolted out of her chair and reached for his arm, boundaries forgotten. "That seems a bit of an overreaction."

"You don't think we should?" Dean seemed surprised at her response. "Last winter the principal at her school asked me to remove her, said she was disruptive. You can't tell me you don't agree. She destroyed your holiday display."

"She squashed a bunch of milk cartons," Callie said as a rush of anger flooded through her. "She didn't hurt anybody."

"Last year she told her classmates Santa was a fairy tale adults made up," he said. "Sent some of them home in tears. A few of the other parents were furious and called her a bad influence."

"Parents don't always see beyond what affects their own kids." And shame on the principal for not delving deeper into Eliza's issues. Clearly, the little girl was struggling with something, but she wasn't talking. Not even to her father. Destroying the mailboxes was a cry for help, even if she wasn't ready to explain herself. "Leaving Christmas Town, especially this close to the holiday, won't do anyone any good—least of all Eliza." Callie squeezed her fingers around Dean's arm, felt the warmth of his body flow into her. "What are you teaching her if every time she does something people don't like, you just pick up and leave?"

"I don't know what else to do." The bitterness in his voice skimmed the edges of Callie's soul, sank in. Settled. "My child hates Christmas. Tell me, Miss Banning, what do I do about that?"

"You already started, Dean." She tilted her chin up and accepted the unspoken challenge. "You brought her to Christmas Town. What do you say we take the next step together?"

CHAPTER TWO

DEAN STARED DOWN at the hand curled around his forearm and felt the tension in his chest loosen. "I don't know what to say," he managed to answer.

He'd walked into Miss Banning's classroom prepared for a disapproving scowl and accusations about his daughter's unacceptable behavior. Hiding his anger and frustration had become impossible, and he'd expected the worst. People had been great about pointing out Eliza's flaws, but no one ever seemed interested in finding a solution. Five schools in fewer than three years had taught him to steel himself against the sympathy-tinged owl eyes and condescending head bobs confirming his worst fears—he was in over his head. Those individuals were wrong, of course, for most of the year. But come Christmastime...

Miss Banning tilted her head to the side and caught his uncertain gaze with her beautiful, kind one. "I don't think I've ever seen someone so stunned by an offer of help." The smile on her face rounded her rosy cheeks and made him smile in return. She was pretty, her expression open and bright. The absence of makeup gave her a fresh-faced look, and her jeans, wool-lined boots and heavy turquoise sweater showed a penchant for practicality over fashion, something he appreciated. For the first time in months, maybe years, he remembered how to breathe, and when he did, he inhaled the scents of ginger and vanilla, as if she'd been dusted by the holiday baking fairies.

"I had mentally packed our bags," he said, trying to accept the fact he had someone to share his worries about Eliza. "I never expected—"

"Yes, I can see that." Miss Banning squeezed his arm and turned to her desk, where she gathered up her papers and shrugged into her navy wool-lined coat. "I like keeping people on their toes." She tossed that smile at him again as she flipped her amber-tinged braid from under her collar. "I heard Eliza and my nephew, Adam, talking about an epic snowball fight in the back playground. I'll show you the way."

Thank you didn't come close to expressing the gratitude stirring inside Dean as he followed her down the hall and into the icy winter air. He'd shouldered the responsibility of Eliza for so long, he'd forgotten how nice it was to have another person to confide in, someone to understand. To listen.

"Oh, blast. Forgot my gloves." Miss Banning hefted her boulder-sized tote bag onto her shoulder as she dug into her pockets. "After living here all my life you'd think I could remember Christmas means snow." She tugged on dark green gloves and shook her head. "At least I remembered them this time. Most days I find them on my kitchen counter when I get home."

"I sewed Velcro onto Eliza's jacket so they'd stick," Dean said, turning up his collar against the blast. "I was tired of having to buy new ones."

Miss Banning inclined her head. "Well, there's an idea. Don't know what I'll do with those extra minutes I spend searching for them. Maybe take a nap." Her laugh made him think of sleigh bells and shooting stars. "Ah, I hear the squeals of snowball pelting. I bet she's soaked through by now."

"That's what dry clothes are for, Miss Banning," Dean said. There were worse things on earth than a sopping, happy child. "And hot chocolate."

"Mmm. You said it." Dean couldn't help but

picture Callie sipping cocoa and sitting in front of a crackling fire with him right beside her.

He blinked and wondered when he'd last thought about cozying up with a woman. Miss Banning's warmth and directness, her concern for his daughter, cleared the cobwebs from his heart. Together they rounded the corner to the snow-covered playground.

"Adam, enough already," she called. "You'll be soaked through, and your father will blame me. Eliza, your dad's here."

The little girl shrieked and stopped instantly. As she spun toward them, a snowball the size of an orange smacked her on the back of her hood-covered head. The happiness shining on his daughter's face froze the breath in Dean's chest. Just like her mother, fire and excitement 24/7, but with a kick of his attitude and penchant toward sullenness.

Eliza scooped up another handful of snow, but before she could launch it at Adam, her friend was out of reach, dashing behind Miss Banning.

"She's gotta try out for the softball team next year, Aunt Callie," Adam said as he latched on to Miss Banning and swiveled her like a shield against Eliza's threatened attack. "She's got a wicked pitching arm."

"So did her mother," Dean said with a touch

of pride. "She made all-state in college. Eliza, come on." He held out his hand. "Time to go."

The excitement on her face dimmed as she trudged over and looked up at her father. "We're leaving, then?"

"Leaving town, you mean? No." Relief surged through Dean once more and he earned a growing grin from his daughter. "Not just yet. I still have my work to finish, and Miss Banning would like you to stay."

"You would?" Eliza shoved her hood off and stared up at her teacher, all blue eyes and blond curls. "But I thought—"

Miss Banning bent down to her level. "I would like you to stay in my class, Eliza, very much. But if you do, some things are going to have to change, okay?"

Eliza glanced around Miss Banning to Adam before she shrugged. "I guess."

"You guess?" Dean placed his hand on his daughter's shoulder and squeezed. "Elizabeth Galloway, there is no guessing. Do you understand?"

"Yes." She frowned, but in the blink of an eye, the melancholy vanished and she turned and leaped into his arms, linking her own around his neck so hard he didn't care if he ever breathed again. "I'm sorry, Daddy."

"I know you are, baby. But you and I need

to have a serious talk. Otherwise we'll be saying goodbye to Miss Banning and Adam here earlier than planned. Understand?"

She nodded against his neck as he rubbed her back.

"Well, Adam, you up for some cocoa before I drop you off at your dad's?" Miss Banning cleared her throat as she glanced away. "I have to pick up more empty milk cartons at The Tea Pot."

"Are you going to make new mailboxes?" Eliza asked, plucking at a loose thread on Dean's jacket.

"I'm hoping to have time tomorrow." Miss Banning stepped closer. "I don't want your classmates to come in Monday morning and not have anywhere to put their presents. The last day before Christmas break is a pretty big deal around here. I'd like it if you came over to help."

Eliza hid her face in Dean's neck.

"We'll both help," he said. "Let me know when and where, and we'll be there."

"Oh, that's not necessary." The startled look on Miss Banning's face made him wonder if she'd forgotten he was there. "I can come pick her up, or you can drop her off—"

"Eliza and I are in this together, right?" He gave his daughter a squeeze. "Besides, I think some photographs of holiday craft projects might add something to the article on Christmas Town."

"Oh, well, then. Sure." Miss Banning tucked a strand of hair behind her ear. "How's tomorrow around three? I should be done with my errands by then."

"Three it is. Now, let's go for that hot chocolate?" Eliza nodded, her smile once again in place as she looked at her teacher. "May we join you?"

Miss Banning let out what sounded like a nervous laugh, and Dean couldn't help but smile at the sound. "That would be nice. Thanks."

He set Eliza on her feet and she zipped back to Adam as if they were tethered. "It's a date," Dean said, and let her lead the way down Main Street toward The Tea Pot.

CHAPTER THREE

"No, Mrs. Banks, I'm sorry, but I can't house-sit for you over New Year's." Callie took a calming breath as she situated her cell phone between her shoulder and ear, and tried to untangle the leashes of Mr. Palmer's toy poodles. She hopped over one and sidestepped the other as the dogs circled her, dancing up on their hind legs. Too bad she'd run out of doggy treats fifteen minutes ago. "I know you'll have trouble finding someone at this late date, but I told you three weeks ago you'd need to look for someone else."

Uncertainty crept into her voice and Callie felt herself waffling. It wouldn't be so difficult to work out. She wasn't going out of town for the holidays, and it wasn't very nice of her to ruin someone else's plans because she'd prefer to spend the time with her family or in her own cozy home. She had to start saying no, but maybe now wasn't the time.

"I think you're being incredibly inconsiderate, Callie." Mrs. Banks's tone took on an edge that set Callie's teeth to grinding. Resolve cemented once again.

"I'm sorry if my saying no ruins your plans, but you had enough warning that I wasn't going to be available. I'm sure if you put the word out—"

Click.

Callie let out a sigh that felt more like a growl as she stared at the bright winter sky. The dogs must have picked up on her frustration because they went silent, plopped their fuzzy butts onto the freezing sidewalk and blinked at her.

"Yeah, I know. I let her down." Callie's stomach pitched. What had she been thinking, picking up where her mother left off as the town's holiday helper? She had enough people on her own list—enough cookie baking, present shopping, gift wrapping, not to mention deliveries. Especially deliveries.

Her parents wouldn't be in town for the holiday, so she'd be doing double duty for them. This was the first Christmas since Grandma had passed, and Callie's father had opted for a change, whisking her mother away on a cross-country RV trip. Her parents wouldn't return until well after the holidays. She wouldn't see them at the pageant or find them waiting by the tree Christmas morning. Callie had hoped helping her mother's friends would ease the ache of missing them.

Instead, she'd seriously overextended herself, and each day turned into a mad scramble to catch up.

People had stopped asking for help and simply expected it. Her current situation was her own fault—she'd let it go on for so long, never saying anything remotely close to "no." Responsibility and helping others was the Banning family motto.

Now the residents of Christmas Town came to her when they needed a pet sitter. Or a run to the grocery store. Or their Christmas presents wrapped. A last-minute trip to the hardware store? Your son left his backpack in the gym? Need an extra three dozen cupcakes for the school fund-raiser? Sure, call Callie Banning. What else does she have to do?

Times like these, she envied her brother Nick. While he'd married and divorced early, Nick had his son, Adam. Even her other brother, Jack, a trauma surgeon who'd recently returned from a stint in Afghanistan, had more of a social life than she did—and that said a lot, considering Jack worked 24/7 in an emergency room trauma center. Bitterness slid in behind resentment, but Callie shoved both aside. Why was she complaining that people thought her reliable? That people came to her when they needed help. At times she wished they'd offer to pay her, even a little, to help supplement her teacher's salary. Goodness, what was wrong with her? Her mother would be mortified.

"Okay, guys." Callie clicked her tongue at the dogs. "Let's get you home." She had fifteen minutes before Dean and Eliza were due at her house, and the thought—no matter how inappropriate—of seeing the handsome single father again was enough to put a bounce in her step and a buzz of excitement in her freezing blood. She tugged on the leashes and angled her charges across the street. Ten minutes later, with a tin of Christmas brownies in hand—Mr. Palmer's thank-you for walking his two furry monsters—Callie was just climbing her porch steps when she saw Dean and Eliza heading her way.

"Come on in," she called, and waved at them, relieved to see the girl break into a wide smile as she ran toward her. "How are you today, Eliza?"

"Daddy took me for pancakes this morning."

"Let me guess," Callie said as Dean caught up and stomped the snow off his boots. "Posey's? Best pancakes on the East Coast if you ask me."

"Chocolate chip!" Eliza said. "They were super yummy."

"Then I guess you've had your fill and don't need any hot cider," Callie teased. "Oh, well, I suppose I can drink it myself. And have one of these brownies."

Eliza's eyes went wide as she looked at her father. "Daddy, can I?"

"'Tis the season, right?" he said. "But one. We don't need you bouncing off the walls all night."

Eliza's giggle erased the final fragments of Callie's bad mood. Or was it the look coming from Eliza's father that set her cheeks to blushing? Oh, this was dangerous territory. She was Eliza's teacher. She shouldn't have thoughts—tempting or otherwise—about a student's single father. Even if he was handsome and attentive. And that voice...

"Well, I've got everything set up." She unlocked the door and let them in, the warmth of her small cottage prickling her cheeks. "You can hang your coats up there." She gestured to her grandfather's coatrack as she unbuttoned her coat and popped off her cap. "And beware of the Sammy."

"What's a Sammy?" Eliza plunked herself on the floor and tugged off her snow boots.

"Sammy is a cat. At least that's what he looks like." Callie grinned at Dean when he arched a brow in her direction. "He thinks he's a dog. If you listen, you'll hear him bark."

"Now you're being silly." Eliza peered around the corner into the kitchen and then padded in stocking feet down the hall. "Cats don't bark. Is he a nice kitty?"

"He's very nice," Callie said. "And he loves little girls, so when he asks to go home with you, you have to promise you'll say no. Otherwise I'll be very lonely without him."

"'Kay." Eliza's attention was on finding the cat, which Callie had hoped for. She didn't want to bombard the little girl with Christmas. At least not until they reached the...

"Wow." Dean followed her into the living room, which was piled high with cardboard boxes marked Ornaments and Decor, and plastic bins stuffed with garlands and strings of beads. "You have a lot of Christmas decorations."

Tissue paper of every color intermingled with gift wrap, and boxes sat topped with wired ribbon bows Callie could make in her sleep. The dining and living room looked as if Santa's workshop had exploded. Labeled packages were piled against one wall, waiting to be delivered to neighbors who'd requested her help with both hiding and wrapping gifts.

"When my parents headed out of town, I

became custodian of the family ornaments. At some point I might actually get them put up." Normally, Callie decorated the day after Thanksgiving, but with everything she had on her plate, including organizing the children's choir for the town's Christmas pageant, the boxes hadn't moved since she'd had her brother Nick bring them down from the crawl space over the spare bedroom. "Eliza, maybe you'd like to come over Monday after school and help me with that?"

The girl shrugged and ducked down to search for Sammy under the metal-and-glass coffee table.

"We'll play that by ear," Callie said as Dean's expression darkened. "One step at a time. Now, let me get that cider."

Alternating hues of yellow and white made the kitchen look larger than it was, but with Dean standing behind her, the room felt like a broom closet. The man made an impression. Rarely had she considered jeans and a black button-down shirt so appealing. With the cuffs rolled up and the open collar, she could see he'd spent considerable time in the sun recently, despite the current overcast weather.

Needing a distraction, Callie lifted the lid on the slow cooker she'd set up this morning, and leaned in to bathe her face in the clove-

and-cinnamon-scented steam. "That smells like Christmas, doesn't it?" She gestured him over as she plucked three mugs from the cabinet. "I keep a pot simmering all season. You never know when you need a dose of holiday spirit."

"It smells wonderful."

Their shoulders bumped as she ladled cider into a mug. Callie pressed her lips together and her face went hot. Surely she couldn't be the first woman in town to find Dean attractive.

"Miss Banning—"

"Please, call me Callie." She handed him a mug. "Miss Banning seems so formal."

"It is formal. You're Eliza's teacher."

"That's right. I am." Good thing one of them remembered. She filled the other two mugs and set them aside as she popped open the brownie tin and inhaled the sweet, rich scent of cocoa and sugar. "Want one?"

"No, thanks. I finished Eliza's pancakes, so I've had my chocolate fill for the year."

Callie grinned. "I don't have a chocolate limit. Especially during the holidays." To prove it, she bit into a brownie, then sighed as she licked powdered sugar from her lips. "The one thing I wish for every year is to make the holiday calorie-free. Then all would be right in the world."

"You have a crumb." Dean gestured toward her lips as his own mouth quirked into a grin.

Callie brushed her fingers over her mouth as the brownie suddenly turned to dust on her tongue. "Thanks." She tried to ignore the prickling of her skin where he might have touched her. *Oh, help.* She almost sagged against the counter as her knees wobbled. Was it hot in here? Maybe it was the steam from the cider.

"I appreciate what you're doing for us. For Eliza," Dean said. "If coming here means figuring out her issues with Christmas, it was worth the trip. It'll make next year, wherever we are, so much easier."

"I'm happy to help." And for the first time in a long time, she knew she meant it. A twinge of sadness struck when she thought of him and Eliza leaving Christmas Town, but there was no regret. Because Eliza mattered. And so did Dean. "But we certainly don't want her getting the wrong idea about…anything." Callie hoped Dean was still following her train of thought.

"No, we wouldn't want that." He picked up his mug and leaned against the counter as he watched his daughter coax Sammy out from around the sofa. "It's been three years since we lost Maura. Some days, I look into my little girl's eyes and all I see is her mother."

"That's understandable." Callie took a gulp

of her hot cider and winced. "We lost my grandmother last year, and while it's not the same thing by a long shot, I still miss her. It's obvious you and Eliza loved Maura very much." No doubt the celebratory mood of the season only magnified their grief over losing Maura. "She loved everything about Christmas—the decorations, buying a tree. She had this one angel. It was white with raggedy yellow yarn hair. She'd ordered it online for Eliza—an angel a baby couldn't break." Dean chuckled. "I remember hoisting Eliza up our last Christmas together so she could put it on the tree. I don't think I'd seen Maura happier. Two months later she was gone. Car accident." He lowered his head, but not before Callie saw the flash of grief cross his features. "I haven't been able to look at that angel since."

Callie wished she had something appropriate to say, but all she came up with was, "Have you told Eliza that story?"

Dean frowned and ran a finger around the rim of his mug. "I haven't told anyone since Maura died. And I know what you're thinking, because I've thought it, too. This time of year, Eliza misses her mom so much she doesn't know how to cope, so she takes it out on the holiday. No matter what I try, she just seems stuck, and she won't talk to me. I even tried bribing her, and when that didn't work I took her to a therapist—which I can tell you was a disaster of epic proportions. I don't ever want to see that look on her face again, as if I'd betrayed her. How does a seven-year-old know to look like that?" Dean shook his head. "I stopped asking. The rest of the year she's fine. We talk about Maura all the time, it's just at Christmas…"

Callie sipped her cider as Dean's voice trailed off. Given the wistful expression she'd seen on Eliza's face whenever the other students spoke about their mothers, Callie couldn't argue with his assessment. But Eliza's behavior wasn't getting better, which meant Dean—and Callie—would have to try something new, and hope Eliza was none the wiser. "Well, let's start on those mailboxes."

"Right. Let me get my camera." He vanished into the hall and returned with what looked like a NASA inspired piece of technology.

"I didn't realize they made cameras this fancy anymore."

"Cell phones aren't all they're cracked up to be," Dean said. "And cameras are their own works of art. Eliza, we came to help Miss Banning, not play with the cat."

"Just a few more minutes," his daughter pleaded as she dragged an errant piece of tinsel around the floor. The pudgy tabby dived after it, missing by enough to make Eliza laugh and dance around the sofa.

"Sammy will wait," Callie said, and called Eliza over. "Now where did I put that glue gun?"

"YOU'RE A REAL pro at this crafting stuff." Dean scanned through the pictures he'd taken as Callie assembled the new mailboxes, gluing five rows of five empty milk cartons together before covering them in glittery red-and-white wrapping paper. He couldn't remember enjoying an afternoon more. Or laughing this much despite Eliza's frown and reluctance to assist.

"Pros don't get third-degree burns from their glue guns." Callie stuck her thumb in her mouth and glared at him. "I notice you were smart enough to stay away from that part of the project."

"A man has to know his limitations. Eliza, you doing okay?" His daughter was unpacking one of Callie's boxes of ornaments, a request Callie had made when it became obvious the mailboxes were a touchy subject.

"These are pretty," Eliza said as she set yet another hand-stitched bear on the coffee table. The collection of stuffed animals was growing. It looked like an audience for the festivities.

"Please be careful," Dean said.

"Stop worrying," Callie told him under her breath as she taped a Santa cutout onto the side of the box. "Those ornaments survived all three Banning children from infancy to adulthood. She can't hurt them."

Dean wasn't so sure. "There's something about large families that's completely foreign to me, but they're appealing all the same. Maybe it's because I grew up an only child."

"The grass is always greener. Now that we're adults, the three of us are pretty close. It was a rough time not so long ago, with Jack in Afghanistan and Nick going through his divorce. This is the first Christmas our parents will miss." Callie popped a Rudolph sticker on top of the mailboxes.

"I'd think they'd want to be home this time of year."

Callie shrugged. "My mom spent the past twenty years caring for my grandmother. She had epilepsy, and the older she got, the more frequent the seizures became. Once she passed, Dad started taking Mom on vacations. They're spending Christmas in Florida. Who would have thought that at twenty-five I'd be sad about my first Christmas without my parents. Silly, huh?"

"There's nothing silly about wanting your

folks with you during the holidays." He glanced at his daughter.

"Thanks." Callie's smile was back, albeit dimmer than before. "It'll feel like they're here once I get the tree up and the house finished."

Dean wasn't convinced that would be possible, given the number of boxes he was seeing. "Just in time to take them all down."

"Oh, I leave them up until Valentine's Day," Callie said. "Besides, it's bad luck to take down your tree before January 1. Didn't you know?"

"I do now." He made a mental note to include that in his article about Christmas Town. "So, are you and your brothers doing a big Christmas celebration? Dinner, presents, the whole works?"

Callie scooped up the leftover glue sticks and tossed them in a drawer, leaving the glue gun to cool on the table. "Good question. We all get so preoccupied with the Christmas pageant, the family get-together ends up being last minute. But yeah, we'll all do something, I'm sure. Which reminds me, I still have to buy their presents."

"You aren't done shopping?" Dean angled a look at the stacks of wrapped and unwrapped boxes along the far wall.

"Oh, those I need to deliver to my neighbors." Callie waved a dismissive hand. "My mom used to be a personal shopper during the holidays, and when she and my dad left, the job sort of fell to me. The boxes will all be gone in the next couple of days. Just in time for my brothers and nephew to invade."

"I'd always hoped Eliza wouldn't be an only child," Dean mused.

"She'll make a great big sister."

He grinned at the flush on Callie's cheeks when she looked over her shoulder at him. "I—I just meant—"

"I know what you mean." Dean turned his attention to his camera so as not to embarrass her. "There's something to be said for never knowing where you're going to be, what adventure lies ahead. I wouldn't want to rob Eliza of that experience, and besides, she loves helping me decide where we're going next. We've made it a kind of ritual."

Not to mention staying on the move meant not dwelling on the past. Moving forward kept him from remembering all the plans he and Maura had made, the life they'd imagined. Eliza adapted well to any situation—as long as Christmas wasn't involved. They'd test run just about every avenue of the educational system, from home schooling—a humbling experience that hadn't proved to be his forte—to personal tutors, but whenever he could, he made certain his daughter attended regular school with other kids. And whenever she was tested, her scores were in the higher percentile. No. This way, his way, their way, was better, wasn't it? "For now it works for both of us." *But for how much longer...?*

"Every family has their definition of stability." Callie placed the final pom-pom on the left corner of the mailbox and admired her work. "Looking back, I wouldn't trade my brothers for the world. They gave me a thicker skin, literally and figuratively. You're giving Eliza the same thing, only in a different way. You're there for her. That says a lot. But right now we need to make sure she doesn't get it in her head to sit on this."

Callie jerked a thumb at the finished stacked containers, one cubby for each of her students. "Eliza! I need your help, please."

"Yes?" The girl stepped out of Callie's bedroom, with Sammy following. The cat stopped beside her and let out an odd sound that made Eliza gasp.

"No way," Dean muttered. "That cat just barked."

"Sure, now you believe me." Callie rolled her eyes. "Eliza, I need you to help me put your classmates' names on these boxes. I'm not sure I remember all of them."

"Okay." But Eliza walked over as if the finished project was a jack-in-the-box poised to pop. "It's pretty." Her chin wobbled. "I'm sorry about the other one."

"I know you are, sweetheart, but maybe you'll help me keep this one safe?"

Eliza nodded and picked up the green glitter pen Callie held out.

"Now, who should we start with?"

"Adam," Eliza announced. "We start with Adam. *A-D-A*—"

Dean watched Callie brush a hand over Eliza's hair, overwhelmed at the gentleness and understanding this woman showed his daughter. She hadn't cast Eliza to the side when things became difficult. Instead, she was determined to help.

Tempting as she was, alluring as he found her, Callie was a hometown girl. She had family in Christmas Town. A life. She had roots. All the things Dean had convinced himself— convinced Eliza—they didn't need.

CHAPTER FOUR

"I'M PROUD OF YOU, Eliza." Dean squatted in front of his daughter and tugged her hood forward, bopping her on the nose with the tip of his finger. "You made up for your mistake and I think Miss Banning appreciates it."

"These mailboxes are much better," Eliza said as if improving the classroom's holiday decor had been her intention from the beginning. She took his offered hand and jumped down from the porch, and they walked into the late afternoon sun. "Miss Banning said I could come back and play with Sammy anytime I wanted. Do you think we could tomorrow? Or Monday after school?" She swung her arms as they headed toward the end of Main Street and the Pine Tree Inn & RV Park.

In a way, the town was a throwback, with Victorian-style lampposts draped with garlands and holly berries, the same garlands stretching across Main Street and between buildings. Lights glistened; ornaments shimmered as they caught either sun or moonlight. Buckets of Christmas candy canes sat on store stoops for eager hands of all ages to grasp as they passed. The roving carolers kept their voices even and steady, bathing the Town Square in gentle, celebratory songs. Everything was so different here, different from the life they'd left behind, different from anything he'd experienced before, and at the center of it all was Callie Banning.

As much as Dean wanted to see the pretty schoolteacher again, he wasn't sure it was a good idea. Eliza might become too attached, which would make this holiday even more difficult for her.

Who was he kidding? Eliza wasn't the only one in trouble. He couldn't remember the last time he'd felt so energized. Excited about the holidays. Happy. Instead of looking uncomfortable when he'd talked about his deceased wife, Callie had listened, asked questions. As if Maura was as important as Eliza.

Before today, any mention of Maura had felt like an icicle to the heart—freezing him from the inside—but now he found himself smiling when he remembered the holidays they'd shared. Her angel. A few moments with Callie had given him a new appreciation for those times.

Callie's enthusiasm for the Christmas season matched Maura's, perhaps exceeded it. Or maybe the town was feeding her excitement. Christmas Town was known for its celebration of all things Yuletide, which was why he was here—to get the real story behind this unique community and help Eliza deal with her feelings about Christmas. He just hadn't anticipated his daughter's objections to the season to be so…destructive. Was he wrong to hope they'd seen the worst of her behavior? That maybe Callie's attention and concern had caught it in time?

Callie…

"Daddy, you're humming." Eliza tilted her stubborn chin up and grinned.

"Am I?" Dean asked. "I didn't realize."

"I think Miss Banning makes you happy. She makes me happy, Daddy. I like her. A lot."

Dean tried not to wince. "She's very nice."

"And I lo-o-ove her cat. Can we get a kitten, Daddy? I'd take real good care of it, I promise!"

"We'll see," Dean said. The thought of having a kitten around was both amusing and terrifying.

"That's what you say when you mean no." Eliza turned her head so he couldn't see her face. Her hand tightened in his.

"'We'll see' means I need to think about it. A cat is a big responsibility, Eliza."

She sighed. "I know. It's okay."

But for the first time since they'd gone off on their grand adventure, Dean wasn't so sure.

"MORNING, GUS, BARTY, MARV," Callie called as she walked past the Christmas Town Workshop, the town's hardware store, early Sunday morning. She was on her way to help with the pageant setup in the town square, and she could already hear hammering in the distance. "Gus, what do you have there?" She detoured up the wooden steps to where the normally cheerful man sat scowling at a notepad. He was bundled in three layers of clothes and a wool hat to cover his bald head.

"We're making a list." He jabbed a pencil against the tablet.

"Checking it twice?" Callie grinned.

Barty chuckled. "Just like her brother. I'm telling you, he's a diamond in the rough."

"Jack?" Callie cupped her gloved hands around her travel mug of coffee and leaned against the railing. "As far as I know, he's all polished."

"No, not Jack, Nick." Marv reached out to snatch the list, but Gus shifted in his rocking chair, moving it out of reach. "Myra Sue Dunnigan announced she's resigning from the town council after the first of the year, which means a special election, and we've been appointed to find candidates."

"Nick came to mind?" Callie must have sounded skeptical, given the disapproving looks she received from the three store owners. "Don't get me wrong," she added, feeling a rush of pride for her older brother. "Nick would make a great addition to the council. He knows everyone and he's down-to-earth, reasonable. But he's going to take some convincing."

"Maybe a word or two from you would help?" Gus waggled his bushy gray eyebrows, while Marv peered at her through thick lenses.

"He knows I'm biased," Callie said. "He'll get my support and my vote, and while I'm happy to broach the subject, it'll be up to you guys to make him say yes."

"Always a catch," Barty grumbled, then adjusted the red plaid hunting cap he'd been wearing since he'd started chemo. "Boy's got some confidence issues. This is just the thing he needs."

Callie couldn't disagree. Nick's life had taken a major detour when he'd married young, had Adam and put his wife through school by working two jobs. When the time came for his wife to return the favor and for Nick to go to college, she'd asked him for a divorce. In one night, Nick had bid goodbye to his dream of a college education and had settled into life as a full-time father and the town handyman. Callie's own college education felt bittersweet— she'd been able to go and Nick hadn't. He couldn't have been more supportive, but Nick seemed to believe he didn't quite measure up to his educated siblings.

Still, he was coming along. She grinned. Her big brother was finally taking charge of his love life and having an anonymous online flirtation with Gina Vernay, owner of The Tea Pot. If ever two people belonged together…oh, Callie had been having fun teasing Nick about his online alter ego, Football20.

"Weather looks like it's going to hold." Callie glanced at the clear sky. Seeing the three men on the porch meant they were in for a warmer day. Normally, this time of year, they'd be rocking away inside the hardware store. "We're setting up the booths for the pageant today. We could always use an extra pair of eyes to double-check everything."

"We'll be there," Marv said as Callie started down the steps.

"You know…" She turned around, tapped a finger against her lip. "I bet if enough of us talk about what a great addition he would be to the council, before we actually approach him, he'd be more likely to consider running."

"You think?" Barty narrowed his gaze.

Callie shrugged. "If there's one thing I've learned living in a small town, it's that rumors can be powerful. I think everyone will agree it's a good idea. Then, by the time word works its way to Nick—"

"Enough people will be behind him that he'll grab the opportunity." Marv snapped his fingers. "I like it!"

"Seems tricky to me," Marv grumbled, but Callie didn't miss the twinkle in his eyes. Marv was former military and no one appreciated a plan of action—tricky or not—more.

"Just a thought. Have a good day." As she made her way to the barn that doubled as community center and town hall, she wondered how long it would take before the Christmas Town rumor mill was running at full speed.

"I should have known you'd be one of the first people here," Dean called as he and Eliza jogged across the street from Posey's. Given Eliza's sullen expression, Posey's chocolate chip pancakes had not worked their magic this morning. "I was hoping to get pictures of everyone setting up the pageant booths."

"Sounds like a good idea. Normally, we set up the morning of, but there's a new band of weather moving in for Christmas Eve. Nothing worse than setting up booths while it's snowing."

Callie stopped babbling and resisted the urge to smooth her flyaway hair, which had come loose from its braid on the walk into town. Windblown looked good on Dean, who gave the impression of having stepped straight off the Emerald Isle in his beige cable-knit wool sweater, familiar leather jacket and worn jeans. Callie's fingers itched to tuck his long bangs off to the side, but even obscured, his gaze had the power to warm her from the inside.

"Pretty much the entire town's going to be out here finishing the decorations," she added. "Eliza, you up for helping?"

The girl shrugged, her flowered pink jacket crackling in the cold.

"How are you with a paintbrush?" Callie tried again. "We need little hands for touch-ups."

"I don't know." Eliza's frown held a tinge of curiosity.

"Well, let's find out. If not, I'm sure there's something you'll enjoy." She hauled open the stained barn door and gestured for them to enter. Dean had been wrong. Given the flood of residents milling about, hammering, gluing and moving booths, she was one of the last to arrive.

"Callie, there you are," Wilson Franks called out, waving a dripping paintbrush in the air. "Just in time. Can you do the rounds this morning and make sure the signs on the booths are straight?"

"Coming. Eliza?" She held out her hand. "I need a reliable helper for the day."

Eliza hid behind her father, peeking around him as if he was the only thing standing between her and the nightmare that was Christmas.

"Go on, baby." Dean brushed a hand over her curls before squeezing her shoulder. "I'll be around if you need me."

Eliza took a slow step forward and grasped Callie's hand. "See you later," Callie said to Dean.

BY THE TIME the last of the booths had been lined up around Main Street and the town square, Callie was sorely wishing she hadn't skipped breakfast. Another few minutes and she might start gnawing on the leftover two-by-fours piled by the barn door.

Eliza had needed a while to warm to the idea of helping set up the Christmas pageant, but she'd come around, at least as far as doing as she was asked. Not that Callie took her eyes off the little girl for long. With all the paint and tools around, she could only imagine the trouble Eliza could get into.

Volunteers were busy moving ladders and dollies out of the way, double-checking lists, running fingers over paint to test for tackiness. Some hauled trash away, while others measured lengths of garland that would drape the front of the booths. Dozens of colorful pots that would house poinsettias during the day were being carried out of Glad Tidings Florist and plopped onto the ground.

"The brochures were right," Dean said from behind her. "This town takes its Christmas pageant seriously."

"Oh!" Callie spun and pressed a hand against her racing heart. "I didn't hear you."

"Admiring your work?"

She turned back to the booths. "I guess. I didn't really do all that much."

"You're kidding, right?" Dean inclined his head and shifted to stand in front of her. "I think you're in at least 90 percent of the photos I took, and in each one, you're doing something different. You, Callie Banning, are a woman of many talents."

"I just do what I'm asked." Callie wasn't sure why she sounded so defensive.

Dean frowned. "Did it sound as if I disapproved?"

"N-no. Of course not." Callie tried to cover with a laugh. "I get cranky when I'm hungry."

"They had muffins and juice going at one point." Dean looked over her head. "I can track some down for you."

"No, that's okay. I'll just grab a quick something while I'm running errands." She glanced around and saw Eliza running a worn and fraying paintbrush over the edge of a booth, giggling with one of her schoolmates.

"More errands?" Dean asked.

"Just a few more things on my list." But Callie cringed, wishing she could take the rest of the day for herself and finish her own shopping before tackling her neighbors' lists. Her mother had always made this look so easy, but Callie wished she hadn't been so quick to assume the role. Abandoning the family tradition of shopping for neighbors—something that went back three generations—had almost prevented her mother from agreeing to go on her husband's proposed adventure. Until Callie promised to step in.

At least all Callie had to do was pick up the gifts and deliver. After wrapping them, of course. She should be grateful she didn't have to shop for them, as well.

She caught sight of her brother Nick hauling his tool bag across the traffic-blocked road to steady the ladder some volunteers were using to string garlands across booths.

Dean murmured something like "hmm" as he fiddled with his camera strap.

Watching the way he cradled the camera, as if it were a child, made her curious. "Why did you become a photographer?"

Her question seemed to surprise him, but he blinked away the expression and replaced it with a coy smile. "Magic."

"Boy, you've really caught the Christmas Town spirit." She laughed, but when he only smiled back, she realized he wasn't joking. "Seriously?"

"Seriously. Come on." He held out his hand. "I'll show you."

Callie bit her lip. "Eliza…"

"Found one of her friends from school and they're touching up Tiny Tim's Toys sign, as you very well know. No one's going to notice if you take a break." He winked and waggled his fingers. "Or hold my hand."

Fat chance of that. Hadn't she just been touting the efficiency of the town rumor mill? She should be grateful Gus, Barty and Marv hadn't mentioned anything about Dean and Eliza spending the afternoon at her house yesterday.

Still…oh, just this once. Callie pressed her lips into a straight line and folded her paint-stained hand into his. "I should grab my jacket."

Dean pulled off his own and dropped it over her shoulders. "I'm not giving you the chance to change your mind." He tugged her down the street. The chill in the air wasn't as intense as she'd expected, and as she and Dean went around the corner of the barn, she felt the town drift away.

Her hand tightened around his, her body warming from his touch, from the idea of being alone with him, even for a few minutes. An escape from reality. "Just a little farther," Dean said. "I found this spot the other day, and I think it's become one of my favorite places."

A decades-old wooden crossbuck fence outlined the back edge of town. On the other side lay one of the largest expanses of untouched snow for miles. "Reindeer Meadow," Callie told him as she kicked her legs over the fence and sank knee-deep. Her toes tingled from the cold, despite her boots. "I can't tell you how many snowball fights were won and lost in this spot."

Dean followed, climbing over the fence. "I'm not surprised. But here…" He tugged her closer. "See the way the sun catches the ice crystals in the snow? The light exploding from all those millions of snowflakes…there's no describing it, Callie. Not to the point where someone would completely understand or be able to see exactly what we're seeing right this minute. Unless…"

He shifted behind her, crunching through snow, and placed his camera in her hands. With his fingers guiding hers, they aimed the lens at just the right angle that the light and sparkle he'd referred to exploded onto the screen. Callie shivered as he whispered in her ear, "Take the picture."

Click.

"See?" Dean's voice made her skin go hot as he brought up the image on the viewer. "Magic. Now you don't have to describe it. You can see it. Forever, if you want. Or if you don't, we just hit delete…"

"No." Now it was Callie who covered his hands. "No. It's beautiful. Don't erase it."

"I wasn't going to." That smile of his was warm enough to melt every inch of snow surrounding them. "But now do you see what I mean?"

"Pictures capture more than just moments, don't they? They preserve memories, too. What you do is capture time." Suddenly every family photograph in her possession felt that much more important. Special. Treasured. "For everyone to see what we do, who we are."

"Exactly." Dean smiled and pulled her around to face him. "I can think of nothing better than capturing this moment, with you, forever." His fingers stroked her cheek. "Callie—"

"Daddy! Miss Banning! There you are!"

Callie yelped and leaped back, nearly losing her balance. Before she could topple into the snow, Dean reached out and yanked her up against him, his low chuckle making her blush and laugh at the same time. She planted her hands against his chest, curled her fingers into the wool of his sweater.

Eliza stood on the other side of the fence, waving her arms madly. "What are you doing out there?"

"Nothing, baby," Dean called, and offered Callie a sympathetic smile. "Daughter calls. Sorry."

"Don't be," Callie whispered, catching his hand in hers for a final squeeze. "Thank you. For sharing this with me."

"You're welcome."

Callie watched him return to his daughter, then hugged her arms around her waist as she followed, knowing she'd never look at this meadow in quite the same way again. She let out a long breath.

"What's going on?" she asked when she reached them. The anxious look on Eliza's face put her on instant alert.

"I, um…" The girl glanced at her father, who shrugged.

"This is your fault, Eliza," Dean said. "How do you want to fix it?"

Uh-oh. Callie's stomach clenched.

"Tomorrow is Secret Santa day and I got Brooklyn's name," Eliza explained.

"Yes?" Callie urged.

"And I didn't get her a present."

Callie kept her stern expression in place. Progress had been made, however, if Eliza was feeling guilty about this. "You mean you drew a name, knowing you weren't going to participate?"

"I didn't want to be the only one who didn't do it," Eliza reasoned, in seven-year-old logic. "But now…"

"Now you feel bad because you and Brooklyn have become friends, and you don't want her to be the only person who doesn't get a present."

Eliza shrugged. It was on the tip of Callie's tongue to ask why she felt the way she did about Christmas, but Callie recognized that stubborn tilt of her chin. Even if she did ask, she wasn't going to get an answer. Not yet, anyway. And not in front of Dean.

"Well, if your father says it's okay, you can come with me on my errands and we'll find something for Brooklyn. Would that work?" She looked up at Dean, who seemed torn but resigned.

"It's okay with me," he said.

"Let me get my coat. Dean, can we meet you back here in a couple of hours?"

"Sure. I want to get some final pictures of the setup. Eliza, be good."

"I will, Daddy." This time it was Eliza who took Callie's hand and tugged her away.

CHAPTER FIVE

CALLIE SORTED THROUGH the papers on her desk before searching her bag. Again.

"Did you lose something, Aunt Ca—er, I mean, Miss Banning?" Adam stopped at Callie's desk on his way out to early recess. His white down-filled jacket and blue ski cap left only his eyes showing, making him look as if he'd been gobbled up by a giant marshmallow.

"I could have sworn I brought the song list with me this morning," she said. "We have choir practice this afternoon and I have to tell Miss Fitz which music we need for the pageant."

"I can help you look," Adam offered as he sneaked a peek at his friends scrambling over each other in the hall to get picked for the daily snowball fight.

"Absolutely not." Callie flopped the papers down and gaped at him. "Did you not promise to lead the charge against the fourth grade marauders?"

Adam's eyes crinkled. "Yeah."

"Well, then, get to it! But eat your snack first!" she called after him, though she doubted he heard her. He was already slamming out the door to the playground. When she started searching again, she caught a shock of blond hair slinking out of the coatroom. "Eliza? I thought you'd already gone outside."

"I'm going now," she said without meeting Callie's gaze.

"Thank you again for your help with the mailboxes." For the tenth time that morning, Callie glanced over at the display by the window. Still in one piece. "I think it made our Secret Santa exchange more fun. Aren't you going to open your gift?" Surely Eliza's feelings about the holiday had to be negated or at least lessened by the promise of presents. But the square box she'd been given was still sitting on her desk, untouched.

Eliza shrugged. Callie couldn't help but wish the happy, carefree child she'd spent time with over the weekend had arrived at school Monday morning. But Eliza was even more subdued than usual.

"Did you eat your snack?"

"Yes." Eliza inched closer to the door, shooting a nervous glance behind her. "I need to go to the bathroom."

Callie stood and leaned into the hall as Eliza

disappeared into the bathroom. "That was even more strange than usual." Worried that the little girl might be sick, Callie followed, pushing open the door and stepping into the girls' room. "Eliza?" She found her huddled on the floor, arms wrapped around her knees as tears glistened in her eyes. "Sweetheart, what's the matter?" Callie sat on the floor beside her. "Are you feeling okay?"

Eliza shook her head.

"Do you want me to call your father? Should he come pick you up?"

"No!" The vehemence in Eliza's voice set off alarm bells in Callie's mind.

"Well, you're going to have to tell me what's going on, otherwise that's my only option."

Eliza dug her finger into a tiny hole in her jeans. "I—I did something bad again."

Not surprised, Callie took a deep breath. "Do you want to tell me or tell your father?"

"Does Daddy have to know?" Overwrought puppy dogs had nothing on the facial expressions of Eliza Galloway.

"That depends, Eliza. I'd like to help you if I can."

"I took something I shouldn't have."

"You mean you stole something?"

Eliza nodded and lowered her forehead onto her knees. "I'm sorry. I know you need it, but

I just got so angry! I don't want to hear all that music. All those songs. I don't like Christmas."

Callie bit the inside of her cheek. *No kidding.* "Eliza, did you take the choir's song list out of my bag?"

Without lifting her head, she nodded again. "I saw it sticking out when you were handing out papers, so when the other kids left for recess and you were standing by the door, I took it."

Callie pressed her fingers against her temple as relief replaced irritation. She wasn't losing her mind. "Where is it now?"

"I put it in my jacket."

"Ah. Well, then. Let's get it."

Eliza lifted her face, tears glistening on her cheeks. "Are you going to tell Daddy?"

"That all depends." Callie got up and held out her hand. "Come on."

"I don't know why I did it."

"Don't you?" Callie led the way back to the cloak room. "I think maybe you thought if I didn't have the list, then there wouldn't be a choir and there wouldn't be a pageant, and maybe they'd cancel Christmas."

Standing in front of her brightly flowered jacket, Eliza pulled out the crumpled piece of paper. "I guess."

"May I have it back now?"

Eliza held it out, but continued to stare at the floor.

"Can I ask you a question?" Callie said as she took the list.

"Yes."

"How would you feel if someone didn't want you to celebrate your birthday because they didn't like the idea of a birthday cake or presents, or a party with all your friends? How would you feel about that?"

She dug her sneaker into a crack in the linoleum. "I guess I wouldn't like it."

"It wouldn't be fair, would it? Not being able to celebrate just because one person didn't want to."

"No."

"You spent a lot of time yesterday choosing just the right present for Brooklyn, didn't you? You didn't want her to be disappointed, and she wasn't. She loved the bracelet and the one you gave her for her sister Madisyn. That's what Christmas is all about. Making other people happy. You did that today, Eliza."

"I guess."

Callie held out her hand again. "Come with me." They returned to the Secret Santa mailboxes and Callie sat down in one of the students' chairs. She hefted Eliza onto her lap and set the song list on the counter. "Do you want to tell me why you don't like Christmas?"

Eliza twisted her hands together, still looking at the floor. She shook her head.

"Okay. That's fine. You don't have to. Or your dad, even though I think you should." Callie tucked a corkscrew curl behind the child's ear. "You know, it's okay if Christmas makes you sad, Eliza. It makes a lot of people sad."

Little hands stilled, her brow furrowed as her nose wrinkled. "It does?"

A spark ignited in Eliza's eyes, encouraging Callie to press on. "Sure. This is the first year I'll spend Christmas without my grandmother, and you know what? I think I miss her more because everyone is so happy and excited about the season. There's nothing wrong with being sad or not liking Christmas because it makes you hurt. But I don't think you should try to make other people feel bad, do you?"

Her answering shrug was slight, but enough for Callie to grasp a glimmer of hope.

"Christmas is a special time of year when we remember how important it is to be kind to one another," she said. "Everything is so pretty and white and sparkling with lights. There's something magical about Christmas that touches people in their hearts. Do you understand that?"

Eliza nodded. "I know."

"But by doing what you're doing, you're making people sad, including me. You're saying that because you don't like it, you don't want anyone else to, and that isn't fair, is it?"

"No. But…"

"But what?" Callie held her breath.

"Nothing. I don't want to ruin Christmas for everyone. I'm sorry, Miss Banning. I won't take the choir list again."

"I know you won't," she said. "And one more thing. Stealing something out of my bag, out of anyone's purse or pocket, is never, ever the right thing to do. I know your dad's taught you that before, right?"

"Yes." Eliza finally looked up, with such raw emotion in her eyes that Callie found it hard to swallow. "Are you going to tell him what I did?"

"I don't think I'm the one who should tell him, do you?"

"You mean I have to tell him." There was that crinkle again, and the way Eliza twisted her mouth as she considered reminded Callie of Dean when he was concentrating on his photographs. "I'll be there when you tell him if you want."

"You will?"

"I will. But you have to promise me no more pranks, Eliza. No more trying to stop others from enjoying Christmas."

Callie had the distinct impression the girl wanted to roll her eyes.

"And I need you to do me one more favor," Callie said. "I need you to help me run and organize the choir. In fact, there's a special song I'm very worried about, and it needs just the right little girl to perform it. I think you'd be perfect."

"If I promise all those things, maybe we don't have to tell him?" Eliza's eyes widened so much Callie could almost see the gears spinning in her mind.

"I can't keep secrets from him, Eliza, and neither can you." At least not forever. "So, what do you say? Deal?" Callie held out her hand, and after Eliza stared at her outstretched palm for a good ten seconds, she shook it, a trembling smile touching her lips. "Okay, then." Callie swiped her thumbs across Eliza's cheeks to wipe away her tears. "Go get your jacket so you can run around for a few minutes before the bell rings. Go on."

She watched Eliza jam her arms into her coat as she dashed out of the classroom. But Callie's own smile faded as she wondered what it would take for Eliza to confide in her. Or her father.

"DADDY, LOOK! THERE'S Miss Banning!"

Dean lowered his camera after snapping the perfect shot of the Yuletide movie theater. The green-and-red flashing marquis advertised the annual holiday film festival, which included nightly showings of *It's a Wonderful Life, Miracle on 34th Street* and Dean's personal favorite, *Scrooged*.

He scratched the landmark off his mental list and shifted his gaze as his daughter dragged him down the street behind her. "Miss Banning!" Eliza called, causing several turned heads and smiles of understanding.

Dean offered a quick wave to Gus, Barty and Marv, who were bundled up in their usual spot outside Christmas Town Workshop. He'd gotten quite a few photographs of the three old men. Dean couldn't help but feel a pang of affection for the lifelong friends who watched over the comings and goings about town.

The roving carolers—whose Victorian costumes must provide some warmth—were moving to the far side of the town square, their songs fading as they went. Dean frowned as he caught the tension in Callie's voice. He looked at the older man she was talking to. Upon seeing Dean, the man straightened and shifted his weight onto his cane.

"Miss Banning!" Oblivious to the tense atmosphere, Eliza threw her arms around Callie's waist and looked up at her with adoration. Dean felt a pang of envy strike, and wished he could throw his arms around her, as well. "How's Sammy, Miss Banning? Can I come see him again? I miss him so so much and I bet he misses me, too!"

"Hi, Eliza." Callie cleared her throat and patted his daughter's back, the strained smile on her face putting Dean on alert.

"Mr. Thompson, I'm so sorry. I completely forgot I was supposed to help your daughter with the festival cookies, but—"

"It's okay, Callie." The older man's voice carried a hint of regret, which shifted Dean to full protection mode as he moved in behind her. "I suppose it wasn't fair of us to think you could handle everything your mother—"

"I'm sorry we're late," Dean said as Callie hugged her arms around her waist. Anger burned low in Dean's gut as he forced a smile in the older man's direction. "I got caught up with my photos and forgot about our dinner date. Dean Galloway." He offered his hand. "I'm working on an article for *US Travelers Monthly* about Christmas Town and its seasonal happenings. Mr...?"

"Thompson." The man pushed his wire-rim glasses higher up his nose and straightened his cap, an embarrassed flush creeping onto his cheeks. "Nice to meet you. I wasn't aware our Callie had another social engagement." His attitude seemed to shift, but not enough for Dean to consider him anything other than a grumpy old coot.

"Yes, well, I—" Callie stammered, her mouth opening and closing like a suffocating goldfish.

"We've only been in town a few weeks," Dean continued, "but Callie's been kind enough to show us around. Help with our Christmas shopping. Introduce me to all the friendly neighbors. But it sounds as if you have your hands full at home. We don't want to keep you. Callie?"

She nodded, as if caught in a trance. "Yes, of course. Mr. Thompson, trust your daughter. I'm sure she'll do just fine and the pageant cookies will be as delicious as always."

"We'll see." But Dean swore the man let out a "harrumph" as he walked off.

"Bye!" Eliza waved at Mr. Thompson's retreating figure as Dean spun them away and down Main Street. "He's cranky."

"He's just concerned," Callie said. "This is the first year my mom hasn't been here to help supervise his daughter's cookie baking—she's older than I am, mind you. I was supposed to step in, and I've been trying to catch up—" Callie broke off, let out a long breath and seemed to center herself. "Thanks for the rescue. I'm not usually so forgetful."

Dean's anger burned fresh at the idea of anyone taking advantage of her generous nature. "I think someone needs a night off," he teased, trying to pull her free of the melancholy. At this moment, he wanted nothing more than to make Callie smile. "I don't think I've seen you stand still for more than five minutes since we met."

"I'm not very good at saying no. My mom is a tough act to follow. She always made it look so easy." Callie's lips twitched, but didn't form the smile he'd been hoping for. "I'm glad you were there."

"We're going to dinner at Posey's," Eliza announced, kicking at a pile of snow as they passed the Bell, Book & Candle Shoppe. White clumps stuck to her bright blue boots. "You can come, too."

"Thank you, Eliza, but I don't want to intrude on father-daughter time."

"You're not intruding. I would've issued the invitation even if I hadn't been trying to rescue you from The Grinch," Dean said, hoping she'd agree to a few hours of distraction. She looked as if she could use a break. "I'd—

we'd—like it if you joined us. Maybe you can convince Posey to let me take some pictures in the kitchen? I'd love to get some shots of her making that amazing peppermint pie."

"Well, I can't refuse the offer of peppermint pie." There was that smile. A flame flickered to life deep inside him, but he banked it with the reminder that Christmas Town was only a stop on his and Eliza's adventures. Instead of reaching for Callie's hand, he kept Eliza between them as his little girl skipped down the street, the holiday lights blinking around them, and he enjoyed the town—and Callie's company—while he could.

"POSEY, YOU'RE ALWAYS saying you'd like to bring in more customers," Callie told the sixty-something woman, whose red hair was piled in a beehive hairdo. "Let Dean feature you in the article. It can't hurt."

"And you always were full of sass." Posey grinned and angled twinkling amber eyes on Dean, who had the good sense to stay quiet while Callie made his case. "You're not fooling me, Callie Banning. You've been trying to get your hands on my peppermint pie recipe going on five years now. How do I know this isn't some kind of put-up to wiggle my secrets out of me?"

"You don't." Callie reached for her hot chocolate, which was topped with a Matterhorn-sized peak of whipped cream. "I guess you'll just have to trust him."

"Were you a Boy Scout?" Posey asked, jotting down something on her notepad—Posey was as old-school as they came—before turning her attention on Dean. "Well?"

"No, ma'am," Dean said, and Callie saw his lips quiver. Eliza watched the exchange from her spot perched between her father and the plate-glass window, blond curls struggling between sodden and frizzy. "But if it'll help, I'll swear an oath to Saint Nicolas not to reveal your secrets. At least not to Callie."

"That's the thanks I get for trying to help you out?" Callie gave him a frown before she winked. "Fine. I'll swear to not even ask him, okay?"

"That'll do." Posey nodded. "I was about to start on tomorrow's pies, anyway. Shouldn't take more than a few minutes to get ready. You got enough film in that thing?" She jerked her wrinkled face toward Dean's camera.

"Plenty," he said, and Callie thought it sweet he didn't correct Posey by telling her digital cameras didn't need film. "Thank you. It's just the personal touch I'm looking for."

Once Posey took their orders and meandered

off to the next table, Dean smiled at Callie. "And thank you. I don't think I would've had the guts to ask, let alone bargain with her."

"Oh, I think you use your charm to get whatever you want. That accent of yours goes a long way, I'm sure."

"Mommy always said he sounded like an Irish poet," Eliza said, before she gulped down her own hot chocolate and ended up with a nose covered in white. "Remember when she'd say that, Daddy?"

"I do," Dean said, and Callie watched as he blinked the surprise away and handed his daughter a napkin. Callie hid her smile behind her mug. She'd been pretty sure Eliza remembered more about her mother than Dean realized. Leave it to the little poppet to prove her right. "That was a long time ago, baby."

"I have an excellent memory. Like Professor Xander on *Proton Patrol.* He is *so* funny!" Eliza squealed as she leaned over the table and grabbed Callie's arm. "Do you watch him, Miss Banning?"

"I'm afraid not." But she knew how popular the superhero show was with her students. Not that she could remember the last time she'd plunked herself down in front of the TV and vegged out. Callie laughed at the shell-shocked look on Dean's face as she stirred the melting puddle of whipped cream into her chocolate.

"When do you watch *Proton Patrol?*" Dean draped an arm over the back of the booth and shifted to face his daughter.

"It's on TV when you're working on the computer." Eliza grinned as her cheeks flushed I-shouldn't-have-done-it pink. "Channel four at seven."

"This is why children should have homework," Dean said with an accusing look at Callie, who shrugged. It wasn't the first time she'd heard the argument, but her classroom, her rules.

"The last thing I want is a class full of students who can't stay awake because they were up late trying to finish homework. Besides, if they sleep on what they've learned, retention is better. Test scores for my students are above average for the county."

"They test second graders?"

"They test kindergarteners," Callie muttered, certain her irritation was showing. But the last thing Dean wanted was an earful of frustration over testing children's aptitude. "But hey, if it wasn't for no homework, Eliza here wouldn't be learning all about science and math with Professor Xander. Sometimes television can be a teacher's best ally."

"Did you always want to be a teacher?" Dean asked.

Callie shrugged. "I suppose. Mom studied to be a teacher. Her father was a teacher. It fit and I love it." For the most part. There were days…

"Daddy, you should watch *Proton Patrol* with me next time. You'd like it."

"It's a date," Dean said, tweaking his daughter's nose before they caught sight of Posey waving him into her kitchen. "Looks like I'm up. I'll be back in a few." He hefted his camera off the table.

"Sure is Christmassy in here," Callie said as Eliza grabbed a crayon from the paper cup beside the napkin holder and started scribbling on her place mat. "What do you think?"

She shrugged and colored in an uneven blue circle.

"I like all the colors and blinking lights. I swear every year Posey finds somewhere new to add tinsel or garlands. You know, there's an elf hidden somewhere in the diner." Callie leaned forward and rested her arms on the table. "I've never been able to find him, but Posey swears he's here."

Eliza wrinkled her nose and added red dots to her circle.

"There's a prize for finding him." Callie picked up the laminated card behind the ketchup, skimmed the list of pies, then flipped it over and looked at the short, stout, red-capped elf dancing a jig. "Here it is. 'Find Elmer the Elf and win a free slice of pie,'" she read. "Says that whenever someone finds him he moves on to a new hiding place. Boy, I sure would like a piece of pie for dessert. How about you?"

Eliza's crayon halted. Her mouth twisted and she peeked up at Callie. "What kind of pie?"

"Any kind, and Posey makes a ton of them." Callie set the card in front of her. "What do you think? Can we find Elmer?"

Suspicion mingled with temptation on the seven-year-old's face. "If we do, can I pick the pie?"

"Of course." Callie nodded and sipped her chocolate as she cheered Eliza's grudging acceptance of anything holiday related. All hail Elmer. "But we'd better hurry. We have to find him before dinner."

CHAPTER SIX

"I HAVE TO ADMIT, I didn't think Elmer would be found this time." Posey set an oversize slice of peppermint pie in the center of the table. Elmer, who looked more like a mutant troll than an elf, perched on the window ledge between Callie and Eliza. At least the little guy had made Eliza smile. "You must be supersmart to have found him on the ceiling fan. It's been almost two weeks since someone spotted him."

Eliza picked up her fork and stabbed through the whipped cream and holiday sprinkles to the creamy candy cane laden filling. "I'm always finding the stuff Daddy loses," she told Posey, before cramming her mouth full of sugar.

"Well, before you go, you need to find Elmer a new place to hide. Bring him up when you're ready."

"Okay." Eliza nodded.

Dean pushed away the last of his fried chicken dinner and plucked a stray fry from his daughter's plate, trying not to get his hopes up about

Eliza's change in attitude. For the first time in years, she wasn't kicking and screaming at the idea of participating in something overflowing with Christmas spirit. Not wanting to make a big deal about her sudden connection to Elmer, he looked over at Callie. "That woman is a marvel with pies. In the twenty minutes I was in the kitchen she made at least four, and each one looked as if it were baked by Mrs. Claus herself."

Callie ate the last bite of mashed potato covered meat loaf, and wiped her mouth, her eyes sparkling like uncorked champagne. "She ran out of pie once and caused a town scandal. Years ago, mind you, but she swore it wouldn't happen again. I've always thought she had little helpers who came in to bake during the night."

"Like the shoemaker and the elves?" Eliza asked.

"Exactly. Hey, do I get any of that?" Callie teased.

Eliza grinned around another mouthful and snatched up a clean fork from the edge of the table.

"Thank you," Callie said. "Elmer here got me to thinking about the elf village just on the other side of the Pine Tree Inn. But I'm sure you wouldn't want to see it."

"Elf village?" Eliza swallowed and looked

at her father before glancing at Callie. "But I thought elves lived in the North Pole with you-know-who."

Dean's spirits dipped. That didn't last long.

Callie shrugged as if Eliza's refusal to use Santa's name wasn't a step backward. "There are lots of different types of elves. Not just the ones who work with Santa. They live in forests, near streams. Elves are everywhere. They're magic." Callie scooped up a forkful of sugar overload and bit into the sweet spark of peppermint. "They see everything," she whispered to Eliza. "But there's a very special section of the park that not many people know about. It's said only children can find their village, and only after the moon is out and the sun is asleep."

"Like now?" Eliza shifted over to the window and pressed her nose against the glass. "The moon is out. Oh, Miss Banning, can you show me where they live?"

"I don't know." Callie grinned at Dean, who gave her a look that said *really?* "Elves are pretty special creatures. They don't show themselves to just anyone."

"What if I'm really careful and quiet? I can be quiet."

"Since when?" Dean asked.

"Daddy, be serious." Eliza tugged her mittens

on and scooped Elmer off the window ledge. "I want to see the elves."

"Now hang on," he said. "We've taken up enough of Miss Banning's time this evening. I'm sure she doesn't want to go traipsing through—"

"I wouldn't have mentioned it if I wasn't willing to go tonight," Callie said with a warning look. "We can see if they're home, but no promises, Eliza. And you—" Callie poked her fork at Dean "—eat your portion. I don't need the calories and this one doesn't need any more sugar."

Not that Eliza was eating any longer, Dean noticed. His daughter's attention had been captured by thoughts of elves in the park as she gazed out the window. Which was entirely, he realized, Callie's intention.

"I BET NO one finds Elmer for weeks and weeks!" Eliza announced as they headed toward the Pine Tree Inn. The enormous tree beside the front door was aglow in multicolored lights.

"Posey said as much." Callie remembered the befuddled look on the woman's wrinkled face when Eliza instructed her on where Elmer wanted to hide. "I don't think anyone's ever wrapped him in mistletoe and hung him on the door chime."

"Posey said if it's more than nineteen days I'll break the record and then I get a whole pie! Can you imagine that, Daddy? A whole pie?"

"My blood sugar's spiking just thinking about it," Dean said. "It's almost your bedtime, so we'd better find these elves quick, okay?"

"Daddy," Eliza whined.

"Your dad's right, Eliza. Besides, the elves don't stay out very long this time of year, so we'll get to look for a few minutes. Come on." She held out her hand for the little girl as they rounded the corner and took a sharp right at the snow-dusted sign marked Mistletoe Park. "That's some RV you've got there," Eliza said to Dean as they passed the glistening gold-and-black vehicle. "Are you a rock star on the side or something?"

"It's nicer than my first house," Dean said, pushing his hands into his jacket pockets. "It is cold tonight. Are you sure…"

"I'm sure. Trust me," Callie whispered as they continued through a thicket of trees and ankle-deep snow. "Get your camera ready, because this is a place you won't want to miss."

"I can't imagine…oh. Wow."

"Told you." Callie took a deep breath as they stood on the edge of the park, a wide-open space surrounded by pines and firs. The pristine white snow blanketing the meadow glistened like a frozen lake. "This is as perfect as winter gets. The silence, the calm. The way the sky arches over and makes you think you're alone in the world. And you know what?" She took Eliza's hands and dashed out into the snow drifts as if lunging into a frothing ocean. "This is the perfect place to make snow angels."

Callie turned to face Dean and, arms out, let herself fall back. A plume of snow burst around her as she waved her arms and scooted her legs back and forth. "Come on, Eliza. You make one, too. The elves love them." Cold seeped in through her jacket, but gazing up at the pitch-black sky, seeing the dots of stars and the full moon beaming down at them, filled her with such happiness that Callie forgot to breathe.

Eliza lowered herself into the snow, looking around as if she were going to step on something or someone—before following Callie's lead and lying down. "It's like a giant pillow!"

"I know." Callie laughed. When she heard the gentle click of Dean's camera, she brought her chin to her chest. "Was I wrong?" she asked, when he lowered the camera again.

"You were not," he said, watching her. "It's

one of the most beautiful things I've ever seen."

"Daddy, I'm making an angel! Look!"

"I see, baby." Dean smiled but didn't move, and Callie, feeling a rush of heat so warm she could have stayed here forever, lay down again and tried to calm her racing pulse. But it wasn't any use. If only...

"Will the elves come now?" Eliza asked as she got to her feet to admire her work. "Oh, Miss Banning, it does look like an angel."

"Let's see." Callie hoisted herself up and stepped away from the indentations. "Very good job, Eliza. The elves will love it. But we have to give them some time to find them. And look." She pointed at the sky as a star shot by. "Quick, Eliza," she whispered. "Make a wish."

The child froze solid in an instant. Her spine stiffened, she sniffed, her jaw locked and she clenched her fists at her sides. "No." Callie's words had flipped a switch inside the little girl and turned off the wonder, not to mention the joy, Callie had worked to cultivate all evening. "I don't make wishes, Miss Banning. Wishes don't come true."

"Sometimes they do." Callie crouched in front of Eliza, but the little girl's jaw was clenched so tight, Callie worried she'd give herself a headache. She'd seen the same expression on Dean's face hours ago when he'd interceded between her and Mr. Thompson.

Scrambling to undo whatever damage she'd done, Callie said, "Sweetheart, wishes are powerful things. Sometimes it just takes them longer to come true."

"Mine never come true." Eliza crossed her arms over her chest, her frown frozen in place. "I'm cold. Daddy, I want to go home now." She stomped away from Callie, leaving the snow angels and any hopes of finding elves in the moonlight behind.

"Eliza," Callie called.

"Enough, Callie." Dean held up his hand and shook his head. His expression was a mixture of disappointment and resignation, but thankfully, no anger. He seemed to understand she'd tried, but once again they'd come up against the brick wall that was Eliza.

Callie ached at the thought of this little girl not believing in magic. In Christmas. In wishes. *Mine never come true.* Callie watched Dean and his daughter disappear around the corner, wondering what Eliza could have wished for that would have destroyed her belief...

"Oh." Callie blinked back the sudden spark of tears as her throat tightened, and she pressed a fist against her heart. No wonder Eliza wouldn't talk to her father. She must have asked for the one thing that could never be—the one thing any child who lost a parent wanted.

For her mother to come back.

CHAPTER SEVEN

"I THOUGHT YOU were going to stop being such a pushover." Gina Vernay scowled at Callie across The Tea Pot's counter as she packaged up Santa cookies in a bright red pastry box. "If you come in on your lunch break one more time to pick things up for someone other than yourself, I swear I'm going to cut you off. Here." Sweeping a hand across long bangs that concealed the thin scar running from her temple to her jaw, Gina reached into the display case and plucked out a carrot cake cupcake. "Eat something, because I bet you don't have lunch scheduled in."

"It's no big deal," Callie murmured, dipping her finger into the thick cream cheese frosting and licking it clean. Her stomach growled, greedy and happy. "Man, you are a baking genius. And carrots mean it's healthy, right? Thanks." Callie breathed in the aromas of coffee, baked goods and toasty warmth. She loved what Gina had done with the place. Between the collection of mismatched wooden tables and chairs, the aged photos, the antique snow-shoes and the crosscut two-man logging saw on the far wall, Callie couldn't help but think of winters and Christmases long past.

"Tell Mrs. Warrington she can send her lazy son in the next time she needs cookies for her bridge club," Gina called. "You're booked."

"Yes, ma'am," Callie said, and resisted the urge to salute. She never should have told Gina about her plans to start saying no. This morning, Mrs. Warrington had caught Callie before she'd had her mug of caffeine-laden courage, and she hadn't been able to form a refusal when the woman had pleaded desperation. "Will we see you at the Christmas pageant?"

Gina glanced over her shoulder toward the swinging door to the kitchen and smoothed a hand over her bangs. "I'm not sure."

Callie bit her lip and offered an understanding smile. When Gina was seven, an accident at the pageant had left her with physical and emotional scars. Callie wished she could help her overcome them, but there wasn't anything anyone could do until Gina was ready to deal with her demons head-on.

"Well, I'll bring you one of Vaughn Craw-ford's handmade candy canes if you don't make it. Thanks, Gina." As she turned to leave, the door opened and Dean pushed through.

"Hello." Callie hoped the flush on her cheeks could be attributed to the icy breeze wafting in, rather than the fact that she hadn't been able to stop thinking about him.

If only she could forget the spark of interest hovering behind his warm and welcoming gaze. The smile that touched her lips felt tight, as if her mouth wasn't sure what to do around him. All she wanted was for him to kiss her.

"Just stopped in for some coffee before heading down Mistletoe Lane to take pictures of the gingerbread houses. Good morning, Gina."

"Would you like your regular?" Gina's gaze darted away and her smile wobbled as if stretched too thin. She turned her back on him and faced the coffee machine.

"Yes, please. Thanks. So—" Dean glanced down at the box Callie held "—I hear you have choir practice this afternoon. Treats for the kids?"

"No." Callie felt her cheeks flame yet again. "I'm running these to a neighbor's house before heading over to the school auditorium."

"At least you got off the hook with Mr. Thompson last night." Dean leaned around her to pay for his coffee.

"Well, actually…" Callie cleared her throat. She could lie, but that was silly. Why wouldn't she just admit she'd…caved? "I did stop by his house on my way home and offer to help them finish up." Guilt had gotten the better of her, not that Mr. Thompson seemed all that grateful. And neither, to Callie's surprise, had his daughter.

Dean accepted his cup with a murmured thanks. "After the way he treated you?"

"It wasn't entirely his fault," Callie explained, taking a step back. "I mean, I did promise to be there, and then I forgot, which left them in the lurch." On the bright side, now she had one fewer family to worry about disappointing. Even better, she'd said no, in a way, and survived the disapproval. Who knew? People could be upset with her and she'd be okay.

"Callie, we're friends, right?"

Friends. That word had never sounded bittersweet before. Callie swallowed hard and tried to shake her thoughts free. They were friends. Even though… "Of course we are."

"Then, friend to friend, have you considered people are taking advantage of your kindness?"

"You think that's what Mr. Thompson was doing?" As if she didn't already know.

"It's okay to tell people no, Callie. In fact, the word is empowering."

"Then it's up to me to use my noes properly." She didn't appreciate him pointing out that she was—in Gina's words—a pushover. He'd found a nicer way to say it, but his words stung more. "I need to go."

"Wait, Callie." Dean followed her outside. "I'm sorry. I didn't mean to upset you, and I suppose this isn't any of my business. I don't have the right to tell you how to live your life."

"No, you don't," she agreed. She turned her face into the icy wind, then found her gaze drawn to his. "But I appreciate you thinking of me. I know I have to grow a spine. I just don't like disappointing anyone."

"We all disappoint people, Callie. I'm just afraid you're disappointing yourself." Dean let out a low whistle when Callie frowned. "And didn't that sound as rude as Mr. Thompson the other night. Okay, truce. I won't mention it again. Your life, your decision. Except…"

Callie couldn't help it; she laughed. "You just will not let this go, will you?"

He warmed his hands on his coffee cup. "I was just thinking you probably would've had time to decorate your own house if you weren't so busy not letting everyone down. I know you said you were trying to pick up where your mother left off, but I don't think she'd like you ignoring your own traditions and life to do so."

"You make it sound as if helping friends is a bad thing." It occurred to Callie to remind him she'd spent considerable time helping him, but she thought better of it. Some things mattered more than others. Instead, she spun on her boots and stomped down the street.

"I'm just suggesting you should help people because you want to," Dean said, catching up to her in a few long strides. "Not because you're afraid someone will stop liking you if you say no."

His words struck like a full body blow, pushing the breath from her lungs. "You think I'm that shallow?"

Irritation flickered across his face. "If I thought you were shallow I wouldn't have spent the past few days finding excuses to see you again."

"Wh-what?" The look on his face told her his words surprised him as much as her. Alarms blared louder than Santa's sleigh bells. "Dean, I—"

"I shouldn't have said that." He cringed. "You're Eliza's teacher and the two of us becoming anything more than friends is inappropriate. Besides, my daughter and I will be leaving soon and the last thing I'd want to do is get your reputation stuck in the rumor mill before we go."

The box in Callie's hands suddenly felt as if it were filled with cement rather than frosting-covered sugar cookies. She didn't need reminding that he would soon be moving on. She didn't want to be reminded. Oh, if he was anyone else, and if Eliza wasn't involved... If he wasn't a man who moved from town to town faster than Santa on Christmas Eve. If, if, if. "I'd be lying if I said I hadn't thought about you, too, but..."

She didn't realize she was seeing hope on his face until the light dimmed in the flecked green depths of his eyes. "Yeah. But." She didn't think she'd ever seen such a regret-filled smile.

Her throat tightened around pain that shouldn't strike this deep this soon. "Dean, *this* wouldn't head anywhere good." She swore her heart was breaking. "As you said, you and Eliza will be moving on, and while that lifestyle works for you both, Christmas Town is my home. I can't leave. It's part of who I am. Just as moving on is part of who you are."

He lifted his hand and brushed chilled, bare fingers against her cheek. "I know. It doesn't mean I don't wish circumstances were different." He moved closer, despite the bakery box between them. "Let's forget I said anything."

"Dean..." Her gaze dropped to his mouth, to his full lips, and without thinking, she moistened her own.

"Oh, sweetheart, don't do that." Dean pressed his forehead against hers and closed his eyes. "Just. Don't."

Callie felt a bubble of laughter—or was it regret?—building in her chest. No man had ever shown such attraction for her, or called her sweetheart in a way that made her feel special. Or made her want to take off at a moment's notice and travel around the country. But it wasn't laughter or regret trying to escape her lips. It was the distinctive pop of hope as it disintegrated inside her.

As close as Dean was, as easy as it would be to kiss him, to let him kiss her, she knew that the moment he did, she'd be lost. And that wouldn't be good for any of them. Not her. Not Dean.

And not Eliza.

"I have to go," she whispered, pressing her cheek into his fingers, then placing a hand against his chest and pushing gently. "I have to get back for choir practice."

Dean took a deep breath and stepped away, the sad smile on his lips tugging at her strained heart. "Have a good evening, Callie." And with that, he headed toward Mistletoe Lane and its gingerbread houses.

Callie watched him walk away, wishing she had the courage to follow her heart.

CHAPTER EIGHT

CALLIE LOWERED HER head into her hands and took a deep breath.

Wrangling fifty second, third and fourth graders the first day of Christmas break had been as easy as corralling ten lords a-leaping or seven swans a-swimming. Whose ridiculous idea had it been to schedule a rehearsal the day before Christmas Eve? Not hers, that was for sure. If Mrs. Moore had listened to her, the kids would have been solidly prepared days ago because of shorter, more frequent practice sessions, instead of the two-and-a-half-hour stretch of strained caroling she'd just endured.

All she wanted to do was go home, take a hot bath and put up her decorations. Except she still didn't have a tree, and the last thing she wanted to do tonight was schlep over to Murphy's Tree Lot and be guilted into buying one that should have been put out of its misery a decade ago.

"I'm sorry if I made you sad."

Callie's head snapped up as Eliza dropped

down beside her on the auditorium stage. She dangled her legs over the edge, her bright pink overalls and uneven pigtails pulling a smile out of Callie despite her somber mood. All her students were special to her, in one way or another. But this little one… Callie blinked away the rush of tears. It was going to be hard to say goodbye to this one.

"You didn't make me sad, sweetheart." She reached out to squeeze Eliza's hand. "I've just had a long day."

"I know you want me to sing 'Joy to the World.' I tried. But the words just get stuck." She pointed a finger at her throat. "They don't want to come out."

Thinking of her conversation with Dean, remembering how she hadn't been able to say what she wanted to, Callie couldn't blame Eliza. But Callie wasn't giving up hope. Not yet. There was a way to save Christmas for father and daughter. All it would take was finding the key to Eliza's locked heart.

"Is your dad picking you up?"

"Uh-huh." Eliza nodded. "As soon as he's done taking pictures of the town signs. We're having spaghetti for dinner. It's my favorite. He usually buys me a cookie for dessert. Chocolate chip." She bumped her head against Callie's shoulder.

Since choir practice had ended earlier than planned, Callie wasn't thrilled with the idea of Eliza waiting for Dean alone. No wonder the little girl had found *Proton Patrol* on TV. "I don't suppose you'd like to come with me to finish my Christmas shopping and errands?"

Callie watched Eliza's trademark holiday pout appear.

"I just thought I'd ask," she added. "I could use the help. You did such a great job picking out presents for Brooklyn and Madisyn, and you could pretend they're birthday gifts. My brothers are pretty hard to shop for."

"I wish I had brothers," Eliza said, plucking at a loose thread in the seam of her overalls. "Do you like yours?"

"I do," Callie said, thinking back to a time when that hadn't been completely the case. Being the youngest of three wasn't the easiest, but it helped, knowing they were always there when she needed them. She still saw Nick all the time. As the town handyman, he was always passing her on the street, and Callie often helped with her nephew, Adam. Jack was another story, however. Being a trauma surgeon meant his life wasn't his own, but this year, they'd promised it would be different, starting with meeting up at the Christmas pageant.

They all lived within a mile of each other and still they had trouble getting together.

If today's practice was any indication, their long-awaited celebration could be a disaster. Boy, she needed to get herself out of this holiday funk. "Well, what do you say, Eliza? Want to do some shopping?"

"I should text Daddy and tell him." The girl pulled out her phone, which Callie knew was solely for communicating with her father.

"I agree. Let him know you might be late for dinner."

"'Kay." She stuck her tongue out the corner of her mouth as she composed a text. The reply came within seconds. "Daddy says it's fine. And I'm supposed to thank you for taking care of me."

"You're welcome." Callie jumped down and reached up to hoist Eliza off the stage. "Now what do you think would be a good present for my brother Jack? He's just impossible to shop for."

"GRANT, I'M TELLING YOU, the Christmas issue next year could be our biggest seller yet." Dean snapped the lens cap back on his camera as he wandered up the road toward Christmas Town. The carved wooden sign across the street glistened in the late afternoon sun, clumps of snow accenting the intricate lettering Dean recognized from the signs hanging above For Christmas's Sake, one of the town's gift shops.

"I have to admit," Grant said, "when you mentioned this town, I wasn't completely sold." Dean could barely make out what his boss, the editor of *US Travelers Monthly,* was saying.

He frowned and readjusted his Bluetooth earbud to hear around the growing static. "What do you mean, when I mentioned it?"

"Yeah, a couple of years ago." Grant's voice faded in and out. "It was a throwaway conversation, now that I think about it, but for some reason the idea of Christmas Town stuck in my head until our last editorial meeting."

"I don't remember," Dean said. When on earth… How would he have come across Christmas Town on his own? His heart hammered an unsteady beat, as if trying to kickstart his brain into remembering.

"Well, glad it's working out."

"Yeah." Dean tried to get his head back into the conversation. "Yeah, I was thinking we might be able to make this an annual piece— come back and visit, see what's new, what's changed?" The idea fell out of his mouth before he had time to think it through. He'd never scheduled something so far in advance, but the idea felt…right somehow.

"We'll see how this one goes and take it from there. So, we've been bouncing around the idea about a Churchill Downs story for spring," Grant said. "How do you feel about Kentucky?"

"Sure." Dean braced himself for the rush that came with a new assignment, a new town, new people. "Eliza and I can be on the road after New Year's." But no excitement followed. He felt a flood of both heat and cold down his spine as a hard pit of regret lodged in his throat, making his next words a struggle. "Send me the information and I'll touch base after Christmas."

"No rush," Grant said. "We're shutting down the offices through the fifth, so anytime after that is fine. You and Eliza have a good holiday."

"Thanks." Dean tapped his ear and disconnected, slipping his camera into its case as he started the hike back into town. The brisk cold wasn't quite as frigid as it had been in recent days. This walk had been a way to clear his head, to try to put things in order. Eliza's behavior had evened out, mostly thanks to Callie, and while his daughter still wasn't ready to embrace the season with a hug and a smile, at least her hostility had taken a backseat.

Dean would take what he could get.

The deserted road and the silent snow-flakes blanketing the street and surrounding trees made him feel as if he'd ventured into another world. The late afternoon long-distance view of Christmas Town became etched permanently in his mind with its gingerbread inspired houses, twinkling lights and snow-capped roofs. Chimneys puffed out cotton balls of smoke, and candy-cane-painted porch rails welcomed every visitor and passerby with cheer and merriment.

At the edge of town Dean stood for a long moment, his memory flickering over something… familiar. He'd seen this view before. A picture, maybe? An article in another magazine? He frowned as he pulled out his camera, popped off the cap and peered into the depths of the town through the lens. Only when he found the right angle, just as the afternoon sun began to dip behind snow-kissed roofs, did it hit him.

"Maura." As the whisper escaped his lips, he turned and raced down the street, past the brilliantly lit ten-foot fir beside the entrance to the Pine Tree Inn. He had his key in hand before reaching the RV. Pulling open the door, he stopped only long enough to put his camera down and toss his jacket onto one of the two cushioned chairs behind the driver's seat. He yanked open cabinet doors, knowing before he glanced inside that he hadn't stored his wife's Christmas ornaments anywhere Eliza would find them. But where were they? He'd set them aside, knowing the day would come when he and his daughter would open those old boxes together. When the pain wouldn't be so overwhelming. Three years was a long time to set the pain aside, however. Three years meant more boxes and organizing, especially in such a tiny space. Where on earth…

"The bathroom." Dean snapped his fingers, ducked behind the door and pulled open the cabinet where they kept the towels and sheets. On the top shelf sat three boxes, one of which had a rudimentary Christmas tree drawn in one corner. Small, so as not to be conspicuous, but large enough for Dean to remember putting it there. He shoved the other boxes out of the way and pulled the marked box free.

His palms were sweating as he set it on the table in the kitchenette. Thankful Callie had taken Eliza for the afternoon—he wasn't sure he could do this with his daughter around— he sliced through the packing tape with a key and opened the box.

Bubble wrap and tissue paper greeted him, along with the handmade tatted snowflake ornaments Maura's grandmother had given them as a wedding present. The painted wooden rocking horse and the nutcracker with a broken arm. An Elf on the Shelf that looked decidedly cranky took its place on the table beside the other memories, until finally, Dean reached into the bottom of the box and…

Maura's angel.

White fabric draped around a cone-shaped form, allowing the angel to settle on any size tree. The round cherubic face was topped with strands of yellow yarn, curling and streaming over gossamer-wired ribbon rings. The blue button eyes and pink cheeks may as well have been an image of Eliza, for all its detail, and Dean smiled, recalling the look of pleasure on Maura's face when she'd opened the box three days before Eliza's third Christmas.

Dean sat down, cradling the angel in his hands as he examined every inch, noticing the attention to detail, the tiny hand-stitching of the gown, the felt hands with tiny dots of colors on the fingers, as if she'd had an angelic manicure. The inside of the cone had been sealed to protect it from age and the heat of lights and… Dean squinted, reached behind him and turned on the light, then angled the angel so he could read the artist's initials. "For Christmas's Sake, Christmas Town, USA, 2010."

Dean's head spun. Maura's angel…*For Christmas's Sake*… It didn't seem possible.

Dean tilted the now empty box toward himself and a card flipped out. He picked it up and turned it over, staring down at the postcard for Christmas Town depicting the exact image he'd seen through his camera lens moments before.

Holding his wife's angel, letting the memories flood back, fired every synapse in Dean's brain, but they didn't slice, didn't burn. Instead they breezed through like a balm, soothing the bruises on his heart he'd feared would never fade.

Maura had been his first love—the only woman he ever considered loving. They'd been together all through college and married for three years before Eliza had been born. He'd never imagined living without her, loving anyone else as much as he'd loved her and yet...

Meeting Callie, even after such a short time, he had to wonder, what if?

The guilt he expected to land on his shoulders didn't manifest. If anything, the smiling image of Maura that circled his thoughts was kind, understanding, a whisper of encouragement even. And he knew, given Maura's kind and generous spirit, she would be overjoyed with the care and attention Callie gave to their daughter.

And yet...

How could he move on? And should he? Losing Maura had been one of the defining moments of his life. The idea of her not being here to watch Eliza grow up was one of his greatest sorrows. Was it possible to overcome the loss and move on?

Except it wouldn't be with Callie. It couldn't be, he reminded himself, as he set the angel on the table and repacked all the ornaments in the box. As disappointed as he was in Callie's reasoned caution when it came to his spur-of-the-moment admission, Dean understood her refusal came from a caring place. Eliza had already lost her mother and she thrived on their travels, their plans. The unexpected adventures. Dean couldn't risk his daughter's heart breaking again when they left. He wrapped the angel in tissue paper and set it on top of the box before sealing it again.

He could live with the regret he'd feel when he and Eliza left in a little over a week. He had to.

For his daughter's sake.

"OH, MISS BANNING! Look! They have *Ferdinand the Bull!*" Eliza dashed between shoppers and employees of the Bell, Book & Candle Shoppe and pushed the hardcover copy into

Callie's hand. "Has your brother read this one? It's my favorite story ever!"

"It's one of mine, too." Callie tucked an autographed first edition by one of Jack's favorite science fiction authors under her arm—she had a feeling it was a better choice for Jack than good old Ferdinand.

"My mommy used to read this to me every night." Eliza ran her fingers over the shiny cover. "I gave her our book when she went to heaven."

Callie heard a soft gasp behind her and saw the store's owner shoot a sympathetic look in Eliza's direction before she gave Callie a sad smile.

"Can I go home and get my money from my piggy bank so I can buy this for Daddy for Christmas? It's their very last one!"

Callie didn't know what stunned her more, Eliza wanting to buy her father a Christmas present or her mentioning Christmas without the slightest hint of anger or disdain.

Not wanting to lose momentum or risk Eliza changing her mind, Callie offered a compromise. "How about you let me buy it now and you can pay me back when I take you home."

"Oh, thank you, Miss Banning!" Eliza threw her arms around Callie's waist and squeezed. "I just know he's going to love it!"

"I'm sure he will. But, Eliza—" Callie bent down to her level "—what made you decide to buy your father a present? I thought you didn't want to celebrate Christmas."

"Oh, I don't." Eliza's voice was emphatic. "But it's like you told me. Just because I don't like Christmas, I shouldn't ruin it for other people. And I know Daddy loves Christmas. Or he did." Doubt crept over the little girl's face. "Do you think he still does?"

"I do." Callie stroked her hand over Eliza's curls. "And I think this is a very nice present. You can even write a message in the front. I think that would make it extra special. We can stop by my house on your way home and wrap it, okay?"

"Great!"

They left the store with the books for Jack and Dean, along with the limited edition Boston Red Sox beer mugs she'd bought her brother Nick, and headed to Callie's house for a round of gift wrapping. Callie couldn't remember having more fun holiday shopping. Eliza's more positive attitude made Callie wonder if the time hadn't come to push a little harder.

She made sure they circled around to the small Santa's village on the other side of the town square, where she bought Eliza a bag of fresh popped kettle corn. Taking a seat on one of the benches overlooking the long line of children and parents waiting to see Santa, Callie drew a deep breath and dived in.

"Eliza, I'd like to ask you a question, but I'll understand if you don't want to talk about it."

The girl's hand stopped halfway to her mouth. "What kind of question?" She dropped the kernel she'd been about to eat back in the bag.

"About Christmas. And how it makes you feel. Would you talk to me about that?"

"Why?"

"Because I'd like to help you enjoy Christmas again. And I think if you told someone why you don't like it, you might change your mind. Or maybe you'd be willing to tell Santa. You know, in Christmas Town, Santa gives very special candy cane wishes. What do you think? Would that work?"

"No."

How could so much anger and resentment be caught in a solitary word? Just as she had the other night in the park, Eliza's body had gone stiff, as if she were frozen, but Callie wasn't willing to let things go this time. Christmas was less than two days away. "No, you don't want to talk to me, or you don't want to tell Santa? I'm sure you can talk to your father about this."

"Santa knows," Eliza said, and angled a furious look toward the man in red across the way. "He doesn't care."

It didn't escape Callie's notice Eliza bypassed her suggestion to talk to Dean. "Of course Santa cares." She slid an arm around Eliza's shoulders and gave her a squeeze. "But Santa can't bring mommies back when they go to heaven, Eliza. No matter how many times you ask."

"I know, Miss Banning." Eliza gave her a look that implied she couldn't believe what Callie had just said. "That's not what I asked him for."

"Oh." Callie couldn't think of anything Eliza might have asked for that would've induced such a loathing of Christmas the little girl would resort to vandalism and theft. "Then what did you ask him for?"

Tears plopped onto Eliza's cheeks and she pinched her lips together so hard they turned as white as the snow at their feet. "I can't say," she whispered. "It would make Daddy sad and I don't want Daddy to be sad."

"I think it makes your daddy sad that you won't talk to him about this, Eliza."

"You can't tell him!" Eliza tossed her popcorn away, scrambled onto her knees and pinned pleading eyes to Callie's. "Miss Banning, you can't tell him ever!"

"Eliza, I can't tell him because I don't know."

"But if I tell you…" Tears spilled free and tracked like icicles down her pink cheeks. "If I tell you you'll want to tell him and—" Her breath hitched in her chest. "Oh, please, Miss Banning, if I tell you, you can't tell my daddy."

"Eliza, listen to me." Callie reached out, pulled her onto her lap and hugged her close. Love for this little girl had come so hard and fast Callie couldn't remember not loving her. Every tear Eliza shed, every sob that caught in her throat cut Callie to the quick, and she'd do anything to take her pain away. "There is nothing you can't tell your father. He loves you more than anything." It was what she loved most about him.

Callie's heart skidded to a stop. Love? Dean? Oh, that wasn't possible. Was it? But Eliza needed her attention now, not her scattered feelings about Dean. "And you're right. If you tell me, then yes, I'd feel as if I have to tell him. Especially if you won't. But I won't lie to you and say I'll keep your secrets. Because secrets hurt after a while." She tapped a finger against Eliza's chest. "You feel it, don't you? That thing that stops you from breathing? That makes it hard to talk? To sing? That's whatever you're keeping to yourself."

"It hurts." Eliza blinked more tears free.

"Sweetheart, trust me when I say your father will understand. Whatever it is, he will never stop loving you."

"But what if he leaves me?"

Callie blinked. She couldn't have heard right. "What?"

"If I tell, he'll leave me and then I'll be all alone, and I don't want to be alone. I'd be so scared."

"Okay. Hold up there, Eliza." Callie hefted her around so she could look into her face. "If there's one thing I can say with absolute certainty it's that your father would never, ever, leave you alone. I promise you that."

"B-but—" The tears started in earnest. "I asked Santa for a real home. One without wheels. I asked him to stop making Daddy move us all the time. I want to go to the same school. I want to have the same friends. I—I want…"

"What?" Callie stroked Eliza's hair. "What do you want? What else did you ask Santa for?"

"A new mommy." And then the dam broke and Eliza couldn't stop crying, as the words tumbled out of her like an avalanche. "I didn't mean to forget Mommy. I love her. But I miss having a mommy, especially at Christmas. And I miss Daddy being happy. He doesn't know I see, but I do. He misses her. They used to laugh all the time, and sing and dance, and oh, Miss Banning, my mommy was so pretty. Daddy says I look like her."

Callie felt her own tears fall, but she continued to hold on to Eliza as the little girl purged herself of her secrets.

"Does wanting a new mommy mean I don't love my real mommy anymore?"

"It does not," Callie choked out. "Of course it doesn't, sweetheart. Your mother loved you very much. She'd want whatever makes you happy."

"Then why didn't Santa make Daddy stop moving all the time? Why didn't Santa give me a real house, and a cat like Sammy? And brothers and sisters? And a new mommy? I've been so good. Most of the time. I try so hard. But Santa doesn't care. No matter how hard I wish, Santa hasn't brought me a new mom."

"Oh, sweetheart." Callie's words vanished. She had nothing to offer to stem the tide of emotions no seven-year-old should have to deal with—nothing except her love and support. "Remember what I said the other night in the park? Sometimes big wishes just take extra time."

"No." Eliza curled into Callie and buried her face in her neck. "I asked for a new mommy too soon, and now Daddy will never be happy again. And neither will I."

CHAPTER NINE

"DID YOU HEAR someone stole the Christmas lights off the tree in front of the Pine Tree Inn?"

"What?" Callie blinked gritty 7:00 a.m. eyes as Posey poured her a second cup of coffee. What on earth had made Callie volunteer to oversee final setup of the cotton candy and Secret Santa booths for the pageant tonight? She should have let them get their own coffee and scones instead of saying she'd pick them up two hours earlier than she needed to be at the town square. After hours delivering all the wrapped Christmas packages, she'd spent a sleepless night wondering what to do about Eliza and Dean's situation. The last thing she should be right now was conscious.

Dean was right. She let people take advantage of her.

She was not her mother. She was Callie. And that was going to have to be good enough. For everyone.

"Not all the lights were stolen, mind you,"

Posey added. "Mostly around the bottom, but they'll have to replace at least fifty bulbs. And you know how many strings fit on that tree? Enough to light up Main Street, I tell you. Your brother's got his hands full today with final pageant prep. Last thing he needed was to add that to his list."

"I'm sure Nick will get it done in time for the pageant," Callie said between yawns. Then she bolted up as if lightning blasted through her. "Wait, what? Someone stole the Christmas tree lights?"

"Oh, honey." Posey patted her shoulder. "Go home and get some sleep. I'll send Devon over with the coffee and scones."

Callie downed the scalding coffee, hissed when her throat burned, and tossed a couple dollars onto the table. "Posey, cancel my breakfast. I have to go." Before the woman could respond, Callie was out the door, tugging on her jacket and racing down Main Street toward the Pine Tree Inn.

Just as she rounded the corner to the inn's front door, she saw Dean approaching from the other end of the street. "Dean, is Eliza up yet?"

"I just dropped her off in the playground at school with Brooklyn and Madisyn. She was awake super early for some reason." He smothered a yawn. "Just like you."

If Callie was right, the little imp had probably never gone to bed. "Can we go inside?" She headed in the direction of his RV without waiting for a reply.

"What's wrong?" Dean unlocked the door and gestured for her to enter.

"I hope it's nothing, but I doubt it." She stomped the snow off her boots before stepping in. Wow. The interior looked like a hotel room, with its warm tones and full-size furniture. "You heard about the Christmas tree lights?"

"Hard not to given we live in their parking lot. Seems odd, doesn't it?" Dean flipped on the coffeemaker. "Take off your coat."

"Dean, I'm going to ask you to do something, and I need you to trust me, okay?"

"Okay." His gaze turned questioning.

"I need to search Eliza's room."

"What for?" That defensive edge returned, along with the protective attitude that made Callie's heart swell. "You think she's stolen something? She told me about the song sheets, by the way." The look he gave her said he wished Callie had, but she ignored him, impressed that Eliza had broached the subject without her.

"Did, um, the two of you talk last night over dinner? About anything special? Like why she hates Christmas?" *Please, oh, please, let me be wrong.*

"Well, she said she wanted to tell me something, but when she looked as if she was about to cry, I changed the subject and told her about Kentucky."

Callie's heart hit the floor and shattered like a glass ornament. "Kentucky?"

"My next assignment. We're leaving just after New Year's."

"Oh, Dean." Callie couldn't see through the tears. She'd known it was coming, but as she heard the words, she wanted to scream. And not only for Eliza. "Oh, no. She'll never forgive me. I told her to tell you. That you'd understand. No wonder she did it."

"Tell me what? Did what?"

"And now I have to break a promise I made to her. Or do I?" Callie tried to find another solution. Maybe she was wrong. Maybe Eliza hadn't done what Callie feared. "No, wait." She held up her hands. "Just let me see her room, okay?"

"Sure. She has the master in back. What is it you're looking for?" He followed Callie down the narrow hall, stood in the doorway as she started opening drawers and cabinets.

She stooped down to the drawers under the

twin mattress, pulled one open and sank down. "Oh, Eliza."

"What did you—"

Callie picked up the bulging, pink knit cap and dumped dozens of colored lightbulbs onto the carpeted floor.

"The tree lights?" Dean stared down, looking both shocked and devastated. "Eliza stole the Christmas lights?"

"I promised her she could tell you first, but you didn't let her." Now it was up to Callie to break not only her promise, but possibly Dean's heart.

"Tell me what?"

She hated betraying Eliza's trust, but she had to put the little girl's well-being first. Eliza was important, not what Eliza thought of her. If she never forgave Callie, so be it. At least Eliza and Dean would be on their way toward healing. Callie was out of choices and time.

"Every year since Maura died, she's asked Santa for a real home. For a cat. Brothers and sisters. And she asked him for a new mommy. She's afraid if she tells you the truth, that she doesn't want to move again…" Callie had to tell him quickly, otherwise she never would. "Dean, she's scared you won't love her anymore and you'll leave her behind."

Callie watched as the color drained from

Dean's face. He lowered himself to the edge of Eliza's ballerina-pink bed.

"What?" he croaked.

"She doesn't think she deserves any of it." Callie couldn't talk fast enough to keep the despair from appearing. "That Santa doesn't want her to have those things, because she asked for a mommy so soon after losing Maura. All this time, all these Christmases, all she's wanted was to find a new home and for you to stay with her in a new family. In one place."

"But— She's always loved traveling," Dean whispered. "Every time we leave for a new place she's excited and happy…"

"Because she believes it makes you happy. She doesn't think you've been happy since Maura died."

"She's right," Dean said. "I don't think I have been. Until we came here. I thought I'd done what was best." He leaned forward and clasped his hands between his knees. "After Maura's funeral, I just packed up what I could, loaded the RV and took off. I did everything long-distance because I couldn't bear to put Eliza in the middle of all the grief, all the things that needed doing."

"You did what you thought was right," Callie said, and laid a hand on his thigh. "Dean, you couldn't have known."

"What? That I was screwing up my daughter's emotional stability? That everything I've done since the day Maura died has been wrong?"

"You did what you could at the time. It's how you survived." Callie tried to soften her voice to take the edge off her words. "No one can blame you for it."

"I blame myself. All this time, all that sadness for my little girl because of what I decided was right."

"But now you know what's wrong, so you can fix it. Dean, this is a conversation you need to have with Eliza. Just the two of you."

"How? How do I have that conversation with my daughter, Callie?" He covered her hand with his and squeezed. "How on earth do I let her tell me I may have destroyed her childhood?"

"You start by not feeling sorry for yourself, and facing up to it." Callie got to her knees and clasped his hand in hers. "You start by telling her that you love her, that nothing will ever make you leave and that nothing she tells you will ever change how you feel."

"I've always told her that."

"But maybe this time, she'll listen."

"Eliza, your father's here."

At just after noon on Christmas Eve, Eliza's

classmates continued to vacate the school auditorium after their final practice. Eliza, who'd remained sullen and silent for the entire session, winced.

"Aunt Callie, what time do we have to be at the gazebo for choir?" Adam asked as he skidded to a halt in front of Callie and Dean.

"Hi, Adam," Dean said. "All ready for Christmas?"

"Yep! I'm going to get my wish from Santa. Dad's picking me up soon. Aunt Callie?"

"Six-thirty, please," Callie called. "And make sure you remember your scarf this time. That's why you got sick last year."

"Nah." Adam grinned. "I got sick because Billy Sullivan bet me I couldn't last twenty minutes in that storm without my coat and gloves. I showed him!" He shot her a grin that was so much like his father's, Callie chuckled.

"Yeah, he showed him," Callie told Dean and Eliza. "That kid was in bed for a week with the worst cold ever."

"Eliza?" Dean said.

"Yes?"

"Come on, baby. We have a favor to do for Miss Banning." He held out his hand. The self-pity that could have crippled him was gone, and in its place she saw a stronger man, a more confident one when it came to dealing with his daughter.

"What kind of favor?" Eliza put her pencil box in her bag and pulled her jacket off the back of her chair.

"Well, I've been so busy I haven't had a chance to get my Christmas tree yet. I was hoping you and your father would pick one out for me." The idea wasn't purely unselfish. At least this way she'd be sure to have a nice, healthy, lush tree to decorate.

"But—"

"Eliza, I think we owe Miss Banning at least this much, don't you?"

"Yes, Daddy." Fear hovered, Callie suspected, because the little girl knew it was a matter of time before her after-dark prank was revealed. But as she passed Callie, the look on Eliza's face called out for help. "Can't you come, too?"

"I have that special present I need to deliver, remember?" Callie gestured to her bag, where her Secret Santa present for her brother Nick was waiting. "But I'll meet you at my house soon, okay?" Hopefully, by then she'd hear from Jack. Her brother hadn't been answering her texts and she was starting to get concerned.

"Okay. Miss Banning?"

"Yes, Eliza?"

Instead of saying anything, the child threw her arms around Callie's neck and hung on. "I'm sorry. I tried to tell him. Please don't be angry that I didn't tell him."

"I'm not angry, sweetheart," Callie whispered in her ear, meeting Dean's concerned gaze over the top of Eliza's head. "But we made a deal, remember? You have to believe me. Nothing will make him stop loving you."

"'Kay." But the sullen tone left Callie wondering if the cheerful, ebullient child she'd come to love would ever reappear.

"We'll see you in a few hours," Dean said as he bent down to zip Eliza's jacket. "I'm so happy we get to buy a tree together, Eliza. This is a wonderful Christmas present."

The sadness cracked—just a hairline fracture—but the tremulous smile Eliza gave her dad seeped deep into Callie's core and took root. She covered her mouth to hide trembling lips. In a few short days they had become part of her life. Part of her heart.

Father and daughter walked out of her sight. And soon... Callie caught the sob before it could escape. Soon, they would walk out of her life.

CHAPTER TEN

"WHAT DO YOU think of this one?" Dean circled the five-foot Douglas fir as Eliza stood and watched, a mingled look of wonder and reservation making her seem far older than her seven years. "I bet Sammy would love climbing in it."

Eliza nodded and reached out a hand to brush the spiky needles.

"You know…" Dean waved the owner over and shelled out fifty bucks, with an extra twenty for guaranteed delivery within the hour. "Eliza, I've been doing some thinking, and you and I need to talk about some stuff."

"We do?" Fear returned and darkened his child's features. Guilt climbed up his spine and threatened to sink its claws into him, but he shoved it away. Callie was right. Feeling sorry for his past mistakes wasn't going to help Eliza today.

"Miss Banning said you like the kettle corn in the park. Want to get some?"

"Yes, please." Eliza was never more polite

than when she knew she'd done something wrong. Dean had settled the Christmas bulb situation with the inn's manager. The grandfather of seven had been sympathetic when Dean explained Eliza's behavior, and had promised to be as stern as possible later this evening when Dean brought Eliza around to apologize.

"It's very pretty here, isn't it? I don't think an article is going to do this town justice."

"What does that mean?" Eliza clasped his hand as they walked across the street to the park. The smell of kettle corn set his stomach to growling. He didn't think he'd ever appreciated the aroma of cooked sugar and freshly popped corn more.

"I mean I think Christmas Town deserves more than just an article in a magazine. What do you think about a book?"

"A book?" Eliza turned a scrunched face up to his. "You want to write a book about Christmas Town?"

"I'm thinking about it." He bought the popcorn and led them over to the bench Callie had told him about. "The problem is it would mean staying longer. And that's not our usual routine, is it?" He'd decided it would be better to open the door for Eliza to walk through, rather than trying to push.

"N-no." She plunked down next to him,

oblivious to the fact she'd spilled half her popcorn on the ground. "You want to stay in Christmas Town? For how long?" Her expression reminded him of a Christmas cracker about to explode.

"Well, that depends. What do you think about staying?" Dean's heart hammered so hard he didn't think he'd be able to hear a response.

"Like stay forever?"

"Is that what you want, Eliza?" He cupped his daughter's chin in his palm and looked into eyes that were so much her mother's Dean almost ached.

"Daddy?" She poked a finger against his sleeve.

"Yes?"

"I did something bad."

Finally. "What did you do?"

Eliza blinked, as if she'd expected him to yell at the simple revelation. "I, um, I stole the Christmas lights from the inn's tree."

"I see." Dean took a deep breath, and as he let it out, he felt three years of pent-up fear and worry that he wasn't the father Eliza deserved evaporate. Everything he'd done, ending with bringing his daughter to Christmas Town, had led them right where they needed to be. Where Eliza might learn to feel safe,.

protected. Loved. "Well." He curled his arm around her shoulders and brought her closer. "Why did you take the lights?"

"Because I was mad at you."

"At me?" Now that was a surprise.

"You said you wanted to go to Kentucky, and I don't want to go. I—" She stopped, as if she'd said too much.

"Eliza, we have to be honest with each other, okay? From here on, we tell each other the truth. And nothing you tell me will ever make me stop loving you."

"That's what Miss Banning said."

"Miss Banning is a smart woman." Dean pressed a kiss on top of his daughter's curls and thanked whatever power had guided him here. "Now out with it."

"I want a house. And a cat. And maybe a dog. And I don't ever want to move again. Ever, ever again. But most of all—" She hesitated. "Mostly I want a new mommy. Even though I still love my mommy. I'd just like a new one. Please don't be angry."

"Do I look angry, Eliza?"

She rubbed her cheek against his chest as she looked up at him. "No."

"That's because I'm not. All I've ever wanted was to give you want you need. The trouble is I never thought to ask what you wanted. So

I'm asking now. Do you want to stay in Christmas Town?"

"Yes." He couldn't remember her looking happier, more expectant, and he took pleasure in reigniting the light in his daughter's eyes.

"You realize that staying here means you're going to have to celebrate Christmas. There's no getting away from it in Christmas Town."

"Daddy, if we stay there's no reason to hate Christmas." The statement was made with a ginormous rolling of eyes. "Because that means my Christmas wish finally came true. Just like Miss Banning said it would."

Callie.

"Okay, then. Let's say we help Miss Banning decorate her tree. But let's keep our staying a secret for now, okay? I think we should surprise her at the right time."

"I love you, Daddy." Eliza squeezed him so hard it hurt to breathe, but he didn't care.

"I love you, too, Eliza."

CALLIE OPENED THE DOOR to find Dean and a glowing Eliza standing on her front porch. "Well, didn't you two do a smashing job picking out the tree. Eliza, I think you've found your calling."

"Has Sammy seen it?"

"Sammy has seen it and peed on it," Callie said. "Which means it's been officially accepted by all those who live here."

"Eww." The little girl scrunched up her nose but dashed inside in a beeline for the living room, where Callie had started unloading her more fragile ornaments. "I practiced my song all the way over, Miss Banning. Daddy says I sound beautiful."

"Does he?" Eliza closed the door behind him as he took off his coat and hung a gift bag on top of it. "She hasn't sung for me, so I'm thinking this is good news for the pageant?"

"She's good to go," Dean said. "We both are. Thanks to you."

"Well, I—"

"Accept the compliment, say thank-you and let's get this place whipped into shape. Eliza? You ready to decorate?"

"Ready! But when are we going to tell Miss Banning... Oh, no! Sammy! Bring that back!"

"Tell Miss Banning what?" Callie blinked up at Dean as Eliza went scrambling after the cat.

"It's a surprise."

"Okay." Callie wasn't sure she was up for any more surprises. "I have to be at the gazebo by six-fifteen to get there before the kids," Callie said. "Earlier if possible, in case I need to wrangle Adam. Nick's going to be pulled in every direction until the pageant actually starts."

"I think tonight might be just the start of him being pulled in every direction," Dean said, ambling into the living room. "Rumor has it he's going to run for town council."

"Well, that didn't take long." Callie grinned and hoped her Secret Santa gift to Nick was the final push he needed. With any luck, her present would be as welcome as the gift she'd found waiting for her when she got home. The small frame housing one of her favorite photos of her parents brought a sad smile to her face. She hoped wherever they were, her mother and father were enjoying the holiday.

The boxes of Christmas paraphernalia never looked more daunting than just before decorating. "Where should we start?"

"Lights," Dean announced. "Find me the Christmas lights."

The smile on Eliza's face, the lack of sadness on Dean's, combined to warm Callie enough for ten Christmases. This day, this moment, knowing no more barriers stood between Eliza and Dean, was the greatest gift she could have received. Anything else… Sadness skimmed along the edge of her smile. Well, she'd deal with that when the time came.

"Box number three. I'll get the cider."

"CALLIE, THERE YOU ARE." Principal Evelyn Moore cornered Callie just after six as she, Dean and Eliza arrived at the town square. "I was telling the other faculty members that since you've done such a wonderful job with the choir and the holiday party the last two years, you can consider the jobs yours from here on."

"Oh." Her heart hopscotched over her last doubt. "I appreciate your confidence, Mrs. Moore, but I'm going to decline. I love working with the kids and the pageant, but it's time for someone new to take over. New person. New ideas. Thanks, though."

"B-but you always..." Mrs. Moore couldn't have looked more stunned if Rudolph had broken loose and was headed her way. "You always say yes."

"Not anymore." Callie beamed as she sensed Dean's approval, and felt a weight lift from her shoulders. "Come on, Eliza. Let's get your fellow choir mates organized."

"Daddy, now?" Eliza's whispered plea, the same one Callie had heard multiple times during the past few hours, had Callie rolling her eyes.

"Goodness, enough already. What is this secret you two are keeping from me? Does it have something to do with that bag you won't let go of?" She headed around the mistletoe-encased gazebo as couples young and old ducked beneath the thick greenery for lingering kisses.

But instead of bypassing the steps, Dean caught her arm and tugged her back. "Not so fast."

"What?" Callie dug her feet into the snow, scrunching her toes in a useless effort to stop from being pulled into a Christmas Town urban legend. Oh, this wasn't good. As she tried to disengage from Dean, she felt as if jumping beans were in her stomach. The thought of kissing him under the mistletoe… "Dean, hasn't anyone told you about—"

"We know all about the mistletoe effect, Callie." His eyes sparkled as he winked at his daughter.

"We have a present for you." Eliza dragged her dad behind her. Then, when he didn't move fast enough, she got behind him and shoved him up the steps. "Come on, Daddy! Tell her!"

"Well, I guess now is as good a time as any. This is from Eliza and me. Merry Christmas, Callie." He held out the present.

"But Christmas isn't until tomorrow." She looked down at the glittery candy cane bag. "I don't open my gifts until Christmas morning."

"Oh, please open it!" Eliza grabbed her arm

and jumped up and down. "Please, Miss Banning?"

"You'd think someone around here liked Christmas," Callie teased, relieved her faith in Dean meant the presents she'd bought for Eliza would now be happily accepted. "There's something extra special about a gift given under the mistletoe. Thank you."

She pulled out a tissue-wrapped object and handed the bag to Eliza as she removed the paper, to reveal a beautiful but worn white fabric angel with bright yellow-yarn hair. "She's beautiful."

Callie frowned, remembering something Dean had said days ago, when they were sipping cider in her kitchen. Something about an angel... "Dean?"

"It was my mommy's," Eliza announced as she patted the top of its head. "Isn't she pretty? I know you have one for your tree already, so you don't have to use it if you don't want to, but... Daddy? Miss Banning, I didn't mean to make you cry." She tugged on Callie's coat. "Daddy, make her stop."

"I'm afraid I'm about to make it worse." Dean cupped Callie's face in his hands. Her heart beat double time. She couldn't think. Didn't dare to hope and yet...a slow smile curved her lips.

"Dean?"

"We're staying, Callie. Here in Christmas Town. It's home."

"It is?" Callie blinked the tears away but couldn't stop them from flowing. "But—"

"There is no but, Callie Banning. Christmas Town is home because that's where you are." He pressed his lips to hers, softly, tenderly, then smiled against her mouth as the sounds of hoots and hollers echoed in her ears. "It's where we belong."

"You mean it?" Callie whispered, and looked into the eyes she hadn't been able to stop thinking about ever since he'd walked into her classroom. Ireland had indeed found her. From that moment, her heart had been his. She reached out and pulled Eliza in for a hug. "Both of you?"

"Both of us," the girl said, bunching her fists in the front of their jackets. "Thank you, Miss Banning."

"For what, sweetheart?" Callie's hand curled in the soft hair at the back of Dean's neck, and she counted herself the luckiest woman in town.

"For making my Christmas wish come true."

"Can I tell you a secret?" Callie brushed her fingers against Dean's cheek before she bent down in front of Eliza, who looked happier than Callie had ever seen her. "You made mine come true, too."

* * * * *

THE CHRISTMAS DATE

Melinda Curtis

Dear Reader,

Local legend has it that a kiss beneath the mistletoe on Christmas Eve in Christmas Town portends a wedding for that couple within the next twelve months. The tradition is only one draw to the town's annual pageant, but it's certainly top of mind for several single residents.

The owner of The Tea Pot, Gina Vernay, has given up on the Christmas pageant, on dating and on dreaming of mistletoe kisses. On a whim, she signs up for an online dating site, but she doesn't post with her real name. Town handyman Nick Banning catches a glimpse of Gina's laptop screen and realizes this might be the opening he's been waiting for.

I hope you enjoy Gina and Nick's story, as well as the other holiday romances about the Banning siblings by my dear friends Anna Adams and Anna J. Stewart.

I love to hear from readers. Check my website to learn about my Harlequin Heartwarming series of romances set in Harmony Valley and to sign up for email book announcements. Or you can chat with me on Facebook (MelindaCurtisAuthor) or on Twitter (MelCurtisAuthor) and hear about my latest giveaways.

Melinda Curtis

www.MelindaCurtis.com

To Nana, who was a crazy-good, made-from-scratch baker, and who gave some of the best hugs, even when she was feeling down. The Tea Pot's pastry case will always be inspired by you.

Thanks to my family, close friends and my supportive husband. A special shout-out to Annissa Turpin-Giannone, who kept me sane during the writing of this novella and the editing of two other books. It was a wild couple of weeks, wasn't it?

Special thanks to Anna J. Stewart, Cari Lynn Webb and Anna Adams for their plotting and emotional support. Next time we'll put out a 4-novella set.

And to my mom, who made Christmas a magical time.

CHAPTER ONE

GINA VERNAY STOPPED believing in holiday magic when she was seven.

She stopped helping to set up the Christmas pageant when she was eight.

When she was thirteen, she stopped pretending to care about the pageant, and at eighteen she stopped coming altogether.

Since then, she'd pretty much stopped stepping out of her comfort zone. Period.

Until now.

In the wee hours of Christmas Eve morning, Gina stood at the edge of the town square and traced the deep, jagged scar that ran from her left temple to her jawline with the tip of a gloved finger, as if her touch could erase the past. The small ball of worry, the one that hadn't let her sleep last night, expanded like bread dough in her chest, pressing against her lungs.

I should have told him.

Snow fell silently, blanketing the square and the balsam firs lining it. The trees, mistletoe gazebo and surrounding quaint old buildings were draped in holiday lights. The town square looked like a snow globe, beautifully pristine and peaceful. The wind swirled around her, stealing her worried breath.

A whistled tune drifted through the darkness. "Jingle Bells."

A block away, a figure appeared on Taylor Street. Nick Banning, the town handyman and whistler.

Gina sucked in cold, much-needed air. There was too much to do today for her to wallow in what-ifs. She hadn't told him and this afternoon she'd face the consequences.

Carefully, Gina walked along the snowy sidewalk toward The Tea Pot. She'd bought the corner shop from her aunt last summer, trading in safe columns of numbers and isolated cubicles for early morning pastry making and running the place where everyone in town gathered.

Arriving at her doorstep just as she did, Nick finished a whistled chorus, his breath mingling with snowflakes. "Morning." He had a boxy tool bag slung over his shoulder. Holiday lights softly illuminated his handsome, reassuring features. Nick was one of the few people in the world who made Gina feel at ease, despite her scar.

She hurried to unlock the door and get them out of the cold. Once inside, she scuffed her boot soles across the extra large doormat, ridding them of snow. "When I asked you to show up first thing, I didn't really think you'd show up this early…whistling."

"No reason not to whistle." He stomped the snow from his feet, first on the outside grill, then on the inside mat. "Big day today."

She had the distinct impression that he knew she had a date this afternoon, and was teasing her about it. Gina flipped on the lights and peered at Nick.

He tugged off his knit cap and slid it into a coat pocket, revealing short dark hair, a gaze that didn't mock and a familiar, lopsided grin.

Nick caught her staring. His grin widened. "What? You forgot today's Christmas Eve? The annual Christmas pageant? The night Santa Claus comes to town?"

"No…I…no." Of course he didn't know about her blind date.

Well, it wasn't exactly a blind date. In her continued quest to de-comfort zone herself, she'd signed up for an online dating service and had been instant messaging a guy named Football20 for a week. He was going to introduce himself to her in person this afternoon. They planned to have coffee together.

That was, if he didn't take one look at her scar and bail.

Worry crowded her lungs again.

"Gina…" Something in Nick's easygoing expression changed. Perhaps he'd noticed her apprehension.

Gina gave herself a mental shake. She didn't have time for distractions. "The dishwasher was delivered yesterday." She removed her own knit cap and unbuttoned her jacket as she led him toward the kitchen. "I'll be glad to get rid of the old one. I'm tired of washing the dishes before I wash the dishes."

Gina's pride of ownership in the shop hadn't worn off. She still enjoyed taking in everything that made The Tea Pot special. The old pair of snowshoes and rusted, two-handled logging saw mounted on one wall. Yellowed photos of original town residents on another. Sturdy wooden tables and chairs from different eras. Fresh wreaths and garlands draped around the windows. The back wall with its collection of teacups and saucers. And the big pastry case at the counter, waiting to be filled.

Gina quickened her steps. She opened the swinging door to the kitchen and flipped on the lights, scanning the room with the same love she'd given the dining room—welcoming whitewashed cabinets, pale blue walls, checkerboard linoleum and…

A puddle oozed in front of the refrigerator. "Oh, no."

Nick came up behind her and leaned over her shoulder. At the subtle hint of woodsy aftershave, and his warmth at her back, her heart gave a mini ka-thump, as if to say *pay attention*. It did that sometimes when Nick was near. She ignored it. Nick was one of her closest friends in town. She'd been back months. If the ka-thump was mutual, he'd have said something by now. The things he most often said to her were *It's broken. I can fix it. Thanks for the cookie.*

She hurried over to the puddle of water. "I don't suppose industrial fridges have a reputation for watering the floor."

"No. Fridge puddles aren't good." He dropped his tool bag to the linoleum, then opened the refrigerator door and started touching things inside—cartons of milk and eggs, cubes of butter. "Everything seems cold. And the motor's running."

"Thank heavens for small favors." Since she'd bought the shop, it had needed one upgrade after another—new electrical, new plumbing fittings, new espresso machine, new dishwasher. And now… "Is it something you can fix? You need a Christmas bonus, right?" She called Nick so often for repairs, he was practically an employee.

"Let's see how serious it is before you go talking bonus." He knelt near her latest catastrophe, removing the grill at the bottom and reaching underneath to pull out the pan.

She hung her outerwear on a hook on the back wall and changed into a pair of soft half boots she kept at the shop. A quick mopping rid the floor of the puddle. "I've got to start baking. When I bought this place, Aunt Martha didn't tell me I'd also inherited the responsibility of serving refreshments to pageant workers this afternoon." So much for her plan to avoid the town's annual tradition. She surveyed the kitchen again, touching her scar.

"Does it bother you?" Nick was examining her, not the refrigerator. "Your scar? You touch it sometimes."

Something about the way he looked at her made Gina blush. "It doesn't hurt." She finger combed her long bangs across her forehead to her left ear, hiding most of the scar. The rest of her hair was in a neat French braid hanging between her shoulder blades.

"I don't notice it," Nick said gruffly. "Haven't since the first day you came back to town."

"That's so…" *Unbelievable*. "…nice." The

scar was long, thick and pinker than the rest of her skin. She might have considered plastic surgery, if the accident that almost killed her hadn't made her fear the sight of blood.

His gaze wouldn't let her go. "I mean it. Noticing your scar is like noticing someone's eye color. After the initial glance, no one can remember."

"Yours are brown," she said firmly, disproving his theory. A nice, warm chocolate-brown.

"And yours are green." He shed his jacket and tattered red scarf, flashing her that lopsided grin. "You cheated. You were looking at my eyes."

She returned his grin, letting him think what he would as she reached for her apron.

"'A hot cup solves everything'?" Nick read her apron. He raised an eyebrow, then pointed to the refrigerator.

"Don't tease the barista." She tucked her cell phone into her jeans pocket. "You want a cup of coffee this morning, don't you?"

"Please." And then his gaze turned serious once more. "Gina—"

"If you've already diagnosed the fridge as dying, I don't want to know until later. I can't take any more surprises until I've done the morning baking. After this, the only thing left to die in this kitchen is the stove. And I desperately need it today." She turned the old industrial oven to preheat. Then she retrieved her cash bag from her purse and hurried to the front of the shop to set up the register, grind beans and start the coffee brewing.

Several minutes later, with the cash register full and two steaming coffee mugs in hand, she backed her way through the kitchen door.

Nick had spread his tools on the floor at the base of the fridge. "You can leave my mug on the counter. I want to see if I can fix this before I install your dishwasher."

She sipped her coffee and then placed her mug next to his. With familiar ease, she dodged around Nick and his tools, assembling ingredients, bowls and utensils on the counter. Her recipes for the day were pinned to the wall—cinnamon walnut coffee cake, blueberry scones, banana nut bread, chocolate chip mini-muffins, frosted sugar cookies. She was making double everything. In addition to the influx of pageant visitors, she expected more town residents to stop in while they set up for the celebration.

Her cell phone announced a message. Almost absently, she pulled it from her pocket. It was from the dating website.

Football20: Would it be all right if I came earlier? At 9:00 a.m.?

A thread of panic stitched her shoulder blades tight at her online date's request. *"Earlier?"*

"What's that?" Nick didn't look up.

"Nothing." She'd hoped for more time to bolster herself to meet Football20 in person. He'd look at her scar, and if he didn't immediately turn away, his first words to her wouldn't be *Let's talk over coffee*. They'd be *What happened to your face?*

"It's not nothing," Nick said, still busy with the refrigerator tray.

"Someone wants to come by this morning and have coffee." Instead of dropping by after work.

"This morning. When you're so busy?" Nick shook his head.

"Yes, it's just…"

"You're busy."

"Yes." Staring at the phone, she sighed with relief that Nick understood, even if no one else seemed to. Not her mother or her aunt, both of whom felt she worked too hard. "I'll tell him no."

"But you're always busy," he added. Nick was bent over the refrigerator pan, fiddling with something in the middle of it. But there was a smile in his voice. "So maybe you should just say yes."

The panic pressed on her again, mingled with the fear of rejection. She drew a calming breath. "Of course. I should get it over with." And get on with her day. Alone.

He raised his gaze to hers, frowning. "You sound like you're the target of a firing squad."

"It's not like that." After a week of online messages, Gina wanted to meet Football20 in person. In their exchanges, he was funny and witty and low-key. She wanted to have someone special in her life. Someone to have long talks with over coffee. Someone to kiss under the mistletoe. If only she didn't have to show him her scar. If only she didn't have to do this today.

"Maybe you should tell him to come some other time," Nick said gently.

Time. That was just it. She'd wasted years already. Many of her friends were married and had kids. "No. I'll tell him this morning works."

She scheduled the firing squad for 9:00 a.m.

NICK KNEW HE should tell her the truth now instead of waiting until 9:00 a.m.

Instead, he clung to the reprieve.

When he'd installed new lighting fixtures in the front room last week, he'd witnessed Gina become flustered when she couldn't remember a password. He'd glanced at the screen of her laptop and saw the dating site logo. A crazy idea had hit him.

He'd wanted to ask Gina out, but any time the conversation turned personal, she clammed up tighter than a hexagon nut on a carriage bolt. She'd disappear into the kitchen or cut him short by offering him a cookie or some other baked treat.

He'd signed up for the dating website when he got home, thinking he'd post a picture and let her discover him. He'd imagined they'd share a laugh and commiserate over coffee, and then later, a candlelight dinner. But before he created his profile, he'd searched for hers. The only woman in his zip code went by a screen name—TeaCupGirl—with a profile picture of Gina. Well, a picture of the unmarked side of her face. She hadn't interacted with anyone online.

Why would Gina go to half measures if she wanted a date?

That night, he'd sat a long time staring out his window, thinking about Gina. Thinking of more than her sweet smile or the soft chuckle she made at his bad jokes. Thinking instead of the nervous way she dealt with many of The Tea Pot's customers—the ones who hadn't known her before the accident. Thinking of the way she averted her face from strangers and covered her scar with her bangs or a hat. She'd bought the place from her aunt, but Martha continued to work there, primarily behind the front counter. No need to wonder why that was. Gina was more comfortable baking than selling.

But he did ponder the dating site. He refused to allow his male ego to be bruised—so what if Gina was seeking a date online instead of asking the man standing right in front of her. If she wanted to find someone, she wasn't trying very hard. Scarred when she was a kid, she'd left town immediately after high school, gone to college and worked several years for a big corporation in Boston. She should be confident and accepting of herself.

And yet with most people this clever, caring woman was withdrawn, wanting to be seen as anything but a desirable woman. She wouldn't let Nick close. Not that he could blame her. Why would she be interested in a guy who'd barely graduated from high school? A guy who patched leaky roofs, repaired rotted floorboards and unstuck clogged toilets? Gina had more in common with Lindsey, his ex-wife, than she did with him. They were both educated, polished and worldly. All things he wasn't.

Nick could have given up. If he'd had any common sense, he might have. Instead, he'd created Football20 and messaged TeaCupGirl that same night, trying to start a conversation. It had taken more than a few tries, a couple patient days and some circling of the truth—about what he did for a living (flipping houses, a dream of his), where he lived (the next town over instead of here) and what he looked like (he'd posted a picture of himself holding a twenty-four-inch rainbow trout in front of his face). Finally, she'd agreed to meet.

And that's when he realized the trust he'd created with her online was based on a lie.

It ate at him, that lie. It sat and gnawed on his gut, especially late at night.

Today, he planned to confess his deception and apologize. She could wrap her arms around him and forgive him, or show him the door. Most likely, this would be the end of his work at The Tea Pot, the end of their easy, early morning conversations, and the end of his dream that his future and Gina's were intertwined.

He glanced up at her, at the white-blond hair that glimmered like tinsel in the overhead lights, at her slender build, at her red T-shirt with a sparkly Christmas tree on the front, partially hidden behind her apron. The way her button nose pinched and her scar accented her cheek as she squinted at a recipe filled him with joy. Not enough joy to erase the nerves that were erratically buffing the lining of his stomach.

Gina turned to him with a smile that was equal parts courage and fragility. "Give it to me straight. I can handle the truth."

She knew he was Football20? He almost said, "Yes, it's me." But he couldn't move. He couldn't speak. He wasn't ready for this conversation.

He should have let drop that he'd signed up for the dating site. He should have casually mentioned, when he'd fixed the wood rot on her back step a few days ago, about a wondrous relationship he was creating via webmessaging. Anything to seed the idea that he was Football20.

"Nick." There was a tendril of worry in Gina's voice. "Is my fridge dying?"

She wasn't *confronting him about Football20? They were talking about her refrigerator?* Nick released a relieved breath. "No."

"Then why are you staring at me as if you're about to deliver bad news?"

Because he was a lying schmuck.

The truth dangled in front of him like a carrot in front of a cart horse, out of reach unless he made one properly timed lunge. He stood and drew a deep breath, intending to tell Gina everything, determined to know if this would rank among the best days of his life or the worst.

Something heavy landed on the back porch, causing them both to jump.

"That'll be the morning paper deliveries. It doesn't matter how well wrapped they are in plastic, in this weather they'll get wet." Gina wiped her hands on her apron and marched to the back door, opened it to a blast of cold air and snowflakes, and dragged the bundles of newspapers into the kitchen. She closed the door and straightened, pausing to take stock of Nick. "You're not telling me something. I can see it in your face."

This was it. *Man up and forget 9:00 a.m.* "Well, um…"

"And don't even think about doing me a favor and repairing my fridge at no charge." Gina shook her finger at him. "I know how hard it is for a small business to make ends meet. Your time is worth something. And someday some lucky woman is going to see it, too."

Whoa. How did they go from repairs to business to dating so quickly? "It's your drain pan," he blurted. "It's clogged. Easy fix. See? I'm almost done." He held up a handful of gunk.

Smooth, Banning. Real smooth.

"No big repair bill? No new appliance?" Before Nick knew what hit him, she had her arms around him, and then just as quickly she was back at the sink, washing up. "Which lucky girl are you taking to the gazebo tonight?"

You, he wanted to say. But the feel of her arms around him had short-circuited his speech function.

"Come on. Callie told me you're smitten with someone."

"Callie doesn't know everything." But his sister knew about Football20.

Callie had borrowed his computer one day this week. She'd noticed the shortcut to the dating website, clicked on it and seen the number of conversations he'd had with Gina. Being Gina's friend, she'd put two and two together. As soon as he'd sworn Callie to secrecy, Nick had removed his log-in and password from his computer's memory so it wouldn't pop up automatically every time he visited the dating website.

Callie may have promised not to tell Gina, but she'd told their older brother, Jack. Nick's siblings were milking this for all it was worth—

teasing, dropping thinly veiled hints when Gina was around, driving him crazy.

He knelt to replace the clean pan.

Gina returned to mixing ingredients in a large glass bowl. "There's no reason you shouldn't be dating."

"You say that as if there's a reason *you* shouldn't date." Might as well talk about the elephant in the room—her scar.

Gina brushed the back of her hand across her forehead, but otherwise ignored his comment. "You're a big catch in Christmas Town."

"Women like having me around when something's broken." And sucker that he was, Nick liked being needed. He stood, moving to the dishwasher in its cardboard box.

"I do like it when you're around," Gina said. "It's just you only seem to be here when something's broken."

"You never invite me over when things are working," he said softly, afraid he couldn't quite disguise his hurt.

"That's because we're both so busy. Me with The Tea Pot. You with your work and Adam."

Adam. His young son, the pride of his life. Lindsey commuted ninety miles to work every day and ninety miles back. It was Nick's responsibility and pleasure to make sure Adam made it to school on time, to his afternoon activities and was fed dinner. Owning his own handyman service meant Nick could make his own hours. Being the only handyman in town meant his hours filled up quickly.

But that didn't mean he couldn't squeeze in a little time to date a special woman. "The shop will be closed for the holiday. You won't be busy later."

"Maybe I'll keep it open," Gina said cryptically. "I could sell a lot of coffee and hot chocolate after the pageant."

"On Christmas Eve?" Despite her holiday-inspired T-shirt, Gina had a holiday spirit deficiency.

And Nick was in possession of a cure—a Christmas date.

CHAPTER TWO

THE FRONT DOOR opened and Gina's aunt Martha called out a greeting. Severe arthritis in her hands had forced Martha to sell The Tea Pot, but she still showed up most days. If Martha wasn't working the front counter, she was gathering with her retired friends at a large oak table in the corner.

Nick was fond of the older woman. She spoke her mind, and they shared a love and concern for Gina. Having two boys who hated being stuck indoors, Martha had taught her niece how to bake, instilling a passion Gina's mother had considered impractical.

Martha entered the kitchen, shedding layers and depositing her jacket, muffler and hat on a hook by the back door. "It's still snowing outside." She shook imaginary wrinkles from an apron decorated with felt holly leaves and glittery red berries. "Do you want me to finish the baking? Or work the front counter? My arthritis is good today."

"I'm in the baking zone," Gina said lightly, but her movements seemed to slow.

Martha exchanged a concerned glance with Nick. "Your customers don't bite, you know."

The front bell rang. And rang again.

"Aunt Martha—"

"Someday, Gina, you'll realize that scar of yours makes you a woman of character and mystery." Her aunt washed her hands and hurried out to the front, where some caffeine-deprived residents of Christmas Town were in dire need of a hot beverage, if the way they were ringing the doorbell was any indication.

Gina's hands stopped moving.

"She's right," Nick said. "You give too much weight to that scar."

"I used to work in Boston." Gina surprised him, jogging the conversation toward a new track.

"I know." He worked at removing refrigerator gunk from his fingers with soap and water. The oily residue clung stubbornly to his skin.

"I learned a lot about myself there," she continued. "There was this one day last winter. It was snowing, like it is now. And I…"

"Go on," he said gently, when her story stopped.

"I was passed over for a promotion. Again." She swallowed, glancing at the items on her mixing counter. "I couldn't understand why. I was meeting my objectives and doing everything they wanted…"

Nick almost said something supportive when she started speaking again.

"I was working late in a remote conference room, trying to prove I deserved that promotion. I overheard some of the management team talking about me. They said I was smart and insightful, a great addition to the team. I was actually glad to overhear them." Bitterness laced her words. "And then my boss said, 'If only her scar wasn't so distracting. If only her scar didn't make clients feel uncomfortable.'"

"That's discrimination!"

"As soon as they'd gone," she continued as if he hadn't spoken, "I gathered my things and ran out of the office. I stumbled out to the curb and hailed a cab. The snow was so thick I could barely see." She stared at the wall, but it was as if she were seeing something else. "When a taxi pulled over, I opened the door. And then this guy came slogging up through the snow, out of nowhere, yelling about how I'd stolen his cab." Her pained gaze focused on Nick. "The wind must have blown the hair from my face. He took one look at my scar, apologized and backed away."

Nick wished he'd been there to protect her.

"Maybe he didn't realize you were a woman until he got close."

"He saw something he should pity," she said, her words a pained whisper. "In that moment, I was a lesser being to him. To everyone."

"That's bull."

She waved off his protest. "I thought coming home would be different. I grew up here. People should be used to my scar. I didn't think about the new residents or the tourists."

He shook his head vehemently. "You're misinterpreting." She was placing her self-worth in everyone else's hands.

"Am I?" The strength in her voice returned, along with something else. Disappointment. Whether it was disappointment in herself or the world, Nick couldn't tell. "I could walk out there now and help a customer. Tourists and those who don't know me notice my scar and pity me. I can tell by the way they stumble over an order or avoid looking me in the eye. I can tell by the generous tips they leave."

"If they make you feel that way, it's because you let them." It was his voice that shook now. He had to make her understand. If all she saw of the world was spoiled fruit, that's all she'd get. "You stand tall in this kitchen, but the moment you step out front you change. You...you shrink. As if you expect you'll be pointed out and shunned…or pitied." His words dropped between them like a thick curtain, dividing the space between believer and nonbeliever, optimist and skeptic, friend and—

Gina's green eyes had widened. Her cheeks paled.

He swallowed hard. He hadn't realized the strength of his emotions when it came to her. This wasn't a good start to the day. "Do you want to know what I see when I look at you?"

"I don't think—"

"I see *you*." He raised his voice over hers. He wanted to wrap his arms around Gina and re-assure her that he was on her side. Instead, he carefully dried his hands with a paper towel. "I see the blond hair first. It's shiny and silky, and makes me want to touch it." He almost reached for her, but she was frozen. "And then I see your intelligent green eyes and I get drawn into the warmth of your smile."

He paused, but she said nothing, so he sol-diered on, his voice dropping low. "To me, your scar accents your expression. When you concentrate on a recipe, it draws down. And when you smile, it lifts up. To me, it's noth-ing more than an eyebrow or a dimple. It's become a part of your face." Her beautiful, beautiful face.

Their gazes connected, as tentative as a first kiss.

She blinked, and looked at her feet. His hopes dropped, as well.

"I remember the day it happened," he said, feeling the need to say something more. "I was already onstage." He'd been standing in the back row of the choir every elementary student participated in. It was a rite of passage. A happy time when the town gathered to sing on Christmas Eve.

Gina turned back to the counter.

He should have shut up, but his lips just kept moving. "I remember the other kids filing in beneath the tree. It was blanketed in snow, but beneath its branches there was shelter from the wind." Just talking about it brought back the chill of that night. "You were a student volunteer, bringing up the rear, behind the kindergarten class. Callie was last in line. She slid on the ice and you helped her up."

His little sister had gone on, leaving Gina alone beneath the snow-laden branches.

"That tree. It was as old as some of the houses on Main Street," he murmured. "Someone should have cut it down years before."

"It was too majestic." She spoke in a voice he had to strain to hear. "There was a quietness there, as if I was alone in one of those snow globes where everything is perfect."

A moment frozen in time, before the branch above her trembled beneath the weight of snow and then cracked. She'd looked up…

Nick didn't remember her screaming. Some kids did. He'd been years ahead of her in school. He remembered blood on the snow and blood in her white-blond hair. He and Ron Umberland had come up to her months later, marveling at her "awesome scar." She'd started to cry. While Nick squirmed, looking for the nearest teacher, Ron had laughed. Gina gave a shuddering sniff and slapped Ron hard. The crack of her palm, the shock in Ron's face, the shrill note of a teacher's whistle. Nick had wanted to say *"Atta girl."*

That stubborn, courageous girl was a rare sight lately. He moved closer and laid his arm gently over Gina's shoulders.

She sighed and leaned into him, warm and soft, and smelling of cinnamon. "My mother says it was the worst day of her life."

"She should say it was the best. You lived. I can't imagine what my life would be like today if Callie had been under that branch." His limbs chilled. His little sister might be nosy, but he couldn't imagine life without her. "You were older and stronger. You're probably stronger today because of it." *Strong enough to forgive him a deception with the best of intentions?*

Just as Nick was about to tell Gina he was her nine o'clock appointment, she stepped from beneath his arm.

"Thank you for that." She wasn't looking at him, but from the side, her expression seemed determined. "I've heard a lot of advice over the years about being grateful and making lemonade out of lemons. But no one's ever put the onus of the scar's residual effects on me before. No one's ever called me a coward."

What? "I didn't mean—"

"It's okay, Nick. I get it. It's like the way you harped on Barty to quit smoking. Or how you helped Clarice through rehab after her hip replacement. I'm one of your projects." She drew a deep breath and took another step away from him. "I know I'm a coward, but I'm going to deal with this in my own way."

Coward.

The word echoed in Gina's head and pooled nervously in her fingertips. She tried beating it out in the mixing bowl, along with any life the dough once held. She tried kneading it out on the breadboard. She tried humming over it. Always the word returned.

Coward. Coward.

It wasn't as if Nick had called her that outright. He'd never be that cruel. But the message was received. She wasn't the only one who thought of herself that way. But his take was unique. If she considered herself broken, presented herself as broken, others would think of her the same way. It was how her employer in Boston had seen her.

What was Nick seeing when he looked at her that she didn't see in the mirror every morning? He didn't understand how hard it was to present herself as whole and strong when she wasn't.

Sugary treats baked in the oven. More sat in pans, ready for their turn. The kitchen smelled of warm cinnamon and chocolate. On the other side of the wall, the murmur of voices increased. Back here, she should have felt safe. She should have felt happy. Everything was on schedule.

Coward. Coward. Coward.

"You're *not* a project." Nick broke the silence between them testily. "And let's get one thing clear. I don't think of you as a coward."

"Maybe not. Maybe it's all in my head," she murmured, nodding.

"I understand," he said, looking relieved. "Have you heard the rumor going around about me running for office. I don't know how it started, but I can't stop thinking about it. I'm the last person you'd think of as an elected official."

She might not have thought of him first, but she wouldn't place him last, either. It took guts to put yourself out there like that. Guts she didn't have.

The clock's minute hand had clicked forward while she'd been lost in thought.

"Shoot," she said. "Look at the time. I need to concentrate on this recipe." A thinly veiled plea to drop the subject.

He complied, working beside her without speaking, sliding out the old dishwasher, wrestling it onto a dolly, taking it to the alley. He wore faded blue jeans and a snug long-sleeved green Henley. When he'd come close, bringing his woodsy scent, he'd lent her strength as she remembered that fateful day.

He'd been unbelievably kind, talking about how her scar was a part of her. And yet he'd also been incredibly frustrated with her.

Because you're a coward.

She didn't want to be broken or a coward. But how could she fix herself? She'd had the scar for twenty years. Just because he believed she wasn't flawed didn't mean she could flip a switch and agree. It wasn't his face people avoided looking at every day.

She glanced beneath the counter where the old dishwasher had sat, and groaned at the mess.

Nick returned to find her cleaning the linoleum for the new dishwasher. "Hey, I can do that."

"It's my dreck." Her embarrassment, more like. Amid the dust bunnies and stray clumps of old dough there was a small Christmas ornament, the size of a domino, in the shape of a Victorian house. She carefully washed the glass ornament in the sink, revealing red-and-gold trim on a white house. "Doesn't this look like Mr. Drummond's place? The white one that's seen better days?"

He leaned over her shoulder to examine it more carefully. Her heart did that funny mini ka-thump again.

"It does," he said. "I want to buy that house. Mr. Drummond is going to put it up for sale come spring."

She longed for a house with history, and a man to help her fill it with children. But whereas she'd been hoping Football20 would be that someone, suddenly, she thought of Nick. Of strong arms, warm brown eyes and gut-wrenching honesty when she needed it. Even if she didn't want to hear the truth. "Wasn't that house one of the original homes in Christmas Town?"

"Yes. I knew last year that was the house for me. Adam and I walked by it on our way to the town square on Christmas morning. Adam swore he saw reindeer footprints on the roof." Nick shifted, his chest brushing against her shoulder, fusing her feet to the floor. "This is the seventh year I've had to put up a cardboard fireplace at my mobile home and leave the back door unlocked for Santa to come in. Next year, my son is going to spend Christmas Eve in a house with a real fireplace." His breath wafted across her neck, sending her blood tingling with awareness.

Awareness of Nick? It was simultaneously thrilling and treacherous. They were friends, nothing more. He wanted her to show more backbone. She didn't want to disappoint him. But chances were she would.

"It'll need a lot of work," she said. More like an entire renovation.

"I'm testing for my contractor's license next month. I want to specialize in restoring these old beauties. I think I can make a go of it. And what better way to learn than working on my own place?" There was pride in his voice similar to the way she spoke of The Tea Pot.

She dared to glance at Nick over her shoulder, wondering at this new feeling of excitement. He'd been helping her for months, and today she felt a slew of sparks? "I want you to take this home and put it on your tree." She turned slightly, holding out the ornament.

"Put it on the shelf for now, to keep it safe." Still in her space, he wiped his hands with a blue rag he took from his back pocket. "Who're you meeting at nine?" His question was 100 percent proprietary male, surprising in its directness and the thrilling tendril of feminine power it created in her.

"It's just a guy I, uh, met online." Her cheeks heated. "I can't believe I told you." The only other person who knew was Callie.

"Maybe you're worried." There was something unreadable in those dark eyes, as if he knew something she didn't. "Do you trust this guy?"

"Of course. I wouldn't have accepted his invitation if I didn't." In the dining room, the sounds of conversation were increasing. She needed to check on Aunt Martha. Gina needed to walk out there as if she owned the place, with a smile on her face, so she didn't negate his faith in her.

Her feet wouldn't budge. At this moment, she didn't have the courage to face them as if she wasn't flawed...and she didn't want to step away from Nick.

"What does this guy think about your scar?" His voice. So close to her ear. Intimate.

Her cheeks were on fire now. She was surprised Nick didn't back away from the heat. "He doesn't know. I—I didn't tell him. Do you think he'll run away when he sees me?"

"Are you kidding? You're beautiful. Why would he do that?"

"You have to say that. You're standing in my kitchen." *With me practically in your arms.* Nevertheless, she hugged his words to her heart. No one had ever called her beautiful before.

"He won't run."

She bit her lip.

"You think he'll look in the front window and bolt." It wasn't a question. Nick was incredulous.

"That's why I replied that coming early was fine. It's best to get it over with."

He made an unintelligible noise, turned her to face him and kissed her.

CHAPTER THREE

HE'D IMAGINED GINA'S lips on his. He'd pictured her smiling as she gazed into his eyes and welcomed his kiss. He hadn't dreamed he'd drop a kiss on her mouth to stop her from speaking nonsense.

She didn't know. She couldn't see. She thought she was worthless.

Nick wasn't always good with words, so he put how he felt into his kiss, being careful not to wrap his arms around her and hang on tight, because he never wanted to let her go.

But he needed to. He also needed to pull back, regain his composure, apologize.

He did none of those things.

"Gina!" Martha called from the front. "I could use some help out here."

Only then did Nick draw away. Only then did he mumble something that may or may not have been an apology, while staring at his boots. Only then did he add, "That guy isn't going to run. He'd be a fool to run." Gina backed out of the kitchen, looking everywhere but at him.

GINA HAD NO idea what possessed Nick to kiss her.

She'd thought they were friends. But friends didn't kiss friends like that.

She'd had only a few dates in college—blind dates, all of them—but she knew the difference between polite good-night kisses and kisses that said *I'm into you*.

She'd never been the recipient of such a kiss. It electrified. It shocked. It drained.

And yet it was as if Nick's kiss was balm to her insecurities. She smiled and looked people in the eye as she hurried about the main room, refilling teapots with hot water, topping off coffee cups and placing pastries on pretty plates. Over the noise of the boisterous and growing crowd, she could hear the occasional bang and bump of Nick installing the dishwasher in the kitchen.

"What's gotten into you?" Aunt Martha asked when Gina darted behind the counter.

"Nothing." *I've been kissed.*

Kissed with wholehearted enthusiasm. Her lips still tingled. Her pulse still skipped happily, longing for more, naively hoping for a kiss beneath the mistletoe. Local legend had it that a mistletoe kiss on the eve of the pageant meant wedding bells in the New Year.

Clearly, it was time to get a grip.

Just a few more minutes.

"You should take a dose of *nothing* more often." Aunt Martha gave her a quick hug. "That's the smile I've been waiting to see since you bought the place."

Gina glanced in the mirror behind the espresso machine. Sure enough, she was smiling, with her scar peeking from beneath her bangs, framing the curve in her cheek and the arch of her brow. Nick was right. Her scar was part of her face, not marring it.

The idea scared her. It'd take time to accept. Maybe even more kisses.

Reality check, girl.

Nick had never shown the slightest interest in her until she talked about her insecurities. He had a reputation around town as something of a life coach, helping others reach their potential.

Aunt Martha stood back, gripping Gina's hands. "You've been far too worried about The Tea Pot and what our customers might think of you. It's the holidays. Loosen up and let them get to know you like I do."

Gina tried smiling in the mirror once more. Really, it wasn't so bad. She went about her work, beaming at Aunt Martha and the customers who met her gaze.

And then she caught sight of the clock. Eight-thirty. Her smile crumbled.

Football20. She felt as if she'd betrayed him. She'd made a connection with a man online and then found that special spark in her own backyard...*er, kitchen?* It was as if she were cheating on someone she'd never met in person. And wasn't that a silly notion?

Silly, yes. But a difficult idea to shake. She felt the urge to confess to Football20.

She slid her phone from her back pocket, intending to send Football20 an instant message via the dating website. But she hesitated over what to say. She couldn't tell him she'd just been kissed. Instead, she babbled: Incredibly busy this morning. Thought refrigerator might be busted (it's not). So grateful my friend Nick is handy and available.

She didn't add he was a great kisser.

There was always a time lag on messages that went through the dating website. While waiting for a reply, she circulated through the dining room, picking up dirty cups and dishes.

The oven timer buzzed loudly, as did her phone with a message from Football20: You're lucky to have such a good friend.

Her date didn't sound jealous. He sounded nice. Did she want him to be jealous?

Gah! She wasn't the kind of girl to pit two

men against each other, as if she was a princess and they were vying for her hand.

She carried a tray with dirty dishes toward the kitchen, testing the idea of her and Nick. He was more involved in the community than she was, more outgoing, and apparently more perceptive than she was about herself. They shared a strong work ethic, a similar sense of humor and a love of country music and baseball. He had a young son who'd perfected the art of the soulful gaze, which earned him an extra cookie when he came into the shop.

As for Football20, she might not know his real name or what he looked like, but they had things in common, too. They were both fond of action movies, old houses and harbored a desire to travel. They both loved small towns, even if Gina wasn't so fond of one small town tradition...the pageant.

Reality intruded when Gina remembered her scar.

One kiss and a few compliments and she was acting as if she had two men to choose from. Two decades with the scar and she knew that wasn't possible. The euphoria of Nick's kiss drained away.

She pushed through the swinging door, prepared to tell him she wasn't interested in being his latest project. "Nick, about what happened earlier..."

But her handyman was gone. The kitchen was empty, other than his tools and the dishwasher, which was parked halfway into its cubby.

A note on the mixing counter indicated he'd gone to the hardware store for a new hose.

Despite her better judgment and the impending awkwardness, Gina was disappointed he'd left.

She removed pans from the oven and set them out to cool. She put another bunch in, then began making the fruit compote for the Danish. But she couldn't escape the fact that she'd been kissed in this room. Never mind her scar or the dishes soaking in the sink. She'd been kissed.

And she liked it.

No matter the reason, she'd never walk into the kitchen again without remembering Nick and his kiss.

Drat.

Callie darted in the back door. "Hey, I'm dying for news of Football20. I have five minutes before I have to be at the town square." She stood on the mat, stomping her boots and shaking the snow off her jacket. "I see my brother's been here and left his usual mess."

"Ain't that the truth," Gina mumbled, although Nick wasn't at all messy—her emotions were the chaotic jumble.

"Is Football20 still coming tonight?" Callie finished her stomping and crossed the room directly toward a tray of chocolate chip mini-muffins just out of the oven.

"No. He's going to be here at nine." In just a few minutes. Gina brushed the back of her hand against her scar.

"The rat. I wanted to see him arrive." Callie snatched a hot muffin, tossing it from hand to hand to cool. "Just my luck I have to be on the square at nine. You'll be kind to him, won't you?"

"Hey, whose side are you on?"

"True love's," Callie said, and darted out the back.

IN DECENT WEATHER, Gus, Barty and Marv sat in rockers on the porch of the Christmas Town Workshop—the local hardware store. From there, they could see the town square and most everything that happened in the community.

When the weather turned inhospitable, the three store owners dragged their rockers indoors, making sure they faced the plate-glass window.

As Nick came across the creaky floorboards

of the threshold, all three men rocked and greeted him.

Nick glanced at the time. He had fifteen minutes to buy a hose, drop off his Secret Santa gifts and keep Football20's morning date with Gina. Her dumbfounded reaction to his kiss was alarming. Was he that much of a disappointment?

"How's that dishwasher install coming along?" Gus asked. His bald head gleamed in the fluorescents.

"Hear tell Yolanda Brewster's porch gave way under all the snow. She call you yet?" Barty scratched beneath the red plaid ear flaps of his buffalo hat.

"Someone said some bulbs are missing from the tree at the Pine Tree Inn. Are you here to pick up replacements?" Marv peered at Nick over round, thick lenses.

He responded to each of them in turn. "The Tea Pot's dishwasher needs a new hose, Gus. Yolanda told me not to worry because her son is coming tonight, Barty. I hadn't heard about the bulbs being stolen." Theft was unusual for Christmas Town. "If you've got a box of bulbs left, Marv, I'll take it."

"There's a box on the counter." Barty pointed. "Hoses are in plumbing, aisle two."

Nick hurried to the rear of the store. Floorboards protested his every step. He'd blown it with Gina big-time, telling her how to behave, what to believe about herself and kissing her... *Kissing her!*

He found the hose he was looking for and returned to the counter, where the rhythmic sound of rockers made a harmony with the creaking floorboards. None of the store's proprietors disturbed their watch to ring him up. Nick added the cost of the hose and the bulbs, calculated tax and rounded up, leaving bills on the counter. "Your floorboards are getting worse."

"Then come by and fix them," Gus said. "We'll pay for your time."

"I'll schedule you for next week." He didn't relish exploring their crawl space, especially in winter, but it was preferable to worrying about boards giving way and friends getting hurt.

Which made him think about Gina's accusation that she was one of his special projects. He didn't take on projects. He helped people. It had started when he was young, the helping. His grandmother had suffered from epilepsy, which meant his mother was on call to help her. All the Banning children learned early to pitch in.

First, he'd been Mommy's Helper, stepping in to make his grandmother comfortable after a seizure, while his mother called the doctor. Then he'd been Daddy's Helper, handing him tools as he fixed everything from cars to air conditioners. Finally, he'd been assigned to keep his younger sister out of mischief. That had been the hardest job of all.

"Who are you bringing to the pageant tonight?" Gus asked, pausing in his rocking.

"Well...I—"

"It's time you settled down." Barty tugged his ear flaps.

"It's time Adam had a baby brother." Marv pushed his glasses up his nose. "In my day, women appreciated a hardworking man. You want to get married again, don't you?"

"Dating is different nowadays." Nick edged toward the door. "Women are complicated."

The three men chuckled, nearly drowning out a gust of wind.

"Women were always complicated." Gus started rocking again. "That hasn't changed."

"But it all boils down to one thing." Barty held up a finger.

Nick found himself leaning forward, cocking his head in order to hear better.

"Just love her." Marv closed his eyes, perhaps thinking of the wife he'd lost to heart disease a year ago. "You just have to love her something awful."

"And then the awful stuff don't seem so bad," Gus said absently, staring out at the swirling snowstorm.

"And making up is that much better." Barty grinned.

Nick was considering love advice from these three? *Time to move on, Banning.*

Marv peered at him over the top of his glasses. "But you have to remember that it's your life. You may love her, but don't ever compromise your dreams for her. Like public office. We hear you're running."

"Yeah, I've been getting that a lot these past few days. It's a rumor." Nick hurried off.

Admittedly, the thought of serving the community officially was appealing. Nick regularly attended as many council meetings as he could fit into his work and parenting schedule. But a seat on the town council would mean less time with Adam. The older his son became, the more complicated his schedule of activities. There'd also be less time to take on historical home restoration jobs. And what if a relationship with Gina panned out? She could barely show her face in her own shop on tourist-filled days. Would dating a politician and living at the edge of the spotlight be too much for her?

He didn't know. The wind peppered his face

with snowflakes. His boots sank in fresh layers of snow.

Nick detoured to Callie's house. He'd taken on his dad's role as the Secret Santa, since his parents were touring the country in an RV. To ensure Jack received his gift, Nick had delivered it earlier in the week. Because of their work schedules, volunteer commitments and Adam's routine, the siblings didn't get together as much as they'd like—what family did?—but they'd promised their parents that this year would be different. Jack wouldn't take a holiday shift at the hospital. Nick would postpone all but emergency repairs. And Callie would focus only on family for the day.

Leaning into the wind, Nick hurried through two feet of snow and stomped up the steps. He retrieved a wrapped box from an inside jacket pocket and slipped it carefully into Callie's mail slot. Nick and his parents had a big surprise planned for Jack and Callie.

On his way back to The Tea Pot, he passed the town square, waving to a few brave souls who were out early, trying to stock their booths despite the snow. His sister was one of them. She gave him a thumbs-up.

Less than two minutes until nine. He'd need all the luck he could get.

Nick paused outside The Tea Pot, peering

in the window at the crowd. Every chair was taken, much of the floor space, too. Any more bodies and the fire marshal, who was at the condiment bar doctoring his coffee, would begin kicking people out.

The bell rang as Nick entered. Gina glanced up nervously, and then away. Her smile was fragile, but she didn't seem as small as usual.

He would have preferred her to run into his arms, but he understood her tension. She was expecting her online date, a stranger, to walk through the door. Nick thought again about saying, *"It's me. Football20."* But she was busy filling orders.

The line ended halfway to the door. Nick hesitated. Most seemed to be waiting for the storm to abate before traipsing out to set up for the day's festivities. He overheard numerous discussions about the snow letting up, and the great snowstorm of 1991.

Gina was filling drink orders from Martha, who was working the old cash register. No way was Gina going to have time to talk to him alone. He'd thought by nine she'd be over the worst of the rush. He hadn't factored in snow.

Now wasn't the time to confess. He'd surprised her this morning with his kiss. Maybe she should understand how much he cared about her before he revealed himself as Football20. Maybe then she'd realize she wasn't a project, and that he'd go to any lengths to win her heart.

He turned and reached for his phone, quickly messaging Gina through the dating website as Football20: Something came up. Can't make it until noon. Sorry.

He knew the moment Gina received the message. She startled and reached for her phone, read what he'd written and drooped.

Nick stepped out of line and headed toward the kitchen, pausing at the door. "Something wrong, Gina?"

It was Martha who answered. "Nothing's wrong. She's…" Gina's aunt did a double take. "Well, I'll be. She was as perky as a well-rested kitten until a moment ago." Then Martha returned to taking money from customers.

Nick leaned closer to ask, "Did that guy show?"

"No." Gina glanced at him out of the corner of her eye. The kiss seemed to have created an invisible barrier between them.

Way to go, Banning.

"There's been a change in schedule. No biggie." And then she mustered a brave smile and met Nick's inquiring gaze. "He's still coming. It's just…he's coming later."

"You bet he is," Nick said firmly.

SHE'D BEEN STOOD UP. Gina couldn't believe it.

Although Football20 had told her he wouldn't be there until later, Gina glanced up every time the bell above the front door clanged. The steady stream of pageant workers continued to congregate in the front room. At this rate, she'd need to bake more of everything for afternoon refreshments.

Nick had finished the dishwasher installation over an hour ago. He'd left to help set up the pageant. They still hadn't talked about that kiss.

It was as if Gina's life was on hold. Her emotional life, anyway. And maybe her business. There was a temporary lull at The Tea Pot.

Her mother barreled in, wearing a zipped up, quilted stadium coat long enough to double as a sleeping bag. She stepped behind the counter to adjust Gina's bangs over her scar.

Gina felt like a fidgety child, but it was easier to submit to her fussing than argue.

Her mom studied her handiwork, then nodded. "I need to finish Christmas shopping this morning. Do you two need me to pick up anything?"

"You're out and about in this weather?" Martha asked. "Where's your common sense, Danielle?"

"I have things to do later." Gina's mother

sniffed, although they all knew she didn't attend the pageant. She'd stopped volunteering after Gina's accident. "You can't postpone Christmas, Martha."

Gina's parents hadn't been excited about Christmas in years. If Christmas Town had a contest for the role of Grinch, her father would have won, hands down.

"Are you doing something special for Christmas?" Martha asked.

"No," Danielle said too quickly.

"Fine," Martha grumped. "Pick me up a box of saltwater taffy at the Sweet Shop."

Her mother made a note on a slip of paper. "What about you, Gina?"

Gina wasn't proud. She could use all the help she could get today. "I bought Dad a book about vintage airplanes. It's waiting at the bookstore." An image of Nick bundled against the cold came to mind. "And if you see a man's red scarf, could you pick one up? It'd be great if you could have it gift wrapped, too."

"Of course," Danielle said. "But your father's favorite color is blue."

"I'm not giving it to Dad," Gina said enigmatically. She looked at the front door, expecting Nick to enter, broad shoulders easily bearing the weight of his tool bag, flashing that familiar, lopsided grin that gave her heart a good ka-thump.

"Gina?" Her mother's brows were knitted, but before she could say anything more, Carol, the owner of Carols and Curls Beauty Salon, rushed in. Everything about her was slick and stylish, from her cute snow boots to her fluffy, highlighted hair beneath her parka hood.

"I need volunteers," Carol said. "I'm cutting hair for Locks of Love. They make wigs for sick children. I promised I'd deliver twenty locks of hair, which means I need twenty people willing to help, and I've stalled at twelve commitments." Her gaze darted about the room, pausing on women with long hair. "I was betting that I could convince some pageant attendees to donate their hair in exchange for a free cut and style, but this snow is making me nervous. What if there aren't enough women out today with long uncolored hair and big hearts?" And then her gaze landed on Gina.

Aunt Martha, who had short gray hair, and Gina's mother, who had short bleached blond hair, looked at Gina, too. She covered her bangs with one hand.

"You can keep your bangs," Carol said quickly.

The light in the room seemed to dim. A determined *whoosh* filled her ears, as if she was walking outside in a heavy snowstorm.

My hair. She used it as a shield. A cowardly shield.

Gina gripped the counter. "Can I think about it?"

"I start cutting at two." Carol nodded, and then rushed toward Holly Mayfield, a pretty brunette with three kids and hair past her shoulder blades.

"Don't do it," Gina's mother whispered, fiddling with Gina's bangs again. "Your hair is your prettiest feature."

"Not my smile?" Gina asked softly.

There was an awkward silence, one that echoed hollowly in Gina's chest. She tried filling it with Nick's pronouncement that she was beautiful, but she couldn't bring to mind the steady, earnest timbre of his voice saying the words.

"Danielle," Aunt Martha scolded.

Gina's mother waved a hand and said unconvincingly, "Everything about Gina is beautiful to me." She distributed air kisses to them both and left, leaving Gina's spirits somewhere in the dank and drafty basement. How could she believe Nick's words or his kiss? Her own mother—

"If one more person comes in, we're going

to run out of food," Aunt Martha predicted gloomily.

One more person didn't come in. A dozen did.

The door to The Tea Pot opened and a troop of Holly Scouts entered, wearing red berets and blue jeans.

Martha tossed up her hands. "Eleven hungry girls. That's it. We need to bake more food and brew more hot chocolate."

"And I thought driving in this weather was stressful." Priscilla, the leader of the troop and one of Gina's childhood friends, gave them a harried smile. "Have you ever tried to keep a group of young girls occupied in a snowstorm?"

Gina shook her head.

"Have your girls earned their cooking badge?" Aunt Martha asked innocently.

"We haven't. We're a new troop from Rebliville." Priscilla herded her charges toward the nearly empty pastry case.

Her aunt cast Gina a significant look.

Despite her doldrums, Gina caught on. "We could use a troop bailout for thirty minutes, or until the snow stops. Are you up for it?"

Priscilla's smile lightened, and the girls whooped.

Soon there were Holly Scouts clearing tables, Holly Scouts refilling coffee cups and teapots, Holly Scouts mixing cookie dough and washing dishes. With their green camp shirts and red berets, they added a festive feel to the shop.

Priscilla pulled Gina aside in the kitchen. "I'm so grateful to you for keeping the girls occupied."

"I'm the one who's grateful. Is one of these girls yours?"

"My niece is washing dishes. My sister is too busy with her career and commuting to organize anything like this. So I make the drive to Rebliville once a week for meetings." Priscilla was a middle school teacher in Christmas Town. "Diana enjoys the Holly Scouts so much, I can't disappoint her."

At the sound of her name, Diana turned, a sweet smile on her innocent face.

Gina suppressed a gasp of surprise. The young girl turned back around, unaware of Gina's shock at seeing Diana's port-wine blemish.

"It's a birthmark," Priscilla explained in a low voice. "My sister always wants to cover it with makeup. But Diana's only eight, and even though it's on her cheek, it's the size of a quarter."

Gina's fingers itched to fiddle with her bangs, even as Nick's words about acting as if she wasn't broken returned. She assembled her lips in what she hoped was a smile. "Good for her. I don't put makeup on my scar anymore."

"I'm glad. Diana doesn't seem to care about her birthmark." She had no hairstyle designed to hide it. In fact, she showed no tentativeness at all. At eight, Diana was more accepting of her appearance than Gina was at twenty-eight.

Aunt Martha poked her head in the door. "It's stopped snowing. Everyone's clearing out."

As the Scouts donned their jackets, hats and mittens, Gina thanked them and reminded them they were each owed a cup of cocoa and a treat later.

Priscilla paused before following her charges into the brisk wind. "Since Diana was born, I've wanted to tell you that I think you were very brave growing up with that scar. And I think..." she looked around the shop "...you might still be."

Gina hadn't been and was far from brave now, but maybe with a little help from friends, long lost and otherwise, she could be. Impulsively, she hugged Priscilla and wished her a Merry Christmas.

The Tea Pot emptied of able-bodied workers. Those remaining were too old or too young to help set up for the pageant. The soft murmur of their voices and the sound of crayons on newsprint was a welcome backdrop after the raucous morning they'd had.

Aunt Martha sat to have a cup of tea with members of her book club. Gina puttered about, cleaning up, removing cookies from the oven, putting Danish in. She paused while wiping down a table to gaze at her reflection in the plate window.

Since she'd left Christmas Town, she'd been hiding, the same as she hid the scar behind her bangs.

For the first time since the tree branch had hit her, she drew her bangs off her face.

CHAPTER FOUR

SINCE LEAVING THE TEA POT, Nick had spent most of the morning volunteering wherever he was needed—replacing missing bulbs in the tree at the Pine Tree Inn, shoveling snow from the sidewalks around the town square, helping carry boxes and bags to vendor booths.

Thankfully, the wind was dying down and the sun was coming out. The clearing weather lightened spirits and made everything seem easier. The town square began bustling with residents and early tourists. Soon Lindsey would bring Adam by. It was time for a cup of coffee and a check-in with his favorite barista.

"Nick, hold up." A booming voice came from behind him.

Nick paused at the corner of Christmas Tree Lane and Jack Frost Avenue, gazing longingly at Gina's shop, before turning to Carlos Yanez, the town mayor.

The older man's breath came in huffing clouds. He landed a gloved palm on Nick's shoulder. "I've been meaning to ask you about the town's snowplow."

Nick suppressed a groan. "Did it break down again?"

"No-ho-ho. But it needs replacing, don't you think?" His faded brown eyes sparkled with inquisitive intensity.

"It does." Nick took a step back, toward The Tea Pot.

Carlos held on to his shoulder. It was a let's-talk-seriously-until-I-have-answers hold, which was odd. Carlos had never bothered with serious talks to Nick before. "And what's your opinion about water resources?"

There'd been a dustup recently regarding water rights on Reindeer River. Several towns downstream claimed shares, but the river's source was the mountain range directly above Christmas Town. "At the last council meeting, you discussed the importance of the existing contract," Nick stated. "If towns like Rebliville need more water, they should look elsewhere. We shouldn't deplete our reserves, even if we could generate more revenue by selling to them."

The mayor nodded. "And education. Where do you stand?"

"Pay the teachers a decent wage. Equip our

schools with the latest technology." Callie had drilled that into him often enough.

The mayor beamed and squeezed Nick's shoulder. "I'm glad you've decided to run for town council. You have my full support." Carlos called to another council member, who'd been adjusting the walls of the face-painting booth.

Town councilman? It wasn't a rumor or a pipe dream. The mayor wanted Nick to run for office, was offering his full support. To Nick. The local handyman who didn't have a college degree.

Things like this didn't happen to him. He was "the other Banning." He'd married young and dropped out of college in his first semester to support his wife, planning to get his degree after she graduated. But then they'd had Adam. And then Lindsey had left him because he was a blue-collar working sap, one she was embarrassed to introduce to her coworkers. It hadn't been the friendliest of divorces, but he and Lindsey had found a neutral zone where she didn't snipe at the sight of paint on his hands and he didn't jab back at how her high heels didn't add to her promotability.

Someone walking past misjudged the space and bumped Nick's shoulder, jolting him out of incredulity in time to notice Adam and Lindsey turn a corner and head his way. "I haven't agreed to run."

Carlos paid him no attention as he called other council members over. Soon Nick was surrounded by councillors and involved citizens.

"Your faith in me is flattering," Nick began, raising his voice to be heard. He could see himself on the other side of the council table, maybe someday even becoming mayor. He could see his parents, siblings and son in the crowd, nodding approvingly to whatever point he was making. Who he couldn't see was Gina.

The sun glinted off a window at The Tea Pot.

Although the idea of serving the community stroked his ego, his feelings for Gina held more sway.

Skinny arms wrapped around his waist. "Dad? Are you going to be mayor?" Beneath a fringe of dark hair covered by a navy stocking cap, brown eyes stared at him worshipfully. "That's cool."

"Let's not rush things, son," the mayor said in his loudspeaker voice.

"He could do it." Lindsey stood at the corner, oblivious to the fact that her comment had rendered Nick speechless. Neutral zone or not, compliments from her were few and far between. She held out her hand toward their son. "Come on, Adam. We have to pick up something at the bookstore."

A group of carolers dressed in Victorian costumes began singing "Deck the Halls" in front of The Tea Pot.

It took Nick a few more minutes to extricate himself from the town's politicos.

Callie intercepted him as he crossed the street, which was closed to all but foot traffic. By way of greeting, she slugged his shoulder, not doing much damage through his thick winter coat. "You didn't tell Gina. She said she was going to meet Football20 at nine, but when I texted her she said it was postponed. Are you chickening out?"

"No, runt." He was trying to untangle the mess he'd made with Gina. "I think she needs to get used to the idea of dating me, before she knows I'm the one who's been getting to know her online." Thankfully, Gina hadn't mentioned to his sister that he'd kissed her. If she had, Callie wouldn't have let him hear the end of it.

"And how do you plan on getting Gina used to the idea when you're out here and she's in there?"

His phone vibrated in his inner jacket pocket. He tugged it out. A smile warmed his cold cheeks. "Here's how. Something's wrong with her stove."

Callie's eyes sparkled. "You better tell Gina who you are before you fix everything in The Tea Pot and she has no more use for you."

Nick hesitated, and in his hesitation his sister must have seen his vulnerability, because she hugged him fiercely. "You're perfect for her."

He set Callie aside, rolling his eyes. "Thanks. Wish me luck."

"Break a leg. I'm off to choir practice." She turned, but he stopped her with a touch to her arm.

"Your plate is too full, runt."

Instead of making a glib retort, Callie bit her lip. "I'm trying to say no more often. You of all people know how hard that is. But you don't just fix things, bro. You also fix people. Please don't tell me that's why you're interested in Gina."

"No!" The word burst from him like a nail from a nail gun. "Why does everyone think that? She doesn't need fixing." What she needed was a supportive partner. Her confidence would grow from a safe place.

Callie narrowed her gaze. "Who is everyone?"

"Just Gina." The admission came out more harshly than he intended. Growing up, Gina had been sheltered in Christmas Town. The barriers she'd erected against the outside world had protected her, but also created boundaries on her life. It was time they came down.

Callie slugged his shoulder again, harder this time. "Don't blow this."

"I'm trying not to."

"You won't." But she looked doubtful as she backed away. "I've really got to go this time. I don't want to hear about any broken hearts. It's Christmas."

"Merry Christmas to you, too." His own sister didn't think he could pull this off? He swallowed back foreboding.

With quick strides, Nick covered the distance to The Tea Pot. When he entered, the town's old guard all turned to him as if he'd been the topic of recent discussion.

Gina was consolidating pastries in the display case. There was something different about her. Different shirt? No. Different apron? No. He couldn't quite put his finger on it.

"I hear you're throwing your hat into the political ring." Martha stood next to a table in the corner with nearly a dozen of the town's retired citizens. "Is it mayor or town council you're running for?"

Ah, that explained their scrutiny.

Gina made a noise behind the counter. He

realized what was different about her. Her hair had been pushed back, revealing her scar.

Everyone in the room seemed to be waiting for his answer, including her. Gina, who hid from the world, was probably erasing their kiss from her memory banks. She brushed her bangs forward, over her scar.

The feeling of foreboding came rushing back, stronger this time. It made unsettling attempts to bore a hole in Nick's stomach. "You know, Martha," he said carefully. "The mayor was just talking to me about it. Surprised the heck out of me. How would I find time for something like that?"

"I think you should consider making time," Martha said. It was a sentiment echoed by her friends at the corner table, along with words like *deserving, new blood* and *about time.*

"Whatever I decide, I appreciate your support." There were too many variables to consider—Adam, the time and financial resources needed to be more than the town handyman, Gina.

Gina disappeared into the kitchen. He followed. She was busy measuring flour when he pushed through the swinging door. The kitchen was warm and smelled like a big sugar cookie. This morning she'd been aglow, but now her light had dimmed. Her white-blond hair seemed as flat as her demeanor.

He hesitated just inside the doorway, trying to choose a topic of conversation. Coming clean about being Football20? Talking about the kiss? Reassuring her he hadn't made a decision about public life? Asking her about the oven?

She might be ducking behind her hair, so Nick chose to dodge behind his tool bag. "There's a problem with the stove?"

Gina arranged her bangs carefully over her forehead before turning to him. Her gaze dropped from his face to his boots. "The knob is stuck on 350 degrees." She produced a large plastic dial broken in two pieces. "I was trying to increase the temperature and it snapped off in my hand."

"Unfortunately, we'll have to order a replacement part." The hardware store and its three wise men wouldn't have that knob in stock. "Until then, we can adjust it with needle-nose pliers. Do you have an oven thermometer?"

She nodded. "I put one in as soon as it happened, in case I adjusted it the wrong way."

"That's my girl." *I wish.*

There was an awkward silence.

He cleared his throat and swung his tool bag to the floor. "About the town council—"

"It's none of my business," she said, but her cheeks pinkened.

"And yet you fiddled with your hair when Martha brought it up." Gina had shrunk. A withered flower on the vine. He wanted to kiss her again to prove she didn't need to do either. "Me, an elected official? Ridiculous." He hated the sound of his hurt-roughened voice.

"I disagree." Her words might have buoyed him if she hadn't spoken to his work boots. "I admit I hadn't thought of it, but you'd be great in public office. You know everyone and you listen to their concerns. You'd have no qualms standing in front of a crowd with all eyes focused on you."

"I sense a *but* in there somewhere." He suspected she was seeing him in a new light, one she'd never thought to shine on him—that of a potential life partner.

Just one problem. Her discomfort reminded him that she shied away from the limelight. His running for town council was likely to be a relationship deal breaker.

"It's nothing." Her smile was so brittle, it almost broke his heart. "Besides, my opinion doesn't matter. Do you want to run?"

Lying would be easier, but he'd already lied

too much to her. "I think I might, I like making a difference in people's lives—whether I'm fixing a leaky faucet or voicing an opinion on a new ordinance. And as the only member of my family without a college degree I would find it…validating." He pondered that for a moment. "I didn't realize that was important to me until just now. I guess I'm not as comfortable in my own skin as I thought, at least not where my family is concerned."

He took a step toward her. "This opportunity in politics—"

"Don't." She held up a hand, preventing him from closing the distance between them.

Something akin to a growl worked its way up his throat. It wasn't a sound he ever remembered making before. "This morning…when we kissed…"

"That was a mistake. On your part." She rushed on. "It was like you were asking a wallflower to dance because you felt sorry for her… *For me.*"

"That was *not* a pity kiss." Frustration made his voice gruff.

She patted his shoulder. "How could it not have been? It came out of the blue."

His fingers flexed with the need to hold her and prove the kiss and the emotions behind it were heartfelt. "I'd been thinking about it for a long time. I'm thinking about it again."

That stalled her. She opened her mouth to speak, closed it, then tried again. "I need to give this guy I met online a chance first. You... you confuse me."

"You're confused?" She had no idea how flummoxed *he* was. He was competing for a date with Gina? With himself? "So you think this guy you just met is a better fit for you? The same guy you believe will run as soon as he sees your face?" Nick had blown this day and it wasn't even noon.

Noon. The appointed time for Football20 to show up.

"It's not about who's more appealing." She pressed her hands to her cheeks. "It's about being fair."

Fair was him telling her the truth about her online boyfriend. Fair was Nick kissing her under the mistletoe later. Chances for anything fair happening to him today were slim. "I'll wait here until this guy makes an appearance," he said, knowing full well her online date wasn't appearing until Nick decided it was time.

He handed Gina the needle-nose pliers and pushed through the door into the dining area. "A large coffee, Martha."

He carried his mug, his frustration and the dilemma of Football20 to a small table by the window and scowled at the world.

"WHAT'S GOING ON between you and Nick?" Martha asked when Gina returned to the front carrying a tray loaded with cookies and Danish.

Several customers heard her aunt's question and halted their conversation for the opportunity to pick up a bit of gossip. A cloud must have passed over the sun, because the shop seemed to dim.

Ducking her head, Gina finished restocking the case before answering softly, "Aunt Martha, leave it, please."

"That's what I say to my dog when he misbehaves. Minus the please." Aunt Martha stole a warm apple Danish. "What's going on?"

Gina sighed. "I have a date today."

"With Nick?" Her aunt held out her hand for a fist bump. "He's adorable and upwardly mobile, what with that political future ahead of him. Not to mention how handy he is around the place. No wonder he shows up so quickly when you call."

Gina clasped Martha's hand with both of hers and lowered it. "That's not… He's not…

I have a date with someone I met online," she finished, exasperated.

"I'm confused. Why is this making Nick moody?"

"Nick caught me at a low moment. Now he thinks he can fix me, like one of his projects. By dating me." It felt like a lie, especially considering Nick said he'd been thinking about kissing her for a long time. Gina knew better. She'd been back for months. If he was interested in her, she'd have sensed something sooner, wouldn't she? If he'd wanted to ask her out, he'd have done so long before this, wouldn't he? That kiss was as unexpected as a lottery win.

"Men don't date women to fix them." Martha tsked. "Honey, if they want to date you, they want to date you."

"You don't understand. I made a commitment to have a date with someone else first."

Aunt Martha's brow clouded. "As in go steady?"

"No!"

Several patrons glanced their way again, including Nick. Gina lowered her voice. "It's my first date with this man."

Martha needed more clarification. "The man who isn't Nick."

"Exactly. I have a first date with someone else, not Nick."

"And already you're exclusive?" Martha's brow remained wrinkled. "That's some man."

Gina considered thunking her head against the pastry case. "Nick's given me no indication that he liked me until we started talking about my scar and my—" *cowardly* "—insecurities earlier today. Don't you think he's the kind of man who listens to you admit your flaws and then helps fix them?" *Whether you want him to or not.*

"Nope." Martha's gaze settled on Nick. She sighed dreamily. "He's a rarity. The kind of man who accepts you as you are."

"We'll agree to disagree," Gina said. "I don't think I should consider dating anyone else until I give the man I met online a chance."

Aunt Martha chewed a piece of Danish slowly, considering that logic. Then she swallowed and shook her head. "Isn't that putting all your eggs in one basket? What if this online friend of yours turns out to be a dud? You may blow your chance with Nick. And who knows? Nick might be mayor someday."

"That's the problem, isn't it?" Gina hung her head. "I've owned this shop for nearly six months and I barely interact with my own customers. I'm not the right woman for Nick. If he's going to be a politician, he needs someone who can stand in front of a crowd without wanting to vomit. Someone more polished, more confident, more—"

"Unblemished and poised? Like her?" Aunt Martha gestured to the door, where Nick's ex-wife entered with his son, Adam.

Lindsey didn't just fit the description of Nick's ideal mate, she was the model the description was based on. Confident, flawless, savvy fashion sense, great hair.

I have great hair, a small voice inside Gina protested.

One out of four is a loss, Gina mentally retorted.

Nick greeted his ex-wife with a reserved nod.

"Gina," Aunt Martha was saying. "Nick's already had high maintenance. I think he knows what kind of woman he wants this time around. Maybe you should think about what kind of man *you* want. I'll give you a hint. He'd look a lot like Nick."

CHAPTER FIVE

"DAD!" ADAM PRACTICALLY TUMBLED through the door and into Nick's arms, bringing the fresh scent of the outdoors and the familiar one of sweaty boy. "I'm here. Let's start Christmas!"

Adam's skinny arms around his neck almost made everything that had been going wrong this morning disappear. "Hey, buddy. I thought you were busy with the choir for another few hours."

"Aunt Callie called an end to choir practice. I need hot chocolate before lunch." He settled deeper against Nick. *"Please."*

"Okay." Nick nodded at his ex. "Merry Christmas, Lindsey."

The soon-to-be bank CEO stared down at him. "I still have shopping to do. Can you watch Adam this afternoon?"

"Sure."

Adam jumped up, kissed his mother goodbye, wished her a Merry Christmas, then scampered to the pastry case. Several Holly Scouts trooped in, making a beeline for the counter. Gina's welcoming smile greeted the children. The last time she'd smiled at him like that was when he'd told her she didn't need a new refrigerator. Was it just the rumor about him running for office that threatened his chances with her? Or did it have to do with his lack of a college degree?

Lindsey turned to go.

"Linds." Nick stopped her. "Can I ask you a question?"

She shrugged elegantly in that untouchable way of hers, so much more distant than any gesture Gina made.

"As a high school graduate and handyman, I wasn't good enough for you after you earned your degree." When she started to protest, he hurried on. "Hypothetically—and this is not a get-together hypothetical for you and me—but, hypothetically, if I was elected to the town council would that have balanced things out for you?"

With a shake of her head, Lindsey sat down across from him. "Nick, I never judged you based on the number of diplomas that hung on your wall. And my opinion of you wouldn't change if you ran for office. We just grew apart."

"That's not an answer, Linds." Not one that would shed light on his current dilemma.

"Ah, but it is." She began ticking things off using her fingers. "You love watching sports. I love going to art galleries. You love interacting with the people in this town, helping them nearly to the exclusion of having a life of your own. I love going to new places and meeting new people. You love everything this town stands for, including the pageant and its celebration of Christmas. I think it's Podunky."

When she put it that way, he understood their incompatibility perfectly.

"I'd much rather live in a big city, like Boston. The lifestyle and career opportunities are ten times better than anything I can commute to from here." Her admission nipped at his fatherly rights, but before he could reply, she added, "Not that I'd take Adam away from you. He needs his dad."

Nick drew a deep breath and shook his head. "Why did I think I wasn't good enough for you?"

"I probably screamed it at you once or twice while I was moving out." She looked contrite. "People say things they don't mean when they're stressed."

Across the room, Gina wore that fragile, brave smile, accented by bangs draped over one eye. She looked more Goth girl than shop-girl as she answered questions from boisterous children about her baked goods.

"Thanks, Linds. Merry Christmas." They stood and hugged, agreeing on a drop-off time for Adam in the morning.

Nick was deserving. After five years of thinking otherwise, he found that hard to believe. Kind of like the way he'd told Gina she was beautiful and not broken, and she hadn't believed him. Together they might learn to believe in themselves. If they trusted each other. He just needed Gina to realize they could move forward together.

And that's when he came up with an idea.

NOON HAD PASSED fifteen minutes ago with no word from Football20.

Aunt Martha was giving her the high sign—fluttery brows and head nods in Nick's direction. She was a proponent of a bird in the hand was worth more than a relationship online. Thankfully, Nick wasn't giving her the I-told-you-so scowl.

Adam pressed his face to the pastry case beside a few of his friends and some of the Holly Scouts, still under the supervision of Priscilla. Adults Gina didn't recognize were coming in, stomping the snow from their boots and singing snatches of holiday songs. The Tea Pot was in for another busy run.

Gina found her gaze drawn to the Holly Scout with the port-wine mark on her cheek. "Is this your first pageant, Diana?"

"No. I've been before." The girl glanced up at Gina, pointing at a Christmas-tree-shaped sugar cookie. "That one, please. It's the first one I'm performing in. Our troop is putting on a puppet show." It was surprising to find Diana was a chatterbox. "I play Mrs. Claus. I only have two lines. Do you want to hear them?"

Gina nodded, realizing that Diana had noted her scar. It didn't seem to change the way the child interacted with her. For that matter, none of the children responded to her awkwardly.

She plated a cookie for Diana, handing it to her with a mug of hot chocolate. The girl kept talking.

"First, Santa comes in after his night in the sleigh and I say, 'Santa, you're home.' And Santa says how tired he is. And I say, 'Once again, you've given the gift of a happy Christmas.' And then we all stand and sing 'Here Comes Santa Claus.'" Diana's big brown eyes sparkled. "Will you come watch?"

Gina didn't go to the pageant. She'd wanted to go on a date with Football20, to avoid the festivities altogether. But now, she wanted to see Diana up on that stage, smiling and singing along with the rest of her troop.

Confound it. Nick was right. She was letting her scar limit the size of her life. Gina squared her shoulders. She wouldn't refuse this little girl. "I'll be there cheering you on." With or without Football20.

She handed Adam a cookie and a mug of hot chocolate. She never charged him, considering the amount of work Nick did for her—not to mention her suspicion that Nick undercharged her for his services.

Gina's mother entered in her zipped-up stadium coat. She darted past the adults lingering in her way as they perused the menu, and came behind the counter. She set a shopping bag on the floor, gave Gina air kisses and then rearranged her bangs over her scar. "I found everything you two wanted."

Despite having his order, Adam studied Gina through the pastry case. She knew he was angling for a second treat.

Diana seemed to be, as well, since she didn't make way for the children behind her. She rubbed her cheek near her birthmark, then grinned at Adam. "Are you having your picture taken with Santa? My mom has thirteen pictures with him, one for every year she was in school."

A picture with Santa. The fallen tree branch had severed any desire Gina had for a picture with the jolly old elf. She had three pictures with Santa, not thirteen. At that moment, Gina realized if she had kids, she was going to be one of *those moms*—the ones who didn't do crafts, didn't fill out baby books and didn't have a history with Santa. All because of an imperfection on her face.

Diana wasn't letting that stop her.

It felt wrong to hide.

But before Gina could come out of hiding, Aunt Martha tugged her bangs out of her eyes. "The girl needs to see, Danielle."

Gina dodged two sets of hands vying for control of her hair. "Hey! Don't touch."

"But, darling, there are a lot of people in here," her mother said.

"You need another dose of nothing," Martha grumbled. "Why don't you ask Nick to fix something in the kitchen? Something only you can show him."

Gina shoved her hair out of her face. "Mom, I don't want to hide anymore. This is who I am. I have a scar. And I'm okay with that." There. She'd said it. Maybe she wouldn't always feel confident about her appearance, but at least she was on record and standing firmly outside her comfort zone. The floor beneath her felt as unpredictable as thin ice. Her gaze sought Nick's.

He raised his coffee mug in salute, that endearing, lopsided smile on his face.

She couldn't help herself. She smiled back.

Aunt Martha applauded. Adam and Diana grinned, lips fogging up the case.

Gina was going to have to clean the glass after this.

"I'm only trying to protect my baby. You'll always be perfect to me." A finely manicured hand reached for Gina's hair once more.

Gina caught it in her own. "Mom, this scar is a part of who I am. You wouldn't love me more if it was gone, would you?"

Her mother opened her mouth, then snapped it shut. Her eyes seemed to tear. She squeezed Gina's hand fiercely. "Is that what you think? That I love you less because of that scar?"

The entire shop seemed to hold its collective breath, watching their family drama unfold in all its messiness.

"No," Gina said in a thin, creaky voice. The urge to retreat to the kitchen was strong. Just as fierce was her need to be someone who didn't let a scar define her.

Her mother didn't hear her. She stared at a wreath on the far wall. "I've tried to be supportive."

"I understand." Gina swallowed thickly. "But…I think I need to be brave."

Her mother scoffed, all traces of hurt eradicated. "As if you weren't brave when you went away to college? Or to Europe? Or interviewed for a Fortune 500 job?" She pulled her into a hug. "You are the bravest little girl ever."

Gina didn't know what to say.

"She's not little," Diana piped up. "Little girls aren't the boss in the kitchen."

"Has she battled a tiger?" Adam asked. "She's not brave until she's battled a tiger."

"Adam," Aunt Martha chided gently. "You're looking at a tiger woman." She pointed to Gina's mother. "And Gina just stood up to her."

Adam scrutinized Gina's mom as if searching for her stripes.

Danielle responded with a subdued half growl, half meow.

Adam's and Diana's eyes widened. The two children turned and fled. Several customers chuckled. It was as if the room sighed with relief. Crisis averted. Holiday merriment to resume.

"Way to scare the customers, Danielle," Martha said.

Gina's mother tugged her stadium coat down. "They enjoyed it. Look at their smiles."

Gina's cell phone vibrated in her pocket. It

was Football20: Maybe meeting today isn't such a good idea.

Gina gasped. Had she been dumped? Had he seen her through the window and rejected her?

She typed out a quick reply. Maybe you're right.

"Men," she muttered. She needed a man just as courageous as she was. Or at least was *trying* to be.

Her mother looked up from pouring a cup of coffee. *"Men?"*

"Don't ask," Martha cautioned, leaning forward to wave to the next little customer. "Merry Christmas! May I help you?"

IF GINA'S EXPRESSION was any indication, she was extremely upset with Football20's request for postponement.

Mad enough to dump her online beau for Nick?

Customers ebbed and flowed about the shop, carrying packages and wearing harried smiles.

Adam slid into a chair opposite Nick, depositing a plate and mug on the table before shedding layers—jacket, gloves, hat—to the floor. He took a big bite of Santa's cookie beard and slurped some hot chocolate.

Nick tried not to grin. The neat gene had skipped Adam completely, much to Lindsey's chagrin. "Adam, this isn't your bedroom." Nick's phone buzzed midlecture. He kept his stern gaze on his son. "Pick up your things before someone trips on them."

While the boy hung his outerwear on his chair, Nick checked his phone.

Gina had sent another message through the website: Are you chickening out on meeting me ever?

There was fire in that question. And in her eyes, which he could see clearly, since she'd pushed her bangs off her face once more.

"I need a refill." He drained his coffee, then hesitated as an idea came to him. "Adam, you like Gina, don't you?"

Red frosting rimmed Adam's grinning lips as he nodded.

"She's been stuck in The Tea Pot all day. She needs to get out. Maybe even see Santa."

"You need my help? To get Gina to Santa?" When Nick nodded, Adam's gaze turned speculative. "Can I have another cookie?"

A Holly Scout with green frosting on her cheek grinned at him. There'd come a day when Adam wouldn't think twice about ignoring his old man for some feminine attention. But right now, Nick's son was oblivious to the girl's wiles, working the woe-is-me angle for more sugar.

Nick heaved a belabored sigh. "Okay. You can have another cookie. But only if you ask your friend if she wants one, too." He nodded toward the Holly Scout.

"That's the deal? Get Gina to Santa, plus me being polite? You're a sucker, Dad." Adam rolled his eyes and wiped red frosting on his shirtsleeve. "Diana, do you want another cookie?"

The little girl's grin widened as she nodded.

Nick caught the eye of the Holly Scout troop leader. He thought her name was Priscilla. "Cookies all around?"

She shrugged. "Why not? It's Christmas."

Nick carried his coffee cup to the counter, waiting for his turn in line. "A dozen sugar cookies and a coffee refill," he said to Martha when he reached the front.

The older woman chuckled. "You're in for a big sugar crash."

"The cookies aren't for me. They're for the kids," Nick replied. He handed his cup across the counter to Gina, trying to infuse his words with spontaneity. "Hey, how about breaking for lunch and walking the square with me and Adam? You've been cooped up in here all day and he wants to see Santa."

Martha didn't give her niece a chance to answer. "She'd love to. Besides, she needs to distribute hot beverages and sweets to pageant workers. Annalise can help me until she gets back." She gestured to one of her book club sisters in the corner.

"Don't I have any say in this?" Gina gripped Nick's coffee cup with both hands.

"No," Martha and Nick said in unison.

"Come on," he added. "I'll help you distribute coffee and sweets, and treat you to a shepherd's pie." He might have imagined it, but he thought he heard Gina's stomach growl.

"Okay, but you can't ask me anything about you-know-who." She shook her finger at him.

Nick held up his hands. "Do you need help preparing things?"

"No." Gina headed toward the kitchen.

Martha waited for the door to swing closed before she leaned across the counter and whispered, "Kiss her under the mistletoe."

Nick gave her a thumbs-up and took a rain check on his coffee. He returned to his table and set the plate of cookies on it. Holly Scouts swarmed him, ignoring the direction of their scout leader to act like ladies.

Adam licked his fingers after eating his second cookie. "Don't forget, Dad, we've got to stand in line to see Santa and make a candy cane wish."

"We have to eat lunch first."

Adam glanced at the clock. "It's already twelve-thirty. Santa only stays until two."

"Plenty of time."

CHAPTER SIX

FORTY CUPS OF coffee. Twenty of hot chocolate.

Four dozen sugar cookies. Two dozen Danish.

Two Banning men.

It almost felt as if Gina should be singing about one shy baker in a pear tree.

She'd bundled up for her rounds. Her stocking cap had earflaps that ended in colorful braids and hid nearly all of her scar. Cowardly, yes. She didn't have to give up all her safety nets in one day, did she?

They worked their way around the square, dodging strolling tourists, harmonizing carolers and scurrying pageant workers. Gina hadn't been to the pageant in years. She'd forgotten the bustling energy of the event.

Gina pulled a wagon loaded with thermoses of hot coffee and hot chocolate. Nick carried a box of sweets. Adam ran ahead to take food and drink orders from workers at each booth.

"How did Aunt Martha do this on her own?"

Gina narrowly missed catching her wheels on those of an oncoming stroller.

"She did it slowly. Took her hours, I think."

"Adam is determined to see Santa." Gina was equally determined to get him there.

Santa sat on a throne on the stage. The line of children who'd come to see him and make a wish stretched more than halfway across the square.

"I've been thinking about this project business you keep accusing me of." Nick tugged one of her yarn braids, then peeled back her earflaps, exposing her scar, if the brisk air on her face was any indication. "And I think you're right."

Gina's feet slid on a patch of ice, leaving her heart somewhere behind her. Miraculously, Nick juggled the box of goodies and steadied her. She hadn't realized until that moment how much she didn't want to be Nick's charity case.

"I've done an evaluation." He nodded a greeting to his cousin, Bill, who was selling gifts for the male with gifting challenges at the Desperate Husband booth. "My conclusion is you need to be taught how to date."

The air left Gina's lungs in a whoosh.

"We'll start with something easy, like lunch. You'll be required to make small talk, of course."

She drew a deep breath. He was joking, right?

"We'll move on to kissing."

Gina's feet planted themselves in the frozen asphalt.

He tapped her nose with his forefinger. "In theory only. The politics of kissing are very important."

She found her voice and her sarcasm. "Really?"

"Yep." He lifted the box lid as his son ran up.

"Just two cookies." Adam reached in. "No drinks."

Nick began walking toward the next set of booths, pausing to look back when he realized Gina wasn't following him.

Don't ask. Don't ask. Don't— "What are the politics of kissing?"

"Well." He rocked back on his heels. "You never kiss in the kitchen unless you mean it. And you only kiss someone beneath the mistletoe if you're serious about them." He sneaked a glance at the gazebo, where couples stood in line for the opportunity to test the local legend. "What are you doing later? We should talk more about this in front of the mistletoe."

Frosted breath stuck in her throat. All her life she'd been waiting for an invitation to kiss beneath the mistletoe. This was red velvet cupcake buried in cream cheese frosting. Irresistible.

"Why in front? Why not underneath?" This last came out on a puff of newfound air.

He tsked. "There are things that need to be discussed before you enter the gazebo. That's where young couples go wrong."

Gina's ribs ached with longing. There was danger here. Danger to her pride and her heart. "What kind of questions?"

Adam called for them to catch up.

Nick tucked the box of sweets beneath one arm, strode back to her and began pulling the wagon, leaving her no choice but to follow. "The same ones you might ask a man you met online. Do you want a family? Are you interested in a large house with creaky floorboards and lots of history? What do you see yourself doing ten years from now?"

She'd asked Football20 those same questions and more. She wanted a family. She wanted that creaky old house. But what would Nick be doing ten years from now? He'd probably be mayor. And she…

Her knees weakened. Right there, at the intersection of Jack Frost Avenue and the Mistletoe Trail.

"Hold up." Nick placed the box with cookies and Danish on top of Gina's thermoses. But instead of steadying her, he hurried through the crowd to a bank of snow left by the morning's plow run. People walked between them, obscuring her view.

Adam returned to the wagon, out of breath. "Two coffees. Black. Where's Dad?"

When Gina gestured toward the snowbank, Adam hurried to his side.

Nick reached into the bank with both hands and pulled out a frail, snow-covered body.

Gina gasped. It was Barty. He listed to one side and Adam propped him up.

"Nick has SOS radar." Callie appeared beside her. "I just wish he could turn it off sometimes. Not that I'm much better." She sighed. "I've got to keep moving or I'll never get anything done. Can you make sure Adam sees Santa?"

"I'm on it already."

"And give this to Nick." She pressed a small wrapped box into Gina's hand. As quickly as Callie had appeared, she disappeared.

When the two Banning men rejoined Gina, she said, "Barty's lucky you saw him fall." She handed Adam two coffees.

"I didn't see him at all. I noticed his walker on the sidewalk, wobbling by itself." Nick shook his head. "He'll be fine. I can't believe people are so busy and rushed they don't see what's right in front of them."

Gina saw what was in front of her. She imagined herself falling forward into Nick's arms. Not busy. Not rushed. His lips would claim hers in a slow, passionate kiss. Her arms would encircle his neck. And everything would be right with the world.

"Not to mention—" he lowered his voice, interrupting her wayward thoughts "—Barty shouldn't be out here at all. He wanted to see how the replacement Santa was doing." Nick spied the gift box in her hand. "What have you got there?"

"It's from Callie." Gina held the box toward him.

"It's from Santa," he corrected, accepting it. "We do a different version of Secret Santa in our family. These small gifts are hints as to what the family got you for Christmas." He unwrapped the box and opened it. "A miniature hammer and a sprig of mistletoe? I'm stumped."

Despite not wanting to pry, Gina peeked. "That's not a hammer. It's a gavel, like the mayor uses at town council meetings." And the mistletoe…

Why did it have to be mistletoe?

His eyes sought hers. His familiar grin softened. "These are two gifts my family can't give me."

"They're giving you their blessing." For love and a public life. The gavel was a reminder of the limits Gina had yet to cross. Baby steps. She was taking baby steps, but Nick's grin encouraged her to grab his hand, hang on and run with him. She gulped back her fears. "Where do you want to be ten years from now?"

Nick looked around the town square. And then his warm gaze landed on her. "Right here."

She shook her head. He wanted to serve. "Nick, I—"

"If I kiss you again, you'll realize there's something between us you can't hide from." His words were gentle, but there was a hint of secrets in his voice, like the subtle, enticing scent of vanilla in an oatmeal raisin cookie. "You can't run from this, Gina."

"Not true." In the past twenty years, she'd grown quite good at hiding.

NICK LIKED FLIRTING with Gina.

He liked kissing Gina.

But that didn't mean she didn't exasperate him.

"You want to go into politics," she said.

"And I...I'm not ready for that. I may never be ready for that."

He'd jumped the gun, as he had with their kiss that morning. There was a serious need for backpedaling. "Maybe I want to run someday. But that doesn't mean I'm going to start in the next year or so. Like you said, I'm a busy man."

"I don't want to be the reason you passed up any opportunity."

"You think you aren't worth it to me?" He resisted the urge to take her into his arms and kiss her, proving how serious he was about making her a priority. Instead, he deposited the nearly empty sweets box on top of the thermoses and cradled her face in his hands. "You've worked with numbers. You've done trade-off analyses." He inched closer, until they were nearly touching. "Sometimes you have to give up something to get something you want more." He knew as he said it that the timing of the mayor's offer was all wrong. Nick needed to be there for Adam. He needed to expand his business to include historical renovation. And he needed to explore these feelings he had for Gina. He stroked his thumb over her scar.

Adam ran up with their last order. He stopped

within hugging distance. "Dad, are you gonna kiss Gina?"

"Maybe," Nick said at the same time Gina whispered, "no."

"Adults." Adam shook his head. "I'll never understand them." He filled a cup with coffee, then rummaged in the box for a Danish.

Gina stepped away and Nick's hands dropped to his sides. "I should get back to The Tea Pot," she said as her cheeks bloomed a soft pink.

"Oh, no. I promised to buy you lunch," he said firmly, tucking her arm in his. "I heard you tell your mother you weren't hiding anymore."

She opened her mouth, most likely to argue further, but he added gently, "Please, Gina. Then we can go see Santa." Together, like the family he hoped they'd be someday.

Adam returned in time to hear Nick's plea. "You can't leave us, Gina. If you go, I'll never get to see Santa."

"You just want to eat the remaining cookies after lunch," Gina said.

"Yep." Adam's grin pulled up on one side, just like Nick's. "But if you eat with us, Dad won't get called away."

Gina sighed.

"That's a *yes*." His son pumped his fist in the air.

"Santa's line is below twenty," Nick said. "Let's eat."

Adam bolted for the shepherd's pie booth. Nick and Gina followed more slowly, arms twined together, while Nick pulled the wagon.

"See," he said. "This is nice."

"Nick—"

Diana ran up to Gina, dragging a woman behind her. "Mom, this is the pretty lady who let me do her dishes. I want hair like hers."

Gina fiddled with one of her hat's yarn braids, as if trying to pull the earflap over her scar. "The Holly Scouts came to our rescue earlier at The Tea Pot. I think Diana earned another badge."

Diana's mother studied Gina's face. Her gaze turned compassionate. "My daughter wanted to show me your special braid. I'm sorry—"

Nick sent a silent plea to Diana's mother: *Don't say "I'm sorry to bother you." Gina needs you to accept her, scar and all, just as you do your daughter.*

"—but I can't see it. Would you mind taking off your hat?"

She did understand. Nick breathed a sigh of relief.

But in order to comply, Gina would have to remove her hat and deliberately expose all of her scar to this woman. It was different than pushing her bangs back when she was standing behind the counter with customers ten to twenty feet away. Gina was opening herself up to close inspection. He knew it. She knew it.

Gina's cheeks paled.

He gave her fingers a reassuring squeeze. She held on. With her other hand, she removed her hat. Her white-blond hair shimmered in the afternoon sunlight.

Within his grip, her hand was as tense as marble, as if she was waiting for someone to point and scream at the horror that was her face. Gina kept her chin up and didn't make a move to adjust her bangs over her scar.

She still didn't understand. "You're beautiful," he whispered.

Gina made a soft noise, like a trapped animal that knew a predator was near.

They stood at the corner of the intersection. People passed by from all directions. Talking, laughing, paying Gina and her scar no heed. They were too busy with their loved ones, with lists of gifts to buy and timelines to be met for the holiday.

"People are so rushed..." Nick murmured close to her ear.

"That they don't see," she finished just as softly. Her hold on his hand eased.

Diana's mom walked around Gina. "Your

hair is a beautiful color. Thank you for sharing with us. I've never made French braids before. Is it hard?"

A small sigh escaped Gina's lips. If Nick hadn't been protectively close, he would have missed it.

"It takes a little practice." She put her hat back on. "Diana's hair is long enough that you could do it. I bet if you stop at the Carols and Curls booth, Carol will show you how."

Adam had reached the front of Posey's lunch line and was jumping up and down to get their attention. Nick excused them, escorting Gina and towing the wagon to the booth.

"You're a brave woman, Gina Vernay," he said.

Gina scoffed. "You don't know how much I wanted to sink into a snowdrift."

"Ah, but I do. Because I know you."

When they joined Adam in line, Posey waved to them. "My generator keeps going out, Nick. Can you look at it?"

Was there anything in this town that wasn't breaking down today? Nick forced a smile on his face. After all, he was holding Gina's hand. Life didn't get much better than this.

CHAPTER SEVEN

WHILE GINA AND Adam sat at a picnic table beneath space heaters, Nick fiddled with Posey's generator. Adam kept casting worried glances toward his father.

"We'll get to Santa right after this," Gina promised.

"Bannings help people," Adam said as if repeating the family motto. "That means sometimes we have to miss stuff."

"Not today. Eat up." She kept an eye on the line for Santa. It was dwindling. And it was nearing two o'clock.

Nick diagnosed Posey's generator as being out of fuel. Apparently the fuel gauge was frozen. He claimed his shepherd's pie and sat down, digging in as Gina and Adam pushed the remains of their meals around their paper plates.

"You're like one of Christmas Town's elves. Or maybe Santa's maintenance man," Gina said. What she really wanted to say was *"Your son is dying to get to Santa. Eat fast."*

"It's always something, isn't it?" Nick reached over to grip Adam's shoulder, giving him a gentle shake.

The wind kicked up, sending a dusting of snow from the trees around the square into the air.

Gina's body seized up. The wind. A crack. Her scream.

Her focus tunneled on Nick's half-eaten shepherd's pie, but in her mind's eye she saw the branch, thick as a man's leg, fall out of the sky. Her back felt the cold, hard ice.

In the present, a scream stuck in her throat.

"Hey!" Nick's voice seemed faraway. "It's okay. It's just the wind. There are no trees around. You're safe." His hand covered hers.

Gina blinked. She was breathing as raggedly as if she'd just run a race. This was why she didn't come to the pageant. She hadn't experienced a flashback like this since she'd left Christmas Town. She stood up, on legs as limp as rolled dough.

"I'm done, anyway," Nick was saying, clearing their table.

"I need to get back to the shop." Where she'd truly be safe.

"Gina, we can't miss Santa." Adam's voice. His small hand trustingly wrapped around hers. "You promised."

Her breathing slowed. She became aware of the noise and activity of the pageant. The carolers singing "I Saw Mommy Kissing Santa Claus." Posey calling an order to her cook. Nick promising to collect his slice of peppermint pie later. The sun sparkling across the snowy square. Children bounding through two feet of snow, their laughter pealing through the air.

Gina grabbed a yarn braid and tugged her hat more firmly onto her head. If only she hadn't paused under that tree twenty years ago. If only it hadn't snowed so heavily the night before. If only she could go back in time and tell herself that her scar didn't matter. That what mattered was in her heart, and who she saw standing in front of her.

Nick moved in close enough to kiss, placing his hands on her shoulders. "Are you all right?"

She hadn't been, but she was now, buoyed up by a child's trusting grip and Nick there to steady her. She could do anything. She could even stand in front of a crowd and smile at strangers while they listened to her husband speak about new policies and changes for the better. She could lift her hatless head and smile, despite them looking at her scar and wondering about the story behind it.

"Are you ready?" Adam jumped up and ran

a few steps, urging them to follow. "Let's go see Santa."

"I'm ready." This bold new woman leaned forward and pressed a light kiss on Nick's lips. She didn't even need a candy cane wish. Hers had been granted.

They left her wagon and thermoses with Posey. Adam held one of Gina's hands, Nick the other as they cut across the town square toward the stage. They were halfway there when Adam made a noise of disappointment.

"Santa's left," he said morosely.

Sure enough, the sign posted on the edge of the stage said Santa had gone to pack up his sleigh.

Gina caught sight of a flash of red behind the stage. There was a possibility she could bribe Santa with the promise of coffee and cookies. "Just a minute. Wait here, you two." She'd learned not to underestimate the power of sugar.

Gina hurried up the stairs, slipped behind the curtain and bumped into her mother.

In a lip-lock with Santa.

The two figures leaped apart.

Her mother was cheating with…

"Dad?" Gina lowered her voice to a whisper. "You're Santa?"

He moved his fake mustache and whiskers

from beneath his chin to cover his mouth. His pillowed paunch had shifted to the left. He straightened it, hefting his girth like a bowl-ful of velvet-covered jelly. "With Barty being sick, someone had to step in."

And her father, who'd played the role of Grinch for years, had. Gina didn't know what to say.

"We figured now that you're back and vol-unteering, we should, too. Your father made a wonderful Kris Kringle." Her mother's green eyes glowed with pride.

"She was the perfect Mrs. Claus," he re-plied gruffly.

"Neither one of you is done yet." Gina recov-ered enough to grab them both and lead them toward the main stage. "There's a little boy out there who's been helping with the pageant. He deserves one of Santa's candy cane wishes. His name is Adam." Something Diana had said earlier tickled her memory. "He'll need a pic-ture with Santa, too."

She half expected her dad to say his time as Santa had expired, but he came along will-ingly, as did her mother, who was wearing a red velvet dress beneath her jacket. That ex-plained why she'd been suited up like a sleep-ing bag. They emerged from behind the curtain and her dad gave a hearty, "Ho, ho, ho."

Adam and Nick had disappeared.

"If that man left to repair something for someone…" Gina mumbled, reaching for her cell phone. She texted Nick: Where are you?

Then she huffed and looked around. "It's Nick's son. Do you see Nick anywhere?" She didn't, but she remembered Adam had seen Mrs. Claus earlier. "Hey, tiger woman. Zip up your jacket. Adam is going to recognize you from The Tea Pot."

"Merciful heavens. That was him?" Gina's mom knelt and struggled with her jacket zipper.

"Danielle is a tiger woman?" Santa chuckled.

"Hush, Howie." The zipper caught and her mother stood, yanking it all the way to her neck.

Gina's phone buzzed. A text message. "It's from Nick."

I think it's better if we don't meet at all.

That was Football20. Wasn't it?

No. It was a text from Nick's phone, not a message via the dating website.

Gina's toes went cold. The tips of her fingers went cold. She was cold everywhere.

Nick was Football20?

Betrayal stabbed at her, deflating her lungs of much needed oxygen. The world funneled down to this one small shard of truth.

Nick was Football20.

It couldn't be. Gina tried to reconcile what she knew of the two men. There'd been the picture he'd posted online. She'd thought his obscured face was fitting, since she hadn't uploaded a complete photo, either. He'd said he lived in a nearby town, that he bought, restored and sold old homes. He'd lied. Football20 had lied.

Nick lied.

Mumbling. Someone was mumbling. Gina wanted it to stop. The rambling words were distracting her from figuring out what she was going to do.

Because Nick had lied.

"You can't kill anyone, dear. It's Christmas." Her mother rubbed Gina's back. "Stop mumbling. Whatever's got you upset, you'll be over it as soon as the choir starts to sing."

Gina sincerely doubted it.

Nick and Adam came around the stage.

Nick. Football20. Liar.

She wanted to back away. She wanted to run. She wanted to cover up her scar and never let anyone see it again.

"There you are." Nick's lopsided smile chilled

her even more. "Someone needed help carrying a Christmas tree to their car."

He was always so helpful. Somehow he'd discovered she was on the dating site. Somehow he'd noticed she'd had no interactions with anyone. Wasn't that just like Nick, to step in and help wherever he saw a need?

Adam's eyes rounded as he caught sight of Santa. And then he was running up the stairs.

Gina gripped her cell phone tighter. "I got your message, Football20," she said to Nick.

His foot slipped on the first step.

"Merry Christmas, Adam." Santa dug into his nearly empty bag for a candy cane. "Lick this three times and make a wish."

Adam slowly unwrapped the red-and-white-striped candy. "I was going to wish for a remote control car." He gazed adoringly at his father. "But…"

"Take your time," Gina's mother said. "It's a big decision and sometimes just the taste of peppermint helps you figure out what you really want."

Adam noticed Gina's mother. "Hey, aren't you the tiger woman? From The Tea Pot?"

"Yep." Danielle sniffed. "You think Christmas Town lets Santa out alone? He needs backup. Those elves are slackers, always singing and sneaking off to play reindeer video games."

Adam grinned, then fumbled with the wrapper. "Can I make two wishes?"

"The rule is one," Santa intoned in his accountant voice as if he was cautioning a client not to cheat on his taxes.

"Santa can make exceptions, can't he?" Nick asked. "After all, you're the big man, the head honcho, the leader of the pack."

Nick liked to make his own rules.

Had anything he'd said to her today been the truth?

If it wasn't for Adam, Gina would have pushed Nick off the stage into the snow.

No, she wasn't that aggressive when betrayed. But she might have stomped her foot and called him a liar.

She sent him a dark look.

"Isn't Christmas the time of forgiveness and second chances?" Nick asked softly.

"We were just talking about that," Gina's mother said.

Santa placed his hands on his knees, lowering himself to Adam's level. "You can make two wishes, but one of them must be selfless."

"For others, not for you," Mrs. Claus explained.

Adam nodded solemnly. He held the candy

cane tightly in one hand and licked it three times, then said, "I wish my dad had someone who took care of him the way he takes care of everyone else in town, because when I'm not with him, he's alone." Adam turned his best give-me-a-cookie gaze toward Gina.

"Better wish again," Gina muttered.

Adam licked the candy cane three more times. "And I want Santa to bring me a remote control car." He smiled at Santa, flashing those big puppy dog eyes.

"Oh, my," Mrs. Claus said. "That's a face that's hard to refuse, even for the tiger woman."

"Tell me about it," Gina said.

Across the square, the carolers started singing "Jingle Bells," reminding her of Nick's whistled tune that morning. Reminding her of how much she liked him. Of how open she'd made her heart to him. And of how much damage he'd wrought. She wanted to cower. She wanted to hide.

Instead, she drew off her cap and pushed back her bangs.

REINDEER DROPPINGS HAD hit the fan.

Gina knew Nick was Football20 and she wasn't happy about his deception. He'd been tripped up by technology, he realized, thinking Gina's text message had come via website to Football20.

"Hey, buddy." Nick took Adam's hand as they went down the stage stairs to the snowy green. "Those were some great wishes."

"You need Gina, Dad. You didn't have to give me extra cookies to help you find a new wife."

Gina, who'd taken the stairs ahead of them, turned and glared at Nick. "It's bad enough you *L-I-E-D*. But you had to resort to bribery? With your own son?"

Adam only briefly tried to sound out the word Gina spelled, before leaping off the lowest step into what was left of a snowdrift. "Parents bribe kids all the time. No biggie."

Gina spun away.

"Yeah, thanks for the help, dude," Nick said, watching his hopes walk off. "It looks like they're starting a snowball fight over at Reindeer Meadow." A safe distance away on the other side of the town square. "How about you head on over there? I'll join you in a bit."

"Snowball fight! Ah-ah-ah-ah…" Adam waved his hands in the air and ran across the square.

The Banning family had enthusiasm in spades. Too bad enthusiasm wouldn't help

Nick make things right with one emotionally wounded baker.

"Gina!" he called after her. "Let me explain. Please."

She whirled on him, her white-blond braid whipping about in anger. "Which was a lie? That I was your project? Or that you wanted to date me?"

"I want to date you. I've tried to ask you out for months."

Her hands fisted and landed on her hips. "How hard is it to say 'Would you like to go out to dinner on Friday?'"

"I've tried. You always cut me off."

"You didn't try hard enough. I can't believe you. It's more believable that I'm someone you think needs a boost to get back on track, like Barty's nervous Labrador or Annalise's failed driving exam." Gina leaned into his space, fire and brimstone, all self-consciousness about her scar gone. "At least you told them you were going to help. You had to lie to me. Why couldn't you just tell me the truth?" The energy seemed to drain from her. "I could have... I would have..."

He was going to confess all now, whether she wanted to hear it or not. "The truth is you've fascinated me since the accident." He looked across the square to the empty spot where the tree that scarred her had once stood. "Before then you were just another girl who loved Christmas. The branch changed all that. And then you slapped Ron Umberland on the playground and looked at me as if I was going to be next. On some level in my little-boy brain, I went, *'Whoa.'*"

"I have no idea what you're talking about," she said.

"You don't remember your mom coming to get you from school? She chewed you out but good, forbidding you to ever attack someone because of what happened. From that day on you hid your scar."

Gina reached up with gloved fingers and traced the jagged line. "I find it hard to believe I was so fascinating, when I can't remember you ever talking to me in school."

"I was a kid. Worse, a boy," he admitted. "When the girl who slapped Ron hid, my fascination faded."

"If you did all this just to get me to slap someone again," Gina muttered, "you've wasted your time."

"You give me such lofty goals. Mine have been more selfish." Nick inched closer. "The little girl who struck back at a boy on the playground grew up. She's still full of spunk, but now she's also hardworking, stubborn and brave. She's the kind of woman I want to take long walks with. I want to kiss her under the mistletoe."

Gina's gaze drifted to the gazebo and the laughing couples.

"I can list a dozen times I tried to ask you out, starting with the first time I fixed The Tea Pot's garbage disposal, and ending with us finding the Christmas ornament this morning."

His smile twisted ruefully as she blinked up at him in wonder. "I wish I had a more honorable motivation for lying to you. I could say I did it to make you see you're a beautiful woman. Or to help you overcome your fear so you won't shrink every time a stranger comes into The Tea Pot. But the truth is..."

Nick had to pause and clear the emotion from his throat. "The truth is I did it all because I'm selfish. I just wanted to earn one date, so I could be with you. I'm tired of being cut off mid-windup for a date request, with a cookie fresh out of the oven. I want to spend time with you, Gina. Time together where I don't have a wrench in my hand and you don't have a whisk in yours."

There. He'd told her all of it. It was up to her now.

CHAPTER EIGHT

GINA WALKED AWAY from Nick.

How could she not? He'd developed a crush on her when they were kids? She'd sabotaged his attempts to ask her out with sweets? It was too outlandish to believe.

She glanced back. Nick stood where she'd left him.

Her heart ka-thumped.

She'd been ignoring her heart for months. Because she couldn't trust it. Because someone interested in a woman who hid and shrank and averted her face from strangers was too bizarre to believe.

"Please tell me you've changed your mind." Carol sat in an empty stylist's chair in her booth, looking glum. "I need one more volunteer to reach twenty."

This was it. Gina could do something really brave and prove the scar didn't rule her life. Or she could spend another Christmas shrunken in fear.

Her phone buzzed. She read a message from

Football20: I know you're disappointed in me. Please forgive me and have faith in me. If you can't do that, continue to have faith in yourself. Merry Christmas.

Forgiveness. Faith. Both took courage. Some people seemed to think she had a lot of that.

Gina gazed around the town square. It didn't seem like a snow globe anymore, but there was a different kind of beauty now. Whereas the silence had been safe and peaceful, the laughter of children, notes of a familiar song and heartfelt greetings for a happy holiday were just as welcoming, perhaps more so.

The Tea Pot stood staunchly on the corner. The wind had softened, blowing wisps of snow across the square. She'd been closed off to nature's beauty, to life's beauty, to her own inner beauty.

Nick wasn't a part of the nearby landscape. No doubt someone had urgent need of his fix-it skills. The scene suddenly felt empty.

Carol sighed heavily behind her.

"Cut my hair," Gina said. And when it seemed as if the woman hadn't heard her, she said again, louder, "Cut my hair."

"Hey, I'm ready whenever you are, girlfriend." Carol rose from the chair. She shook out a green drape decorated with prancing reindeer, including Rudolph.

Gina entered the booth and sat. The shepherd's pie she'd eaten earlier decided it didn't like the cookie she'd sneaked in the kitchen. Or maybe it was just nerves.

Carol brushed out her braid, fastening the gleaming length with a ponytail holder at the nape of Gina's neck. "When I cut this off, I can trim the rest into a bob. You can keep your long bangs, but... Never mind. I shouldn't say anything."

"You've been encouraging me to cut my hair short since last summer." What did it matter if Gina put her scar on display for all to see? It was time to embrace herself, scar and all. "I say let's do it."

"Do you mean it? Oh, Gina. It'll look beautiful. You'll be so happy, I promise."

Her stomach churned once more. "I'm sure I'll love it."

She couldn't help but wonder if Nick would, too.

WHEN GINA ENTERED The Tea Pot, most of the crowd had cleared out. Her mother and father sat at a table, holding hands and snuggling. They'd changed out of their Claus costumes into jeans and sweaters.

Her mother and Aunt Martha gasped when they caught sight of her.

"Oh, Gina," her mom said, turning in her chair. Her hand drifted over her mouth, no doubt holding in all the remarks about how Gina should never have cut her bangs.

The style was flattering, even if it was shockingly different from her long, tamed tresses and bangs. It suited her angular features, making her eyes look huge. The short locks twisted and curled and drifted on the breeze, as if happy to have such a weight lifted.

But if her mother didn't like it...

"Darling, it's beautiful." Danielle rushed to hug her. "You're beautiful."

"She's perfect in every way." Aunt Martha wrapped her arms around the pair.

Not to be outdone, her father enveloped them all in a warm embrace. "What a lovely Christmas present."

"Speaking of which..." Aunt Martha slipped behind the counter, then held up a small wrapped package.

"You brought my gift here?" Gina asked. "I thought we were exchanging presents tomorrow morning."

"This isn't from me. It's from your Secret Santa," Martha said slyly.

"I don't have a..." Gina glanced around, half expecting to see an unfamiliar man in the shop. But there were no mystery men in her life. It must have come from Nick. "When did he drop it off?"

"About thirty minutes ago." Martha set the box on the counter and pushed it across to Gina. "Open it."

She edged closer. "It's not a Secret Santa gift. It's just a gift."

"No. He said to specifically tell you it was from your Secret Santa," Aunt Martha insisted, her faded green eyes sparkling. "Why don't you open it? It's probably *nothing*."

"Who dropped this off?" her father demanded.

Martha and Danielle both shushed him.

Gina picked up the box. Shiny green paper. A bright red bow. It was large enough to fit a softball inside. "It can't be a Secret Santa gift." That implied Nick had gotten her something else and this was just a hint at a more important gift.

Slowly, she removed the wrapping. A white box from the card shop told her nothing about what was inside.

"You were never like this as a girl," her mother said. "You ripped the paper and tossed the bow like that was the best part of opening presents."

But this was different. This was from Nick.

Gina lifted the lid. Inside was a snow globe. A beautiful Victorian house, white with red trim. Above it, Santa and his sleigh rode off into the night. There were even tracks on the rooftop. "It's perfect."

And then she saw the small note card beneath it: "In ten years."

Her phone buzzed with a message from Nick: I'm here. In front of the mistletoe.

Gina's heart pounded. This was one of those moments in life when everything slowed down and things changed. It was the branch dropping toward her. The man shouting she'd stolen his cab. Nick turning her around and kissing her.

"The way she opened it, I thought it was an engagement ring or something." Her father sat back down. "It's just a bauble."

"It's more, Dad. It's so much more." It was an apology and a promise. A hint at the true gift only Nick could give her. One that couldn't be bought or boxed or wrapped. He was offering her a chance at love.

Gina set the snow globe on the counter and went into the kitchen, retrieving the wrapped red scarf her mother had picked up for her. At the last minute, she embellished the plain box with a little something extra.

"DAD, WHY ARE WE waiting here? This is where people kiss." The disgust in Adam's voice was palpable.

The sun was setting. The crowd was moving toward the stage. On the perimeter of the square, only vendors packing up their wares and a few couples waiting their turn beneath the mistletoe remained.

"You like Gina, don't you?" Nick asked.

Adam bobbed his head. "She's as cool as Aunt Callie."

Speaking of his sister, Nick was testing Callie's patience. Adam should have been lined up with the choir behind the hardware store five minutes ago, but Nick was hoping Gina would walk out of The Tea Pot at any minute.

And then there she was, with a gift in hand. Her short hair blew in the breeze, glinting like silver beneath the sparkling lights that were just beginning to come on. Her scar was no longer hidden. She smiled. At him. It wasn't a fragile smile. It was a smile brimming with confidence and joy.

Something warm burst in his chest, a jumble of emotions he didn't dare trust but couldn't bring himself to suppress. Love and hope and happiness.

"This is for you," Gina said when she reached them.

"Usually, kids get gifts on Christmas," Adam said reproachfully.

She turned that brilliant smile on his son.

"I know what you like, and that comes out of the oven, not the store." She handed Adam a frosted Rudolph sugar cookie.

Although he thanked her for the treat, Adam tugged on Nick's hand, clearly nearing the end of his patience. "Aunt Callie's gonna come find me if we don't go soon."

Nick accepted the small thin box from her. "Can you forgive me?"

Gina nodded. "Open it."

The sky grew darker. Street bulbs blinked on. Strings of lights twinkled. But it was Gina who glowed.

He reached for the bow and realized she'd attached the Victorian ornament they'd found in her kitchen that morning. He chuckled.

"That's the reindeer house." Releasing Nick's hand, Adam claimed the ornament, crumbs falling from his mouth. "Cool."

"Open it," Gina encouraged again, smiling at Nick

He drew away the ribbon and opened the box. It was a red scarf. Just like his tattered, faded red scarf.

"It's something to keep you warm while you work on your house. I suspect I'll have to buy you another one in ten years." The welcome in her voice wrapped around him, cradling Nick and his dreams.

Adam backed up. "Dad, I have to go. You know, choir?"

"Adam…" Nick wasn't sure how to include his son in this special moment. If all went as planned, he'd be embarking on a new life. Tonight. Beneath the mistletoe.

"Dad, Aunt Callie told me you'd probably be kissing Gina under the mistletoe. It's okay. I'm a kid. I don't need to watch that." Adam kicked at a drift of snow. "Can I go line up for choir now?"

"Yes." Nick held out his hand to Gina as Adam tromped off.

Gina slipped her palm in his and gave it a reassuring squeeze. The last couple cleared out from beneath the gazebo. Vaguely, Nick registered that his sister, Callie, made up half of that dazed and distracted-looking couple. It didn't matter. The gazebo was all his and Gina's now.

Together they walked toward the mistletoe. Their boots crunched on ice and snow. Across the town square, a crowd had gathered around the stage.

"I'm sorry I lied to you," Nick said.

"I'm going to look back on Football20 as a romantic gesture by a man who found it difficult to get my attention."

"I've fallen for you hard, Gina. Smart, forgiving and a good cook. I'm a lucky man."

They stopped at the entrance to the gazebo. He claimed her other hand.

"Who said I was a good cook?" She grinned. "I can bake anything, but cooking? That's an entirely different skill set."

He drew her closer, guiding her arms around his neck, slipping his around her waist. "Lucky for you, I'm a man who loves to grill." There was one more thing they'd needed to discuss before they entered the mistletoe gazebo. "About my future in politics—"

Gina shushed him gently, taking a step into the gazebo. "Don't treat me with kid gloves. Haven't you heard? I'm a brave woman." She tugged him forward, until they were standing beneath the mistletoe. "If our relationship leads somewhere…we'll go forward together."

That was good enough for him. Nick pressed his lips to hers. Their first kiss had been unexpected, and filled with angst and longing. This one offered a promise and—

"This is a surprise." His dad's voice. "Who knew our son had plans beneath the mistletoe this year?"

"Dad?" Callie said, then louder. "Mom? You're supposed to be in Florida."

"They weren't due to arrive until tomorrow." Nick rested his forehead on Gina's. "That's what your Secret Santa gift meant." A small photograph of the family on Christmas.

"Your mother couldn't stand the thought of Christmas without her babies," Matthew Banning deadpanned. "We drove all night and all day to get here."

"At least you weren't the only ones driving the snowy Massachusetts roads," Jack said. He held the hand of a pregnant woman. Gold glinted on his finger. His *left* finger.

Nick kept his arms around Gina, but he couldn't resist a jibe. "I always thought I'd be your best man."

"You'll have to settle for me being yours." Jack's bride was blushing.

His dad surveyed his progeny. "I think congratulations are in order. I'm just not sure who to congratulate first."

"I told you we needed to come home for Christmas." His mother clapped her gloved hands. "A mother always knows. Welcome to the family. All of you."

"Just one more kiss," Nick whispered to Gina. "For luck."

"You can kiss her later," Callie exclaimed. "Adam, hurry. We're late."

"Don't worry," called a masculine voice with a hint of an Irish brogue.

"Careful of that icy patch, Sophie," Jack said.

"I'll be careful if you will," she replied.

"Hurry up, Dad!" Adam's voice, farther away now.

The sound of footsteps departing indicated Nick might finally have Gina to himself.

"We should go," she said.

Neither one of them moved.

"Just one more kiss before we go on our Christmas date." And then Nick closed the distance between them.

The announcer called all children to the choir, adding that Callie Banning was needed immediately backstage.

The world seemed to drift away, or maybe Nick and Gina rose above it, adrift on the warmth found in each other's arms, the joy of their heart-thumping kiss, and the promise of the mistletoe.

* * * * *

LARGER-PRINT BOOKS!

GET 2 FREE
LARGER-PRINT NOVELS
PLUS 2 FREE
MYSTERY GIFTS

Love Inspired

Larger-print novels are now available...

ReaderService.com

Manage your account online!

- Review your order history
- Manage your payments
- Update your address

*We've designed
the Harlequin® Reader Service
website just for you.*

Enjoy all the features!

- Reader excerpts from any series
- Respond to mailings and special monthly offers
- Discover new series available to you
- Browse the Bonus Bucks catalog
- Share your feedback

Visit us at:
ReaderService.com

RS13